STEVE JACOBS was born in Port Elizabeth, South ..... , 1955. He studied Law at the University of Cape Town, and after a year spent working on a kibbutz in Israel he practised as an Advocate in Johannesburg. After leaving the legal profession he worked as a journalist, a bookseller and a property manager. He also worked on a photographic safari camp in Botswana.

He is an active campaigner for human and animal rights, and has been a Trustee of Beauty without Cruelty, worked with squatters at the Crossroads township, and been a member of Koeberg Alert, an organisation opposing a nuclear power station.

He is currently sub-editor of the *Straits Times* of Singapore in their office in Sydney, Australia.

A collection of his short stories, *Light in a Stark Age*, was published in 1984 (Ravan Press). This was followed by two novellas, published as *Diary of an Exile* (Ad. Donker, 1986), and the novel *Under the Lion* (Heinemann, 1993).

This book is great.
features: - scene of Mandela's release
- multiplicity of perspectives: Jew, Afrikaaner, black, ruling class + dominated
- difficult love story
- the complexities & contradictions of an oppressed society (how to think about vio of the oppressed class)

STEVE JACOBS

THE ENEMY WITHIN

Heinemann

Heinemann is an imprint of Pearson Education Limited a
company incorporated in England and Wales, having its registered
office at Edinburgh Gate, Harlow, Essex, CM20 2JE.
Registered company number: 872828

www.heinemann.co.uk

Heinemann is a registered trademark of Pearson Education Limited

First published by Heinemann Educational Publishers in 1995

British Library Cataloguing in Publication Data
A catalogue record for this book is available from the British Library.

ISBN: 978 0 435909 98 7

Cover design by Touchpaper
Cover illustration by David Axtell
Edited by Victoria Ramsay

Typeset by CentraCet Ltd, Cambridge
Printed by Multivista Global Limited

08 09 / 10 9 8 7 6 5 4 3

For Yvonne, Vicki and Alexia

'But what if I should discover that the very enemy himself is within me, that I myself am the enemy who must be loved – what then?'

C. G. Jung

PROLOGUE

The thumping in David Tshabalala's head was making him mad. It had been there since the hammer attack; it got worse when he was excited. He pulled the baby tightly into his chest as the growl of the old Valiant grew closer.

Curled into her blanket, the child whimpered, almost lost in his broad labourer's hands. A trail of spit dribbled from the corner of her mouth on to the sleeve of his lumber-jacket, but in the night the small stain was almost invisible. The baby arched her back as if she were building up to scream, but then seemed to think better of it and relaxed with a gurgle into the safety of his embrace. Her tiny fist beat against the air for a moment before the miniature fingers unclenched and the angry gesture turned into a wave.

The Valiant was bearing relentlessly down the tarred road which separated the brick houses of Nyanga from the squatter camp. Its headlights drove nets into the darkness, snaring the dark shapes of pedestrians. Its occupants scanned faces, seeking to fix on the scarred forehead of the man who had stolen their baby.

David Tshabalala reached into his jacket pocket and his thick fingers closed over the comforting length of the Okapi pocket-knife. Its blade was out for quick use: the steel's keen edge bit into the palm of his hand. His foot scuffed a clod of mud and he stumbled. If he could just cross the road without them seeing, he'd escape into the alleys between the squatter shacks. In the darkness no one would find him there: the car could not follow, nor would Gloria and her father pursue him on foot. And in the morning? Well, that could take care of itself.

David shambled past a shack where squatters were selling fruit and vegetables and he heard the babble of customers haggling over prices. They were all too preoccupied to notice the stocky man half-walking, half-running down the smoky township street, bent over as if in pain, with the red car stalking him.

A thin wind, born on the marshes of the Cape Flats, slapped a misty

1

hand against David's face. Two sheets of corrugated iron in the shackland clattered together with the sharp retort of gunshot and he stiffened, squeezing a yelp out of the baby. He hoped the witch-doctor's medicine had cured the child's diarrhoea; the last thing he needed was for both of them to be covered in shit.

He sneaked a look over his shoulder at the Valiant. Mr Kekana was driving, peering short-sightedly over the top of the steering-wheel. Gloria sat tensed beside him, right up against the windscreen, her head moving frantically from side to side, her bottom lip sticking out in her agitation.

David tried to hide his face in his collar, but the streetlight betrayed him. He felt their eyes find him, pick him out of the dark. The car grumbled closer, accelerated, paced him. How could those two harm him? A woman and her old father! And yet he was unable to control his fear. He was catching gulps of breath in his mouth because his nose could not take in sufficient quantities of air. The quick inhalations made his chest heave and rocked the baby girl in the cradle of his left arm while the blunt fingers of his right hand once more sought the reassuring menace of the knife.

The blade was so sharp that, at the *braai* with his friends earlier, it sliced through the tough, dry steak as if the meat had been tenderised. David had chewed slowly, not listening to the chattering of those around him, looking forward to seeing his wife and baby at the witchdoctor; his anticipation made the bitter meat taste sweeter. He drank a few beers and lay back under the weak midday sun, hoping that things between them would improve. But their meeting was disastrous.

She was so beautiful. Her round face, plumper since she had had the child, was the picture of good health. Gone were the furrows of worry that had crossed her face when she lived with him, even when they had made love and she should have forgotten everything else. Her full breasts and wide hips made him ache with desire; the need was not sexual, he just wanted to hold her in his arms and take solace from the mother of his child. His stomach churned as her big brown eyes fluttered. 'Come back with me,' he pleaded, but she shook her head as if from a great height.

'I have to go to choir practice,' she said in her husky voice.

'To see the priest's son?' he responded bitterly.

'No. To sing.'

'Your father always wanted you to marry him!' David cried and grabbed his daughter from Gloria's arms, expecting his wife to follow, but she did not. She stood still for a moment, quivering like a rabbit, then turned and fled. He also ran, confused, stumbling like a drunken man, although the effect of the beers had worn off. The stale taste of the meat lingered in his mouth.

And then the car closed in and he tried to use the bulk of his body to conceal the little bundle in his spade-like hands. 'Shsh, don't cry,' he begged as the cowrie mouth opened to emit a howl of protest and the tiny fingers closed over his thumb. Then the pain erupted in his head as it always did when he got angry, ever since his uncle had struck him with a hammer.

The Valiant passed by and David broke into a trot, but the flash of pain scorched his eyes so that he lost his balance instead of escaping across the road into the squatter camp. The tarmac rushed up to meet him as his knees buckled and his only thought in that split second was to protect the baby. But his legs recovered before the fault in his brain caused the whole edifice of his body to collapse. It was, he thought later when he replayed the events in his mind, a fatal slip; his uncle's hand had reached across the years, a hammer flailing in his thoughtless grip.

Kekana tried to make a U-turn but the street was too narrow and instead he mounted the pavement on the squatters' side of the road, a little way ahead of the fugitive. Gloria jumped out first, while the car was still moving, but her father ordered her to wait; he would deal with this unpleasantness.

The baby was screaming relentlessly, signalling David's position no matter which way he turned. He hauled up the squirming bundle in his arms, suddenly smelling the sharp whiff of urine, but he could not stop the noise.

And there was Kekana. His little grey beard trembled in righteous anger as he crossed the road which flowed like a black river between them. He had on his church clothes – smart brown pants and shiny shoes, a black and white checked jacket and a red tie.

'Give me the baby,' he shouted, arms outstretched, 'or I'll report you to the People's Court again! Do you want more lashes?'

The words seared into David's head, compounding the agony that already existed there. He felt again the *sjambok* blows that had whipped down, arm after arm, on his unprotected back under the hot midday sun while his stomach bit into the edge of the table over which they had forced him. From the depths of that remembered pain, which had buzzed in his ears like flies, he was aware of this man of the church standing by, watching kangaroo justice being done to his son-in-law.

'Give Gloria back her child and crawl home like a dog,' the old man spat. 'You're drunk again.'

And Gloria was beside her father, fear and anger in her eyes, her mouth opening and closing, showing her flickering tongue as she spoke. But Tshabalala did not hear what she was saying for he shoved the baby at Kekana and then the knife was out of his pocket and performing its magic dance of light through the chilly township air. He heard people screaming but their noise was disembodied: it came from the souls in the black river and he could not connect the voices to any particular person.

Kekana put out his hands to take the baby as if he were receiving a blessing, and the beloved little pawn crossed the gulf between them. As the child came to rest on the old man's fingers, the knife began its arc and sliced where it landed – David did not know where – and Kekana's mouth fell open in shock and pain. He grunted like a pig and David struck again. A pair of hands took the infant – David did not see whose – the blinding light in his brain obliterated his vision. Kekana dropped to his knees and then sank on to the road, making gurgling noises, but David's attention had shifted to his wife.

Gloria was running towards the car. She did not cry out; her breath was trying to heave extra energy into her pudgy legs. But she carried too much weight to move quickly. In a few steps, David caught up and tripped her to the ground. She fell on her stomach and air exploded from her mouth. He smelled her perfume, mixed with the tang of terror. Then the knife plunged down again to free this beautiful woman from the old man's evil that was trapped inside her. She was squealing as he knelt beside her and drove the pocket-knife into her back, releasing years of frustration at both of them. The blade plopped into the flesh through the material of her white church blouse and a dark spurt of blood flooded over his hand: it was like slaughtering sheep in Transkei. She moaned as if she were trying to

4

say something, perhaps to plead for her life, and she covered her head with her hands. Her blood was balm for the scars on his back which had burned every day since he had been lashed. Through his madness, he knew he was killing the woman he loved, in an arena cast by the streetlight, watched by a circle of strangers.

When he straightened, Gloria had stopped twitching and was lying quite still. Her brown and red print skirt hugged the backs of her thighs; it had crept up over her knees, revealing her naked legs to the prying eyes of the onlookers. One of her shoes had come off in the chase and the grazed toes of her bare foot bled into the tarmac. Her head was buried under the pillow of her arms as if she had, at the last, tried to retain some privacy during the intimate act of dying. Blood was spewing from her back and turned the road into a bright, bubbling river.

David looked for the baby but she was gone and a crowd of men was closing in on him. He began to run and his steps took him into the alleys between the shacks. He leaped over a cooking fire and ravaged someone's small vegetable garden, pushing past groups of startled squatters who got out of his way because, when a man ran like that, there was trouble.

Slowly, colour returned to the blank space in his mind where blood had washed out the imprint of what he had done. Then the horror crowded in; he heard a thin wailing noise carried on the wind and he recognised it as his own voice. He was standing alone in the bushes beyond the shacks amidst the rubbish of tangled metal that not even the squatters could use. A half-moon winked at him; by its deranged light, he saw that his sticky hand still clutched the knife. He drew back his arm to fling away the weapon, but he realised they might find it, and instead he let his hand fall to his side. For the second time that night, he dropped to his knees in the antithesis of prayer.

As a Boeing roared above the level of the Port Jackson trees, liberated from D. F. Malan Airport, he gouged out a hole in the dirt with his bricklayer's fingers and shoved in the knife. Then he washed the blood off his hands using the coarse white sea-sand. As an afterthought, he pulled himself out of his bloodstained lumber-jacket and buried that in a separate hole. He stayed on his knees, swaying in a mockery of prayer, between the cage of the township and the cars flashing by on the freeway; he was in no-man's land, beyond the influence of all their lights. How the drivers would have accelerated past this spot had they known a killer hid in the undergrowth!

Wearily, he lifted himself to his feet. He knew this place; it was the way he walked home when his boss dropped him off after work. He followed invisible paths, skirting this ditch and that clump of bushes, putting up his hands to protect himself against the head-high bushes that whipped his face when he took a wrong turning. The wailing had stopped by itself – he had no control over the trapdoor which allowed that noise to switch on and off – and the Boeing had been swallowed up by the empty half of the moon. David Tshabalala wandered through the night, utterly alone.

Except for the elderly man who detached himself from the side of a rock and limped towards him, completely visible even in the semi-darkness. The old man's eyes no longer laughed as they used to when he returned from work in his overalls and gumboots, set David on his knee and told his son stories of the tribal ancestors in Transkei. He was not the vigorous young man that David recalled; the years had dug their claws into his crippled figure. He wore a balaclava, rolled up so that it covered his head only as far as the wrinkles across his forehead. Patches of grey hair sprouted randomly down his cheeks, culminating in a thicket on his chin. When he blinked, his eyelids were so heavy that his eyes struggled to reappear. It was a sad, neglected face above a dark shirt, buttoned up to the wings of his battered collar.

'You were always a quiet boy,' he said. 'Do you remember when you used to go and sit by yourself and talk to the spirits?' Despite his bedraggled appearance, his voice enfolded David in a coat of the warmest skins.

'Yes, Father, but everything has changed.'

'Your mother and I, we thought you were sick. Sometimes when you sat in the corner by yourself, you laughed or shouted. We took you to the witchdoctor and she gave you medicine . . .' He caught his son staring at the open flies of his black trousers and he reached down, with a trace of embarrassment, to zip them closed. 'I forget sometimes,' he apologised.

'We all forget,' David consoled him. 'Don't worry.'

'*Aau*,' the old man said, 'you were so quiet then. What's happened to you? Why have you become so mad?' He looked up at his tall son, and David saw the cut on his neck which had been stitched coarsely, as you would stitch a horse.

'Father, it began when you were already gone. I was staying with Uncle Mkele. One Saturday he was playing music very loudly on his radio because he was drunk. He kept us up all night. The neighbours were scared of him so they complained to me but I didn't say anything until Sunday.'

The old man scratched his wrinkled neck with a thin finger and seemed to loosen one of the stitches as blood began to ooze from the wound.

'I asked Uncle Mkele to turn off the music in the afternoon when we were all sick and tired of the noise,' David continued, 'and he picked up a hammer from the floor and he hit me on the head.'

'Your mother's brother did that?' the old man wheezed, but it was clear that he was only half-listening; he was much more concerned with his neck. He studied his bloodstained fingers, then dabbed the gash ineffectually with his fist.

'The ambulance came and they took me to Victoria Hospital,' David insisted; he had to explain. 'Look, you can see the mark on my head. That's when I started getting the headaches. It was before I met Gloria.'

His father was leaning forward so that the blood, pattering from his neck, did not fall on to his shirt. He seemed mesmerised by the dark globules that drained away his life as they escaped remorselessly, and his broad nostrils flared as if he were trying to sniff the sweet, rich liquid.

'That's when I started to fight with everyone,' David said. 'I used to drink a lot . . . to make the pain go away . . .'

His father sighed. 'You were always so quiet and now look what you've done. I can't understand you, my son.'

'You did not know me when I became a man! You did not see me grow up or where I worked or how I met Gloria and the problems I had with her. You left even before I was circumcised. How can you now judge me?'

'I'd like to listen to you,' the old man shrugged, 'but I'm sorry. I don't have time, my son. Maybe I'll come back again. Then we can talk.' He hunched his frail shoulders, crossing his arms over his chest as if he had suddenly become very cold. He shivered as he asked: 'How did I get this wound?'

'I saw them kill you,' David sobbed, 'the *tsotsis*. You were standing at the front gate and they ran past and they stabbed you in the neck with a *panga* for no reason. I was six.'

Then a cloud blinded the moon and his father was gone. David rubbed his eyes, but he could not resurrect the memory. He stood, alone again, in the bushes, fear seeping into his chest as his anger drained away.

Dread welled up in his throat and burst like a fountain in his mind. It drove his feet back across the wasteland towards the township's demon lights which had borne him and from which death was the only escape. He had freed Gloria. They couldn't live together, nor could they live apart . . . didn't she once say that she would rather die than be without him? Kekana had torn her away and now he had paid the inevitable price.

'Father, I'm sorry!' David cried. 'I've made a mess of my life.' But the old man had already entered that zone occupied by the ancestors. The silence of the bush was only punctuated by the cars on the freeway, their speed cocooning them from the violent township streets where life was as cheap as a packet of Lucky Strikes.

Nobody looked twice at him as he tottered back through the squatter camp on watery legs. No one came out screaming: 'Murderer! You've killed your wife and her father!' His heartbeat almost returned to normal as his panic subsided.

A group of youngsters ran past, barefoot and clothed in rags, chasing one another in childish games, as he used to do when he was their age. But tonight he had cut himself off from society; he could never rejoin the company of normal people. No more could he have *braais* with his friends or play soccer on Sunday afternoons; he had become an outlaw.

'Father, why didn't you listen to me?' he shouted, knowing that now he would never have a chance to put his case to the person who mattered most. 'Why didn't you wait?' The youngsters danced out of the way of this half-running, half-stumbling madman with blood on his jeans, as they would avoid broken glass in the path before them.

David's shoe caught on a piece of concrete and he swore as he fell on his hands in the rubble in this cursed place where the whites had forced the blacks to live. Struggling to his feet, his palms scraped, he lurched past dwellings made of cardboard and corrugated iron and black plastic stretched over wattle frames until he reached the fatal road.

There was no activity, no sign that he had killed his wife and her father. There were no police, no ambulances, no sobbing concentrations of relatives. For a moment he wondered if he had, in fact, done it at all, or if it was just a dream.

By the streetlight he could see a single ragged tree near the place where his knife had ripped out his old life and savagely substituted the unknown. The pavement, opposite a house with a wooden fence, where Kekana had stopped his Valiant, was empty; the car was gone. Keeping his head down, his pent-up breath steaming from his pursed lips, he crossed the empty road into Nyanga. He turned a corner, setting off a chain of barking dogs, jumped over a fence and crept past the shack in his backyard where two families lived.

No one saw him push open the back door as he let himself into the smoky kitchen. His mother was sitting at the rickety table, her head buried in her hands, her body shuddering as she sobbed. She glanced up when he entered, and in the candlelight her thin face danced and disappeared and her eyes dissolved into melancholy shadows. The kettle whistled on the primus stove in the corner.

'Mother,' he said hoarsely, 'don't cry. I'm here.'

Thelma Tshabalala's mouth fell open and she looked so startled that he added hurriedly: 'Don't shout! I don't want them,' he pointed to the door leading to the sitting room, 'to hear '

But she could not restrain herself. 'What have you done?' she shrieked.

He put his hand, defensively, over the bottom half of his face as if to shield himself from her distress. 'Where is everyone?' he asked uneasily. The house was too quiet; no one had come to investigate her screams.

'They're looking for you,' his mother replied, straightening her scarf before crying again: 'What have you done? I suffered so much to bring you up after your father died and how have you repaid me? You drink and you fight and now you've murdered your wife!' She sniffed. 'Gloria is dead and you killed her.'

'They were making me mad!' he exclaimed. 'They've been making me mad ever since I met them. I'm sorry, Mother. What about Kekana? Did I kill him too?'

'They took him to hospital. Pray for him, my son. Pray that he lives. You don't want two deaths on your head.'

He studied her as if she did not belong to him, this gaunt, unhappy woman. She wore a white jersey over her dark dress; a crucifix rested on her chest and a single earring punctured the lobe of her right ear. She had on her smart black shoes as if she were expecting important visitors. A Bible lay open before her at a passage that he did not recognise. It kept at bay the shadows of the devils which the candle threw on the unpainted brick walls.

'Why?' she asked after the silence between them had grown unbearable.

His eyes rested for a moment on the meagre ankles that had carried her thin frame through the rich houses of the white people for all the years of his childhood, while her bony fingers had washed their dishes and shone their silver; he felt no love for her, only a vague distaste.

'What do you mean?' he asked irritably.

'Why did you do it?'

'I'd stolen the baby,' he said, 'and they were chasing me.'

'So what?' she screamed. 'Why didn't you give it back to them?'

'I was scared,' he said truculently. 'I thought they were going to attack me.'

'How can they attack you? A woman and an old man! What nonsense!'

A dog bayed in the yard as someone walked past with a radio blaring. David wondered if they were broadcasting details of the wanted killer. He was stupid to have returned home. This was the first place they'd look.

A photograph of his father as a young man, proud and clean-shaven, stood in its battered frame on the sideboard. He was staring ahead, beaming with confidence as he plotted the course of his life; how could he have known that a death sentence had been handed down on him and was just waiting to be imposed? The guttering candlelight curled his lips into a sneer as he contemplated the disgrace his son had brought on the family name.

'I saw my father in the bushes,' David said. 'I was happy, but he could not stay to talk to me. He had to go back to the ancestors. They were calling him.'

'You're mad!' Thelma clucked. She began to cry again, with the abandon of a baby. He went to her and, bending his long torso, put his arm around her shoulders. She tried to shake him off, but his arm was too heavy and after a short struggle she succumbed and allowed him to comfort her.

'What did I do wrong?' she sobbed. 'What mistakes did I make when I brought you up?'

'Mother, shsh. You did nothing wrong. You tried your best for me. It's not your fault that I did this thing.' He rested his head on her shoulder in the crook of her neck and smelled the sweat that had collected in her hairline.

'You must go to the police,' she said at last in a voice of brittle reeds. 'Otherwise they'll hunt you down like a dog. You must say you are sorry.'

He raised his head sharply and his dark eyes threw back the candle's fire. 'They won't just let me go!' he exclaimed. 'They'll put me in jail.'

'Yes, my son.' She laid her hand, nails bitten, on the open page of her Bible as if the comforting words might penetrate the skin of her fingers and be delivered straight into her bloodstream. 'It's better than if they chase you and shoot you.'

The tap was dripping; the sound perforated the space behind their words. On the other side of the fatal road, the squatters had no running water. They had to take their buckets and queue at a communal tap. This was the cage the whites had forced them to live in; like rats they ate one another.

Thelma wiped her eyes with her handkerchief and blew her nose loudly, and continued sobbing, while her son squeezed her slight body.

'Mother, I must run away now.'

She lifted her hand to touch the indentation on David's forehead and for the first time in years spoke of the hammer attack. 'Your uncle was a gangster,' she said, chewing her top lip. 'You were a good boy until he scrambled your mind. It's good that he's dead,' she added sourly. 'He was no use to anyone.' She rubbed the scar as if she could cure the sickness inside her son's head by polishing the surface. His eyes closed and a blessed relief filled him with utter weariness. If she had not continued to speak, he would have fallen asleep, crouching beside his mother's chair while her fingers massaged away the hurt.

'You shouldn't have got mixed up with the Kekanas,' she said. 'They were too proud and too greedy. You didn't have enough money. That's why Edward Kekana hated you.'

'He said he would report me to the People's Court again,' David said quietly, remembering. 'I got a fright . . .' He squinted into the tumult of that moment when his Uncle Mkele had reached through time with a dark brush and daubed black paint across his future, but his eyes could not focus on the horror of what he had done. '. . . I was trying . . .' his voice stretched until it broke and he could not go on.

'Go to the police,' she urged. 'Tell them the whole story.'

'I don't know,' he muttered. 'The police don't care about our stories.' But she continued to stroke his head as she used to do when he was a child, and his eyelids grew heavier while she crooned a lullaby which could have been a prayer.

The door to the sitting room burst open and David leapt up in fright, his hands groping for the knife that he realised he had buried in the bushes. Naked, he faced the threat from outside, with only his broad hands to protect him, heavy and blunt as shovels; his muscles trembled.

In the hysterical candlelight appeared a teenage boy with huge eyes. As soon as he saw the fugitive, he skipped into the room, slammed the door behind him, and leaned against it.

'We've been looking for you!' he panted. 'Everyone is looking for you!'

David's hands dropped and his head slumped on to his chest. He could not hide the blood that soiled his jeans. Gloria's blood. She had stained him; forever he would bear the mark of shame for what he had done.

'Are the police looking for me as well?' he asked gruffly.

'Yes . . . yes.' The boy was blinking and nodding; his words tripped over his lips in their anxiety to be free. 'The policeman . . .' he stuttered, 'the policeman who took Gloria away, he said you were very dangerous . . .'

David glanced down at his body as if he were not sure they were talking about the same person and his lips parted in a mirthless smile, showing his teeth. He took a step closer to the boy and pointed to his chest with both hands. 'I'm not dangerous!'

The boy tried to retreat, but he had nowhere to go. He squeezed himself against the door and protested: 'The police said no one must go near you.'

'Well then you'd better run away!'

'You don't understand,' the boy said urgently. 'Mr Kekana has a lot of power. If you don't give up, the police will shoot you. They will say you tried to attack them. That's why we've been trying to find you.'

The throbbing returned to David's head as if all the hammers in the world were competing to deliver the fiercest blow. He screwed his eyes shut and had to hold on to his mother to keep from falling. Gloria was staring at him sorrowfully, reproaching him for his violence. As if they had not been violent towards him . . .

'Your cousin is right. Go!' Thelma commanded.

'Yes, Mother,' David said softly, suddenly losing the will to fight any more. Defeated, he allowed them to lead him out into the black township.

PART ONE

PART ONE

1

Womb

Jeremy Spielman pushed back his chair from the dining-room table and sauntered towards the sliding glass doors. The sunlight cast glitter on the late afternoon sea, the heat sucked sticky sweat from his armpits. Dressed in a white cotton shirt and cream-coloured slacks, he stood on the balcony, his fingers clenched on the railings, and observed the Sea Point promenade from ten floors up. Young couples were walking babies and dogs, the inevitable drunkards lolled on the grass, lovers huddled earnestly over coffee at outside tables as he and Elmarie once used to do. A ship was gliding through the misty join in the blue where the sea and the sky met. Out of sight of his eyrie, whites sprawled on the golden sands, trying to tan to the colour of those who, until recently, had not been allowed on the beaches because they were too dark. But the black tide of Africa had begun to breach the dam of white exclusivity; apartheid was crumbling.

'I wish they wouldn't come here,' his mother had got into the habit of complaining as bands of blacks increasingly congested Sea Point's streets. 'They've got their own beaches to swim at. I'm afraid to go out these days. We don't go to their areas. I don't see why they should come to ours.'

It was no use explaining that she wouldn't want to go to their areas. Nor that the Jews were lucky the Afrikaner government had chosen to classify them as white so that they had had access to the best areas for so long. Nor that she had no option but to adapt to a changing political landscape.

'Come for tea!' she called and Jeremy turned, reluctantly, back to the table where she presided with the weight and authority of a Jewish Buddha. Her chubby fingers beat for attention on the stained white tablecloth, then began to tap out a tune while a dreamy expression softened her features.

'I played for the old people last night,' she said. 'They loved it. But their piano was out of tune.'

'I'm sure they didn't mind.' He was continually amazed that those

17

short, fat fingers could move with such agility over a keyboard. 'Do they pay you?'

Esta looked at him with a glance of amused contempt. 'How can I take money from them?' She beat her fist against her breast. 'I play from here, from the heart! Not for money. They're poor old people.'

'Sorry,' he muttered. 'I just hope they would do the same for you if you needed them one day.'

'Of course they would,' Esta said stoutly, then cried: 'Come, Vivian!' This provoked a rattle of cups in the kitchen, and the maid entered, carrying a tray. She wore a placid, glazed face, common to domestic workers who mask their feelings in a potentially hostile environment; she did not utter a word.

'Put it down here!' Esta ordered, adding to Jeremy when the black woman was hardly out of the room: 'She steals from me left, right and centre. I have to buy a new packet of sugar every week. Where does all the sugar go, I ask you?' And with venom in her voice she provided the answer: 'To the location, that's where. To feed God knows who.'

Jeremy cast an embarrassed look after the retreating Vivian. Her huge bottom, wobbling beneath her powder-blue uniform, disappeared silently into the kitchen. She gave no indication that she had heard or had been affected by the comment in any way.

'You can't say things like that in front of her, Ma. She's a person, with feelings . . .'

'She's a thief. And stupid!' Esta raged on. 'Yesterday she broke the vacuum cleaner again. Give them anything to work with and they break it.' Her big bosom heaved with the strain of her indignation, sending shivers through the bold flowers on the front of her fake silk dress. 'Come. Sit.' She pointed to one of the ugly brown dining-room chairs that he had grown up with. 'I'll pour.'

In despair, but choosing not to pursue the subject, Jeremy scratched the top of his head where the hair had begun to thin these last few years; it was alarming how easily his fingers penetrated right through to the scalp. What would that surface look like when all the hair was gone? He took a biscuit from the plate that Vivian had brought: they looked pale and uninspiring. Esta, forgetting her tirade, beamed and slapped her son playfully on the upper arm with the back of her hand. 'Eat! You're so pale. What's wrong? Doesn't she feed you?'

'Relax, Mom. I eat enough and anyway she doesn't have to feed me. We're not married. We don't even live together.'

'What can you expect from a *shiksa*?'

'Mom, you've met her and you liked her, remember?' He chewed noisily to drown out his annoyance. He shouldn't have come. He knew it the moment he had stepped out of the lift and smelled the mustiness that clung to the chunky furniture of old people, that seeped under the door of her flat and filled the foyer.

'She's pretty,' his mother conceded. 'Is she going to become Jewish?'

'We haven't discussed that yet, but it's her decision; I won't put any pressure on her.'

'If your father was alive . . .' Esta clicked. 'He must be turning in his grave,' she added darkly, pouring the tea. 'He wanted Jewish grandchildren. And so do I.'

'Dad was very happy with whatever I decided,' Jeremy protested, watching the thin brown bow of hot liquid that arced from the spout of the teapot into his cup. 'He didn't care whether my friends were Jewish or not. That's *your* problem. Even those old people – you wouldn't entertain them if they weren't Jewish.'

'And you?' she replied, stung by his bitter words. 'You'll do anything to upset me. That's why you chose a *shiksa* to go out with.'

'A very beautiful *shiksa*,' he retorted.

'So, aren't there any beautiful Jewish girls?'

Jeremy did not reply. A few drops of tea spilled into his saucer as Esta's hand shook. His father stared down from his frame on top of the piano, a benign, perhaps even weak, man with grey hair receding from his forehead, in short trousers, with a rucksack on his back and one of Table Mountain's waterfalls behind him. In a younger photograph, thin father and bulbous mother posed, smiling for the camera in somebody's garden – they held hands and seemed very much in love. Her nagging had killed him, of that Jeremy was certain. He died of leukaemia while she nagged him to get better. There were no pictures of Esta on the mountain.

Jeremy sipped his tea – his mother made it strong as he liked it – while the sunlight lapped at the clawed feet of the oppressive imbuia dining-room table, dark wood furniture that was now out of fashion.

'How is your work?' Esta asked, and before he could answer, said: 'I'm so proud of you. All my bridge friends know about my son, the

19

lawyer. They agree with me, mind you, that you'll only really be happy when you settle down with a nice Jewish girl. Mrs Feitelstein's son, Brian, you know him, he's a dentist, he got engaged last Sunday to a lovely girl from Canada.'

'Mother!' he said sharply. 'I don't want you to discuss me with your friends.' But he knew that her husband's death had left a hole which she had tried to fill largely by interfering in her son's life. Playing the piano at the Jewish old people's home was a way of sharing her loneliness, but not suppressing it.

And now, again, she was hovering between the present and the past. 'Your father was a wonderful man,' she said wistfully, brushing away a tear with a hand flecked brown by liver spots. 'He was so good to me. No woman could ask for more.' She tried to put on a brave face; the muscles at the corners of her mouth twitched but gave up the struggle to smile, and instead her lips turned down sourly. 'His family came here from Lithuania as immigrants with only the clothes on their backs . . .' She rubbed the diamond of her wedding ring absently as if she were able to communicate through it with the dead husband who had surmounted poverty to buy it for her.

'I know, Mom,' Jeremy said, 'I've heard this story a thousand times.' But he could not stop her excursion into family history, where memories cosseted her from the intolerable present.

'They were businessmen. They started the shop . . .' She found a tissue and with it tried to staunch the flow of tears that blurred her eyes. '. . . They built something out of nothing. Day in and day out your father was on his feet in that shop. Him and your grandfather and Uncle Hymie.'

'They cheated their customers,' Jeremy said meanly, trying to prick the bubble. 'That's how they made their money. I remember how my grandfather sold jackets to the blacks. He used to hold the material in at the back so the poor man looking in the mirror thought it fitted . . .'

'And you lived well because of it,' Esta chided. 'We sent you to university, we gave you everything you could have wanted. Even a house when your father died.'

Her son shifted uncomfortably, clenching his fist in unconscious imitation of that small, grey Lithuanian in the gloomy shop with its high dusty counters and hat-filled shelves, going all the way up to the ceiling, and full-length mirrors in which ignorant blacks were duped.

'We got rich on the backs of the poor,' he mused, contemplating the hideous furniture. Was it worth being one of the oppressors in order to buy the rubbish with which they cluttered their lives? He shared the guilt.

'Your father worked himself to the bone,' Esta replied, sounding hurt. 'He deserved all the money he earned. Come,' she said, regaining her control, 'do you want more tea? Vivian!' she yelled. 'Bring hot water!'

Jeremy sat back and his gaze fell on his graduation photograph that was turning to the colour of rust on the wall above the piano. Everyone had been entranced as the law graduate held his scroll like a shining wand in fingers that were now as pale as the marble of the pillar against which he was leaning. The black gown gave his torso a false bulkiness; the face, with its thick boxer's nose, was more rugged than the often-wounded features which met him in the mirror these days. With hard black eyes, the young Jeremy Spielman was staring up to heaven.

How ironic! His privileged position had been bought at the expense of the blacks; now he spent his days trying to save them from the gallows.

Vivian returned with a steaming pot. Jeremy had seen fat black women like her at the head of marches that got broken up by the police, supporters of the banned African National Congress, working for Sea Point madams who were oblivious of the tarnish inside their well-polished silver.

'Thanks,' he said, and her round, inscrutable face broke into the smile that she took out when it was appropriate, behind which she buried the years of insults. She put the pot down on the table and once more left the room without a word.

'So,' his mother asked, dipping her beaked nose back into his business, 'have you got any big cases?' Her elbows rested on the table top and she held her cup in both hands near her mouth. He could see the flabby muscles hanging from her arms where they entered the sleeves of her floral dress.

'Things are going steadily,' he answered cautiously, measuring the word for negative connotations, deciding that it was neutral and he could use it without lying.

'What's "steadily"?' she asked suspiciously.

He studied his nails as if the answers were to be found in their pink hemispheres. 'Well, I'm handling an unopposed divorce this week and I've got a few more *pro deos* lined up. It takes a while to break in,' he confessed. 'The attorneys must get to know me better. Advocates have to be very confident and aggressive. And,' he added, 'they have to have analytical minds. They have to be actors and gladiators. But I'll get there.'

'You should be more social,' Esta answered, giving the impression that she had neither heard nor understood a word he had said. 'Play golf. That's what Uncle Hymie says.'

'Mom, I'd never be able to do business on a golf course. I'm such a lousy golfer, they'd lose confidence in me.'

'How do you know? You've never played.'

'I've got no co-ordination for ball games. Remember I played hockey at school? I only got into the second team because they had no one else. It was embarrassing whenever I tried to hit the ball. It's your fault,' he said, trying to make a joke, but she frowned when she perceived herself to be under attack. 'Some people are born to be sportsmen,' he explained, 'others don't have it in their genetic make-up. My ancestors spent more time running away from Cossacks than smacking balls. I'm the result: a moderate jogger but a terrible golfer.' He finished his speech with a smug turn to his lips; he had shifted the blame elsewhere.

'Well if you get married to her, God forbid, you'll have to support her. So you'd better make money.'

'Who said anything about marriage?' he baulked. 'Anyway *pro deos* pay two hundred rand a day – that's not too bad if I can get a few other matters as well.'

'What are all these *pro deos*?' she asked, wrinkling her nose as if the word had a bad smell.

'I've explained to you. It's if someone faces a death sentence and he can't afford to pay a lawyer. Then the State pays.'

'Oh yes,' she said without interest. 'I just wish you'd get some nice cases. We didn't put you through university for nothing.' She found a crumpled tissue in a pocket and studied it, looking for a piece which had not been used. 'Your father slaved in that shop for you. And did you appreciate it? No, you just gave him heartache. And you don't care about me either. Your own mother.'

Jeremy flicked his wrist suddenly and looked at his watch. 'I've got to go!' he exclaimed. 'I'm late. Elmarie is waiting for me.'

'Are you coming for supper on Friday night?' There was a touch of desperation in her voice. 'Uncle Hymie will be here. He'd like to see you. You can bring the *shiksa* if you have to.'

'I'll call you,' Jeremy promised.

'Just don't phone tomorrow night – I'm going to a concert at the City Hall . . .' she paused, leaving an invitation open to him, although she would have already bought tickets. He did not respond, but put his hands flat on the table as a prelude to getting up. She wiped her sagging cheeks with her tissue. 'It's so hot,' she grumbled, 'and I've got a pain in my arm.'

'You've had it for ages,' Jeremy said unsympathetically. 'You tell me every time I see you. Go to a doctor.'

'Doctors!' she thundered. 'What do they know? We took your father to a doctor; it wouldn't have helped if we'd taken him to a hundred doctors! Could they save his life?' She tucked her tissue under her watch-strap and pushed the plate of anaemic biscuits at him. 'Don't you want something to eat? You're so thin. Go on, take them with you. I'll tell Vivian to put them in a packet . . .'

'No, Mom, I'm fine,' he answered irritably; it was no use trying to have any kind of discussion with her: if he had a lawyer's analytical mind, he certainly had not inherited it from his mother.

On the white wall behind her was an oil painting of an Eastern Cape scene, with a corrugated mud track running past aloes towards a range of purple mountains: the kind of cloying, unimaginative art sold on Sundays at the roadside on the way to Hout Bay. To Jeremy that track represented his parents' narrow Jewish-orientated world view. He had got off it within the first six months of entering university, as soon as his new nihilistic friends with John Lennon glasses and scruffy beards had pointed out its intellectual and spiritual poverty. He stopped going to synagogue, found that he had nothing in common with the conservative Jews on campus and sought his friends among the radical intellectuals; he even stopped fasting on Yom Kippur, a direct cause, according to Esta, of his father's death. Jeremy had consistently bucked the pressure to return to that constricted trail, although the illusion of security in those hazy mountains sometimes seemed more appealing than rambling aimlessly in the intellectual wilderness.

He escaped from the flat and took the lift down ten floors into the withering Sea Point heat. Crossing the road, he walked across the grass to the sea-front and leaned against the railing. The waves shattered on the rocks below and he breathed in the fresh air greedily, washing out the mustiness that was clogging his lungs. His mother made him feel guilty for just being alive. Behind him, joggers puffed past, golden medallions bouncing on their bronzed chests, while on the beach, centre-spread bodies, abandoned to summer, stoked up desires that Elmarie would have to sate.

Jeremy had come of age suddenly in a ward at Groote Schuur Hospital when his father, red-faced and vomiting from the agony of a brain haemorrhage, sank into a coma and then curled into a foetal ball. Son and wife kept the bedside vigil, taking turns to go home to sleep, while a rabbi came to say a prayer for the dead. For twenty-six hours, Selwyn Spielman clung stubbornly to this world. His fingers had grown so thin, as the muscles withered from lack of use, that his wedding ring – which had been too tight to remove – fell off and Esta put it in her pocket. With the sound in his throat of raging mountain rivers, which he loved so much, Selwyn's face turned silver and his head rolled over the pillow as he set off on his last journey.

Despite Jeremy's lack of belief, he said *kaddish* at the funeral and at two nights of prayers held in the Sea Point flat. Not long after, he left the firm of attorneys where he had been working and set up practice as an advocate at the Cape Bar. It was a lonely, frightening jump from another secure track to another wilderness that he would have to seed and nourish perhaps for years before it bore fruit.

A seagull cried. On the sand below, a tanned young woman with the figure of a model, her face partly hidden under a wide-brimmed straw hat, undid the straps of her bikini top which then rested unsecured on her breasts. She wriggled her shoulders as she settled back into the languor created by a long lazy day on a thick pink towel in the sun. Jeremy pushed against the railings with a longing so deeply embedded in his chest that he felt he would never be able to reach in to plug it.

He turned slowly and walked back across the grass to his car, eyes down on the lookout for dogshit.

2

Memory's Smile

It was one of the hottest weeks of the summer. Lightning struck the dry vegetation above the Cecilia Forestry Station and the fire raged on the mountain for three days, working its way from Kirstenbosch across to Devil's Peak in the City Bowl. The air above the city was brown as the sun filtered through the sweet-smelling smoke. Charcoal flakes drifted down from the mountain like black snow, tinkling malevolently on the roads. Ash carpets formed on window-sills and floors, and hair was impregnated with soot. Helicopters made noisy sorties with water buckets into the battle-zone but achieved nothing. At night, fiery rings branded the darkness and mountain ridges became flaming swords, pointing accusingly at the city.

A white tramp in a nondescript suit and red shirt was stumbling down Long Street. He tottered through the cone of light built up by a streetlamp and was illuminated for a moment before the darkness once more grabbed him and pulled him in. He had a full black beard of wiry hair, white-streaked, and bloated corpse fingers with dirty bitten nails. A bottle, still in its brown paper packet, stuck halfway out of his jacket pocket. Sighing for breath, he made it to the next streetlamp where his strength gave out and he dropped on to the pavement. His grubby fingers tore at his shirt – the redness was blood – forlornly trying to stop up the hole in his chest. But the gang of thugs that was after him caught up, circled like dogs, and their knives glinted and flashed as they plunged down. A crowd of prostitutes and taxi drivers, sailors and street people gathered round and clapped, passing beers with frothing lips, joking at the spectacle of the tramp's death. An ambulance siren wailed closer; its caterwauling was dented by the tolling of a bell: '*Dolente! Dolente!*'

Jeremy stretched a sleepy arm across his pillow and slapped down the switch on his alarm clock, mercifully silencing the hysterical noise. The eyes of the tramp pleaded from the depths of his dream, begging the lawyer to save his life. With horror, Jeremy recognised the fallen man under all the grime and facial hair: it was himself. He wiped his hand over his face and lifted his body wearily from the sticky sheets; his head ached as if he had just run a marathon. The bedclothes had scorched his skin; the cottage retained heat like a greenhouse. He blundered to the bathroom, avoiding his image in the mirror, and switched on the bath tap. Then he sank into the lukewarm water, washing away the clammy night, and submerged his head, trying to drown out the vision of the terrified hobo reflected in the mirror of his unconscious mind.

The phone shrilled. He cursed as he pulled out the plug and then stood up, wrapping a towel around his waist. He left a trail of wet footprints from the bathroom to the lounge and dripped water on the carpet as he manoeuvred the receiver to his ear with slippery fingers.

'It's all happening in town,' Elmarie said.

'What is?'

'They're going to march. There're thousands of people on the Parade. I'm watching from the office. Why don't you come and join them?' she taunted.

'Because I'm in court today,' he said tartly. 'Besides it wouldn't help my practice if I was seen on the streets with the great unwashed. It was OK to march when I was a student. But I'm respectable now, part of the Establishment.' He added in a softer tone: 'Just be careful if you go out.'

'I'm not leaving the office,' she answered. 'It's mainly blacks down there.'

'I'll see you later,' he snapped, upset at the racist overtones of her comment. 'I've got to go. I'm late.'

He dropped the receiver and switched on the television set, but he did not pay attention to the talking heads. Instead he hurried to his room where he wriggled into the trousers of his slightly rumpled grey suit which he had worn every day this week; the other one was at the cleaners. He wondered if anyone noticed that he had on the same clothes day after day. The Bar was such a conservative place, its members so obsessed with appearance, that he could imagine the sniggers behind his back in the common room during afternoon tea. He buttoned up his white shirt and tucked it into his trousers, then searched for his tie.

The mountain fire must have died down because the sun streamed cleanly through the kitchen window on to the white walls and green tiled floor. Jeremy folded the perforated edges of a coffee filter bag and smoothed it open into the brown-stained funnel that fitted over his cup. He spooned a measure of the fine soothing powder from its Tupperware container into the bag, aching for the first cup of the day. While the coffee dripped, releasing its rich russet aroma, the words of the television newsreader percolated through the house.

Friday, second of February, 1990 . . . State President F. W. de Klerk opening Parliament . . . the anti-apartheid Mass Democratic Movement preparing to march to protest against the exclusion of blacks . . .

Jeremy sipped his coffee. When he was on campus, political gatherings were banned. Attempts by the students to demonstrate brought out the police in baton-charging madness. But de Klerk had changed all that. Soon after forcing P. W. Botha from the country's top job, he gave the go-ahead for peaceful marches if permission was obtained from a magistrate. And the first of these processions was getting ready to set off from the Grand Parade in Cape Town.

The world's press waited for de Klerk's speech like vultures for a sickly beast to slip. If the message did not satisfy demands for further relaxations in the policy of apartheid, the beaks would plunge in and viciously gouge out what remained of international confidence in the country; there could be no recovery.

Jeremy straightened his tie in the mirror, but did not put on his jacket; it was too hot for that. He switched off the television, checked that all the windows were closed and went out, locking the door. Old Mr Pretorius was straining up Ivy Street to his house on the corner, a yellow carrier bag heavy with shopping hanging from each hand, balancing him.

'Terrible fire,' he said, stopping to rest. He put down his bags and straightened, looking not at Jeremy, but, with an immense sadness, at the mountain that had welcomed his ancestors as their ships entered Table Bay three hundred years before.

'Yes it is,' Jeremy answered, his mind elsewhere. 'How are you?'

'Ag, you know how it goes,' Pretorius said in his rough accent. 'With leukaemia some days you don't feel so good. But other days it's better. I'm going to hospital for a check-up on Monday.'

'I'm sure it'll be all right,' Jeremy said with the slightest trace of resentment. 'You look fit and healthy.' His father had surrendered and died a week after his leukaemia was diagnosed. But this old man

27

had been sick for as long as Jeremy had lived in the cottage and he was still alive; he was strong as an Afrikaner ox.

'*Ja*,' Pretorius replied. He bent and scooped his big hands through the handles of the carrier bags, then added: 'Last week my eye fell out.'

The lawyer's forehead crinkled in astonishment; he thought he had misheard, but Pretorius did not explain the remark. Perhaps one of his eyes, behind thick spectacles, was false. The old Afrikaner stood tall and slightly stooped but still proud, a battered white hat protecting his head from the early sun, reaching as low as the tops of his jumbo ears. Despite the heat, he wore a tweed jacket, like a gentleman farmer. Wordlessly, he began the rest of his journey up the hill.

'Goodbye,' Jeremy called after him. 'Keep well.'

Pretorius nodded as if he had forgotten that he was in the middle of a conversation, and continued stubbornly towards his cottage where his two fox terriers waited, yapping and bouncing against the gate; they loved him unconditionally even though he was old and sick. Apart from the dogs, he lived alone; his family occasionally came from the country to visit, especially on weekends when Western Province were playing rugby at Newlands. Then they would take his faded brown station-wagon, which he seldom drove (he preferred to walk): husky father, grimly quiet mother and a clutch of barefoot farm children.

Old age is a tyrant in our society, the lawyer reflected. It casts you out, makes you repugnant to the army of youth, not because you have done anything wrong but because, simply by being alive, the disease of years has crept up on you. It does not have to be like this: other communities integrate their old people, keep them in the family and the workplace. He felt sorry for the old man; somehow he could not find any similar sympathy for his mother who was also old and lonely.

The short drive down Kloof Street to town in the oven on wheels that was his car left Jeremy soaked with sweat even though all the windows were open. With relief he reached Huguenot Chambers, the building which housed Cape Town's advocates, and pushed his plastic card into the slot of the machine that guarded entry to the four floors of parking bays. The barrier arm swung up and Jeremy ascended the ramp to the second floor. Most of the other bays were already occupied, and the sickly smell of car fumes from the morning influx was still trapped between the concrete walls.

He stepped out of the lift on his floor into the welcome chill of the air conditioning. Fatiema, the receptionist, smiled with genuine affection as she handed him his post with slender brown fingers. Gatekeeper to twelve advocates, she was unflappable under pressure. She knew that he had been involved in the anti-apartheid struggle before he came to the Bar, and, although she never discussed politics, the special warmth in her smile revealed her gratitude to a white for taking up the cause of the black oppressed.

'Good morning, Mr Spielman.'

'Good morning,' he said, taking the letters, and because there was no one else in the foyer he added wistfully: 'I've heard they're getting ready to march in town. What a pity I'm in court.'

Her teeth had flashes of gold as she replied: 'Your luck's in. The judge is sick. Your case has been postponed to next Wednesday. You've got the day off.'

'If I don't work, I don't eat,' he said, and his mouth twisted down at the corners. 'Can I have a cup of coffee, please?'

'I'll send it through.' The switchboard started buzzing, a messenger from a courier service appeared with a parcel and the lift disgorged five men in suits, someone else's clients. With a magician's sleight of hand, the phone gripped between her ear and the shoulder of her white blouse, Fatiema dispatched them all. Her imitation pearl necklace hung slightly skew; otherwise her appearance, from the scarf wrapped like a turban round her head to her cream slacks, was impeccable. She could have stepped out of the pages of the magazine that Elmarie worked for.

Excited at the news that he had a free day, Jeremy walked down the corridor with a spring in his step until he reached the door with his name on it. His key searched for the lock and he twisted it. He pushed open the door and entered his office.

His whole legal practice existed in this little room. If he fell ill, it all came to a stop. There was no infrastructure, no one to help carry the load as he'd had when he was an attorney. Advocates worked alone, those were the rules: you lived or died by your own wits. What could he offer Elmarie if they were to marry now? No more than a hope for a better future. Every matter that he gave up was money lost. And he had taken no other work for today because he was supposed to have been in court. No wonder she was suspicious of his involvement in politics: it deflected him from the role of provider.

He took off his jacket – he had worn it while he made his grand entrance, although only the receptionist was there to notice – and hung it in the cupboard next to his black court gown whose ominous dark shadow was offset by a ludicrously frilly white bib. One of Fatiema's assistants brought his coffee and he took a sip, contemplating the few thin briefs that mocked him from a corner of his desk. Some of his colleagues believed you should sit in your office all day and wait for work: you might pick up the scraps that one of your busier brethren on the floor had discarded. But it was demoralising. For Jeremy, a bonus of the job was that, as your own boss, you could come and go as you wanted: the reward for insecurity was freedom. The coffee was cold and flat. In disgust he pushed away the thick white cup and dialled a number.

'Hello, can I speak to Elmarie please?'

'I'm sorry, Jeremy,' the secretary answered. 'She's in a meeting.' The woman knew his voice although they had never met. 'Do you want me to page her?'

'No thanks, Gail. Just say I called. I'll get back to her later.'

The pine bookcases, all he could afford, contained a full set of law reports, the tools of his trade. Half of them were brown leather-bound volumes that he had bought for a fraction of their retail cost from the estate of an ancient member of the Bar who had died leaving behind no one remotely interested in law. The rest he had made up from the library of a young advocate who had surrendered his practice because he could not make a living. These were unbound still, naked in their blue quarterly paperback volumes. But where the law reports ended, the shelves were empty. The senior advocates had plush offices, their wall-to-wall, floor-to-ceiling bookcases bursting with the latest editions of expensive titles. The juniors had to use the library.

To inspire confidence, he had tried to create a learned ambience in his office: the walls were covered by a wallpaper that artfully resembled wood panelling. To his right hung a photograph of his graduation class, a few old maps and his framed law degrees. On the wall facing his chair was a print of Magritte's 'Memory' which he had picked up cheaply at a poster shop and had box-mounted. It was the only unconventional item in his office, but he was so intrigued by the incongruous juxtaposition of serenity and violence that he had to have it.

Should he take the opportunity of a day off and go into town to join the march? Was it the responsible thing for an advocate to do? Or should he sit in his office like a beggar waiting for crumbs to drop off the tables of his colleagues? He knew what his mother would say. And Elmarie. He looked into Magritte's painting as if the answer were to be found there.

The statue's white head stood smiling on the flat top of a stone wall – perhaps the window-ledge of a villa – with a cloudy sky and calm blue sea as a backdrop. A curtain, hanging behind her, obstructed part of the view with its brown folds. A withered leaf lay on the cold stone between the statue's long, graceful neck and one of Magritte's mysterious spheres. The statue had an alarming splotch of blood on her temple which belied her peaceful expression. The painting seemed to interpret the times; it mirrored the chaos of transition in South Africa. By mistake, Jeremy took another mouthful of the vile coffee and grimaced as he swallowed.

On the floor, a pot plant, its gnarled tendrils wrapped around a supporting stick, complained of thirst. But water just ran uselessly through the sand, leaving it as dry as before. Elmarie said it looked poor and he should throw it out, but he had a sentimental attachment to the plant; it had travelled with him since he was at university. He could not discard it, ugly as it was.

With a sudden rush of exultation, Jeremy Spielman unknotted his tie. He *would* go into town; he wanted to recreate in the streets the excitement of his student days, the freedom from the stifling responsibility of his job and the expectations of the women in his life. He ceremoniously draped the tie over his chair and almost ran out of his office.

Lewis Singer was waiting for the lift, shifting his weight from foot to foot. The rotund, pale-faced advocate was gowned and carried a square brown case which would have contained the books necessary for his day in court. 'Have you left your jacket at home?' he asked; the question was supposed to be a joke, but it sounded like an accusation.

'It's a glorious summer's day,' Jeremy said blandly. 'I'm going for a walk.'

'Oh well, unfortunately I'm in court,' Singer said pointedly, 'or I might be tempted to join you. It's too nice to be indoors really.'

'The sun would do you good,' Jeremy teased gently, then turned to Fatiema. 'If anyone calls, I'll be back by lunchtime.' The woman smiled conspiratorially; she knew where he was going.

The lift was full of lawyers and litigants and Jeremy felt vulnerable without his jacket and tie. He parried a few curious glances and nodded to one or two people he knew. Lifts were uncomfortable places at the best of times because no one knew where to look. But Lewis, who took up too much space, made it worse. Jeremy found himself pressed close to a tall, neat man who smelled of a viciously sweet aftershave, and he hoped for a quick descent without a stop at other floors. When the lift doors finally opened on the ground, the passengers burst into the arcade and the forgotten heat of the day. Lewis scurried left towards Keerom Street, Jeremy went right.

Police waited on the corner of Queen Victoria and Wale Streets, opposite St George's Cathedral. Jeremy heard a distant ululating that raised the adrenalin in his blood and made him want to run to join the action. How times had changed! In the bad old days, the police, now so restrained, would have been tearing through the streets like wild animals. But now they stood impassively, some holding shotguns, their dogs grinning at the recollection of former battles and the expectation of another today. Could these beasts and their masters shrug off a lifetime's training in a few months? A policeman had been quoted in the newspaper saying: 'It's very frustrating. One minute the guy is your enemy. The next, you have to risk your life to save him.'

The previous week, an intended march to protest against the conditions in black schools had gone horribly wrong. The organisers refused to apply for permission, saying it was their democratic right to march. Black teachers and pupils emerged from a meeting in the Cathedral hall to find that the police had cut off the way into the city; coils of razor-barbed wire had converted the church into a concentration camp. Between five and eight hundred protesters, banked like a choir on the Cathedral steps, chanted threats at a police water-cannon, which was eventually goaded into spitting back, blasting schoolchildren into the blades. Then the furious mob erupted, hurtling down St George's Street, flinging bricks through shop windows, smashing cars and overturning tables at pavement cafés.

But today's march was different: it was majestic and peaceful. A huge black, green and gold banner of the banned African National Congress openly taunted the police, who, this time, did not react. Smaller banners and posters, bobbing above the heads of the crowd, demanded that Nelson Mandela be released from prison and proclaimed that the 'people' would govern.

Jeremy waded into the crowd, into the slow-moving current past the banks of marshals who wore red and white T-shirts and yellow headbands. It was like being in a mighty river, flowing through the ravine of the street between the cliffs of the buildings. It surged and buffeted him: every now and then there would be a crush from the rear, propelling him forward, hands in his back; then it would suddenly slow, leaving him in a calm, open area in which sweating and shining people huffed and grunted in that township shuffle-cum-war-dance, the *toyi-toyi*, which terrified most whites and stirred most blacks to joy or revolution. Office workers sprouted out of windows, over balconies, from rooftops, like bushes and grasses clinging to the sheer faces of the ravines through which the black waters of the march inexorably flowed. One of those faces must have belonged to Elmarie, filled with fear and loathing at the massed ranks below. The rumbling thunder of thousands of mouths and feet filled the space between the buildings, trapped in the well of the street.

At the top of Adderley Street – the closest point to Parliament – the marchers paused and whistled and jeered. The marshals, hot and anxious, channelled the stragglers back into the main flow. Foreign journalists, hoping that the protest would degenerate into chaos, were dressed in heavy flak jackets despite the heat. Weighed down by their video cameras and sound equipment, they were ready to convey to the world's television screens any indiscretions committed by the State in upholding apartheid. A yellow police helicopter with a blue belly clung tenuously to the steaming air, provoking a salvo of angry black fists.

Exulting at his new freedom, a black man had climbed up on the statue of General Jan Smuts. He straddled the head of the prime minister who was toppled from power by the Afrikaner nationalists in 1948; his feet clad in running shoes were planted firmly on the statue's green shoulders. His mouth was open in a smile that showed off both rows of teeth, as white as the cricketer's hat that topped his round face. While the marchers clapped and stamped their approval, he levelled a wooden rifle and sprayed them with imaginary bullets.

The sun glared down. Jeremy wondered if it would ever be cool again; irrationally he feared that the sun would scorch the earth beyond its ability to recover. The fire on the mountain was the precursor of hell on earth. His wet shirt stuck to his body; he would have to go home after the march – he certainly could not return to work. He squinted as the pitiless white heat assaulted his eyes. Feet kicked his legs and, when other bodies got in the way, he struck out with his elbows. But no one seemed to care; the excitement acted as an anaesthetic.

The march ended where it had begun, at the Parade, empty of the cars that usually parked there. The leaders climbed on to the back of a flatbed truck which was to be a makeshift stage and the thousands who had followed fanned out to hear them speak.

The City Hall presided over the square, divided from it by a street and a row of palm trees. The grand old sandstone building was golden in the brilliant noon sunlight; its clock tower had timed the events of the city from 1905. It had counted the hours since the ANC was banned on April 8th, 1960; now the people were demanding that it be witness to the reversal of that decision. A black trade unionist had the microphone and was threatening F. W. de Klerk, who was at that moment speaking in Parliament, not more than five minutes' walk away. 'If you don't lift the ban on the organisations, release political prisoners and Nelson Mandela today,' he railed, 'we will do it ourselves with our struggle in the factories, trains, *shebeens* and churches . . .'

What chance of that? It was surely just more rhetoric, wishful thinking with which oppressed people kept their spirits and their rebellions burning. A seagull circled and screeched mockingly from its blood-red mouth.

Jeremy realised he was continually glancing over his shoulder, expecting the worst, waiting for loose-limbed police dogs to come loping over the tarmac and crazy trails of teargas to zigzag from the parking floors of the Golden Acre where the riot police hid. He remembered how he once sat shivering in the passenger seat of a friend's car on the university campus while a policeman flexing a *sjambok* stalked outside, not sure whether Jeremy was one of the crowd of demonstrators into which he and his fellows had charged. Their eyes met – it was like staring into the emotionless face of a prowling lion, intense with concentration as it searched for a sign of weakness. But the law student did not blink and the predator moved on. P. W. Botha had frowned down from the teargas haze that hung over the rugby field that day.

And now, a youth leader was continuing the meeting, addressing the alternative Parliament on the square. Using information to which the inner circles of the anti-apartheid groups were perhaps privy, which had not yet been released to the public, which de Klerk was possibly even now announcing in Parliament, he declared: 'The ANC is unbanned.'

The statement could easily have been passed over, misinterpreted as just another demand. Jeremy heard it with disbelief, especially as the speaker did not amplify his remark, but followed on with more political bombast.

'We do not mince our words when we say that we have always been the ANC,' he declared. 'Our task is to intensify the struggle. F. W. de Klerk must resign and Nelson Mandela must be the State President. Our marches,' he concluded, 'must now address the question of storming the Bastille.' He pointed at the Castle, headquarters of the army in the Western Cape. The crowd roared like a lion, chanting: 'ANC! ANC! ANC!', dredging the bellow from deep inside lusty chests, perhaps not fully comprehending what the speaker had said, but instinctively knowing that the dream was coming true.

Cold slivers of emotion pierced the heat that had stifled Jeremy's body; icy needles penetrated the muscles of his shoulders and neck. The day before, it had been a criminal offence to promote the aims of the ANC; now its leaders were standing up in public and freely extolling its virtues as if the law had been replaced secretly overnight. Jeremy closed his eyes and the sunlight seared through his eyelids, driving out the shadows that had been hidden there for years.

A former treason trialist had taken over the microphone. He wore a politician's dark suit and adjusted his gold-rimmed spectacles on his nose, practising for the day when he would speak inside the Hall of Power instead of denouncing it.

'Today,' he said, 'thirty years after the banning of the ANC, this march is of special significance. In 1960 the ANC was banned and there was a march on the Parade. Now, thirty years later, the ANC is unbanned and there is another rally on the Parade. The people,' he stated ambiguously, 'have unbanned the ANC themselves ...' He wiped his sweating black face with a handkerchief. A small white boy with long blond hair stood on the truck next to him: a symbol of the new non-racial South Africa, the hope for the future.

In the heat, the golden walls of the City Hall, now a library and home of the orchestra, beamed down gently on the proceedings. At one end of the Parade were a row of stalls selling Muslim foods and Coca-Cola to a mainly coloured and black clientele. And at the opposite end the 'Bastille', built in the shape of a five-pointed star, crouched like a spider, ready to dart in and nullify the decisions made in Parliament and on the Parade, the two centres of power today.

The crowd was baying for Winnie Mandela, the Mother of the Nation, to speak. She gripped the microphone with one pudgy fist; the other was clenched defiantly to the sky. She was the embodiment of the ANC: she wore a gold and black suit, a green blouse and a green military beret on which blossomed ANC and Communist Party badges. 'We are not prepared to accept a bone without meat!' she proclaimed. The public address system, which had been playing up throughout the meeting, cut out and Mandela's words were eaten up by crackle.

'Sabotage!' someone cried.

'It's the Government!' yelled a hoarse voice from the crowd. 'They want to silence you!' And then a chorus broke out: 'Viva ANC! Viva South African Communist Party! Amandla! Power!'

'We want power!' Winnie Mandela shrieked. 'Unbanning the ANC is no deal. This is not what we expected today. We expected de Klerk to tell us we must go to Victor Verster Prison and fetch Comrade Nelson.' The cheering lifted her up into the hot sky, fist raised like a black Statue of Liberty, until she spun out of sight. Only a matchbox marked the spot where she had stood. The woman chairing the meeting brought the celebrants back to earth, asking everyone to return home in a disciplined manner.

'Where are you going?' asked a young black man with a squint which must have distorted his view of the world to such an extent that he believed Jeremy would take him back to his township.

'To my office,' the lawyer said, and the supplicant, until then riding high on an illusion that everyone at the meeting had been suffused with goodwill, turned away, deflated, to join the surge for the trains.

The crowd spurted across the footbridge over Strand Street. Vendors at the entrance to the station had hidden their banks of fruit under black plastic sheets. One of them, a middle-aged man with a wrinkled oriental face and a permanent stoop from bending to dig in fruit cartons, was slapping his flat hand on the lid of a rubbish bin like a cheerleader urging on his team. '*Viva* ANC!' he shouted whenever someone strayed too close to his fruit, and, pointing to the stairs, he ordered: 'Go!'

A teenager in a black leather jacket and with trousers rolled up round his ankles had got through the defences. He sauntered off insolently, his face buried in a stolen mango. The vendor watched, silent for a moment, without trying to intercept him. Jeremy, who had been swept out on the current of excitement, stopped and then turned back, followed by the fruit-seller's voice, more insistent than before as he desperately tried to save his stock from nationalisation by the masses.

Before stepping off the pavement into Strand Street, the lawyer had to wait for a jubilant group brandishing ANC flags in a victory salute to dance past. A black mama, with MARSHAL printed on her T-shirt, shuffled and bobbed beside them, her watermelon breasts heaving the letters in waves across her chest. The right side of her mouth was paralysed; from the cavernous left escaped a chilling cry of 'To Sea Point!' and the dancers *toyi-toyied* towards High Level Road, a police van pacing them at a distance, well behind.

Newspaper posters confirmed the message from the Parade: FW UNBANS ANC. How had those orators known? Had there been secret discussions beforehand between the Government and the liberation movements? Had the press, in collusion with the ANC, leaked the news? Clusters of people huddled around early copies of *The Argus*. As Jeremy walked past the Supreme Court, the red-eyed doorkeeper with a gloved right hand and tobacco-leaf face was saying to a policeman: 'It's going to be like Rhodesia.'

'*Ja*, the *kaffirs* will take over,' was the gloomy rejoinder.

'It's the beginning of the end.'

The cell of cold air at the entrance to Huguenot Chambers was as exhilarating as a splash of cold water from one of the chilly mountain rivers that his father had loved so much. When Jeremy stepped into the lift, two young white lawyers, wearing trendy ties, entered with him.

Red tie said in Afrikaans: 'It's a carnival in the street. They're really making merry.'

Green tie replied: 'They've got rocks in their pockets.'

To which his friend answered with a snort: 'They've got rocks in their heads.'

Jeremy butted in. 'I saw no rocks,' he said in English.

'Their pockets were bulging,' green tie said apologetically, uncomfortable that the conversation had been overheard and disapproved of.

'Maybe with copies of the Freedom Charter,' Jeremy retorted, getting out of the lift at his floor. So much for ever receiving work from that firm, he thought wryly.

Lewis Singer was picking up a brief at the reception desk. He greeted Jeremy pensively, like a mole emerging from a murky hole. It was only midday and a shadow was already starting to darken his chin, undermining the softness of his baby-pale face.

'Did you hear the news?' Jeremy asked. He had to talk to someone about the morning's excitement, even if it was only to Lewis.

'No. I came back from court straight into a consultation. What news?'

'F.W. unbanned the ANC and the PAC and the Communist Party,' Jeremy announced triumphantly, as if he had had something to do with the decision and was also due some credit.

Singer, his thick glasses hiding his expression, said solemnly: 'I feel very emotional as I stand here. What about Mandela?'

'There's no word yet about his release. But it can't be too long now.'

'I've always liked F.W.,' Lewis said. 'I thought he'd do the right thing. Now sanctions must end. There's nothing to stop investment from flowing into the country.' He turned and made for the toilet, shaking his head in wonder. 'Who would have guessed?'

That's the only reason you're happy, Spielman thought, opening his office door. Not because of the millions of black people who'll begin to taste freedom at last after three hundred years of colonialism and then apartheid, but because your bank balance might improve. He regretted now that he had chosen to share such a special event with such an unsympathetic audience.

He flopped into his chair and sat back staring at the Magritte for a long time until the blood seemed to well and flow over the white brow and to spatter on the cold stone below. The heavy brown curtain was being drawn open behind that placid head, but the sky was full of clouds: the storms that had been covered up for so long were yet to break.

3

Fallout

Jeremy's cottage welcomed him with its usual sweet, comforting smell. The light on his answering machine was flickering and before he put down his briefcase he pressed the play button. Elmarie spoke to him as he raised the blinds and pulled up the sash windows. She was so cheerful on the phone; sometimes he thought he had fallen in love with her voice and not with her in person.

'Hello, it's me. Are you OK?' He could hear deep concern. 'I called you at work but they said you were out. In court, I suppose. I didn't leave my name. I've been in my office all day; it's too hot to go outside. Please give me a ring when you're free.' There was a click, and then Elmarie again: 'Are you still not back?' She paused as if she were not sure what to say next, and concluded: 'I worry about you. Please call me.' There were no other messages.

They did not discuss politics on the phone unless she was being mean, as before the march. Phones were tapped, and why give the security police ammunition to use against him, even if all he did these days was to attend a few political meetings and appear in the occasional political trial?

In 1988 a car bomb exploded outside the Ellis Park rugby stadium in Johannesburg after a big match and two spectators were killed. Soon afterwards, a security policeman knocked on Elmarie's door and asked her questions about Jeremy's activities as a member of the small anti-apartheid group, Jews for Justice. It must have seemed a wonderful opportunity for them: here they had an Afrikaner with access to the heart of a group they could not otherwise penetrate. She assured the policeman – a clean-cut executive with a briefcase, not the thug one might have expected – that Jeremy was not involved in any violence. He appealed to her 'as a patriot' to pass on any information 'which may be of interest'. It was a chilling interview, she sobbed when she told Jeremy (in person, not over the phone): she felt dirty, as if she were a criminal. When the man left, she sat in the bath and scrubbed her skin until it was red. But the invasion, short and polite as it was, festered in her mind – she could not erase it by washing. (How brave the black activists must have been, Jeremy thought, they who were not protected by white skins from the fury of the rulers.)

He made a decision then. Rather than have Elmarie choose between her safety (and sanity) and her loyalty to him, he phoned a few of his fellow members to announce his resignation from the organisation: he gave no reasons and of course they were shocked and did not understand. It was a bitter decision to give up a cause in which he believed because he loved her. But Elmarie was not harassed again. Perhaps relationships are strengthened by such moments of trauma, Jeremy thought, a shared danger that you have survived together. She had stared into the cold white eyes of apartheid and the experience had shown her an ugly picture of herself and left her utterly distressed. But instead of confronting the beast, she had withdrawn even further into the fearful territory of the white *laager*. And she had tried to take him with her.

Jeremy peeled off his clothes which clung to his wet body like a second skin. He walked naked to the kitchen to switch on the kettle, reflecting how easy his life was compared to that of the blacks. He had only to put up with the discomfort for the duration of a five-minute drive from the centre of town; the blacks, forced by law to live in far-flung corners of the Cape Flats, had to travel home jammed into hot, sticky public transport.

He sank into the bath, nursing his coffee, while the healing waters soaked the grime out of his skin. When he felt better, he partially drew the lounge curtains to conceal himself from the view of the block of flats that loomed over his yard; sometimes he forgot, to the probable amusement of the tenants. With a bow to modesty, he wrapped a towel around his waist and dialled the number of the magazine where Elmarie worked.

'I'm well,' she said brightly. She spoke English with that rounded, cultured tongue so often used by Afrikaners trying to disguise their home accents. 'And how was your day?'

'I went to a function,' he said, using one of their code words. Who was he fooling? The security police had the whole march and rally on video surely, and were, even now, poring over the pictures, identifying faces in the crowd. 'I'll tell you later. Should we go for supper?'

41

'I'll be too late,' she said. 'I'm working on a story. Come over at eight and we can go for a walk.'

Disappointed, he said: 'Fine', and put the phone down. He had forgotten how to be alone – an art which he had learned when he left his parents' home and moved into a rented flat in Vredehoek. He had had casual relationships (names half-remembered) with long months between, during which the cold pages of legal textbooks substituted for the passion that Elmarie eventually fired into his life. When his father died, Jeremy had used his inheritance substantially to pay for his house in Ivy Street in which his mother believed he was going to produce Jewish grandchildren. But, instead of the Jewish wife, Elmarie appeared, a volatile, beautiful Afrikaner who breached the fortress of sadness into which Jeremy had withdrawn. She mothered him when there was no one else to do so, when his own mother was so in need of comfort that she could not get out of bed and relied on Vivian, the maid, to feed her. Elmarie sat with Esta's son and held his hand while he grieved, laying the foundation of the relationship that was later to become so turbulent.

Suddenly at a loss, Jeremy clicked open his briefcase and took out a new law report which he had not yet read. He turned the pages, staring at the blocks of type, but they refused to yield their meaning. Instead, his eyes projected images of a sea of people on to the fussy pages, and they swept away the words. Elmarie was there, on one of the balconies, looking down at him, disapproving.

Outside, the lid of the post box thudded and Jeremy pulled on his jeans and a shirt to fetch the evening newspaper. Ivy Street had not changed since de Klerk's speech; it had not developed ruts, nor had the tar melted – it sloped down gently and unremarkably as before. As usual, the Muslim fruit-seller had parked his lorry on the corner under the oak tree. Mr Pretorius was leaning against the rusty passenger door, chatting to the foxy-faced merchant whose sons were playing cricket in the street with a tennis ball and an apple box as the wicket. The old Afrikaner would not have sought out company like this in his healthier days, but, as he neared death, perhaps skin colour did not matter as much as having somone to talk to.

Nor had the world beyond been altered violently by de Klerk's announcement. Late afternoon cars crawled up Kloof Street, heading home as normal. No one was panicking. Hordes of blacks were not rioting, nor were whites shouting at looters from the barricades of their homes. But the headline in the newspaper drove home the irrevocable change in the political order as surely as a spear launched into the heart of white suburbia: ANC UNBANNED. The subhead quoted from de Klerk's speech: 'The season of violence is over. The time of reconstruction and reconciliation has arrived . . .' The events of the day had indeed not been a dream.

Jeremy read on his way inside, feeling a warm glow of pride at having played a part, however small, in this momentous day. He put the newspaper on the floor, the law report a forgotten blue cone on the coffee table, and absorbed the experiences of the journalists, comparing them to his own. Perhaps he would now be able to speak on the telephone without fear. He should call his mother and welcome her to the new South Africa, opened up by the most unlikely of gatekeepers, the National Party, which had slammed the door of apartheid shut forty-two years before. A new man, not bred in that earlier generation, had forged the keys.

Jeremy dressed quickly, burning with the fires of change, hopeful in a way he had not been from the time he became aware that he was white in South Africa and that blacks were oppressed. Now, at last, a future was possible, free from the old strifes and hatreds. Now all those parents who wanted to leave 'for the sake of the children' could store away their emigration applications and settle down to build a new country.

The road to Sea Point sang under the tyres of his car. Crowds of people exulted at street corners, spilling out from the Muslim Bo-Kaap suburb which bordered the city centre, and gathering in pockets along his route. Whoops of joy at liberation entered the car through the open window.

It was too early for Elmarie so he parked outside his mother's flat. He stood before the security door in the foyer, his finger poised over the buzzer next to her name. But an image of her jowled face appeared in the glass and her mouth opened to unleash a tirade of anger at the black mobs who would now invade her white world. Suddenly weary, he turned away and went down the steps to the street. The maids in Sea Point seemed as yet untouched by the unbanning. A group sat or lay on the lawn of the flats, probably to escape their oven-rooms during this fiery summer. They were chatting loudly; one or two had wide-eyed babies who would know a freedom that had come too late for their mothers. Vivian was not among them.

Jeremy walked along the promenade as the mist skimmed the cool sea and Lion's Head reared above Sea Point, dominating the skyline with its olive-green slopes. Nearly all of his friends had left the country to escape the turmoil of the blacks' struggle against the white minority government – they could see no hope of a peaceful future. But Jeremy had stayed, and now his decision to stick it out had paid off; and the mountain seemed to be saying thank you. A single tree near the top hung on stubbornly at an impossible angle, appearing to exist against all odds up there, until you realised how solid a base it had: its position in the world was all a matter of perspective.

He leaned against the railing, staring out to sea, over the jagged rocks, bared like eager black teeth at the white-owned land. He watched a ship glide into the mythical blue country where the sea and the sky met, leaving a smudge of smoke as its signature on the still air, the only proof it had passed this way.

He wanted then, desperately, to share his joy with Elmarie, to walk with her, feeling her hot young skin under his fingers. He would lay his arm across her strong shoulders, descended from those of pioneers who had tamed the South African wilderness and farmers who had turned the angry dry land. His thin hairy white arm came from generations of merchants who had spent a good deal of their lives fleeing from Jew-haters in Europe and Asia. It was ironic that he, from immigrant stock, was committed to Africa, rooted in the land like that flimsy tree on the head of the lion. On the other hand, she, from a line of fighters, was struggling to come to terms with the power of the conquered nations who had risen from the dust, demanding their land back. Lion's Head had watched over the conquest three hundred years before; now it was presiding over the wheel's full turn.

Two tramps, reeking of the sea, rolled by on rubber legs as if the promenade were the heaving deck of a ship in a storm. 'Ag, Nelson Mandela will never be released in his lifetime,' one said. The other replied: 'You never know. Negotiations are still taking place.'

Jeremy smiled. The current political jargon had even sunk to the level of the meths drinkers. But their more notorious ways of interacting had certainly not been erased by the sudden freedoms of this extraordinary day. A shrivelled man and woman, eyes reduced to slits in bloated red faces, had detached themselves from the benches where they probably spent most of their time. For no obvious reason, they began to flail at each other in dreamlike slow motion, their language as putrid as excrement under the noses of the prim whites walking their perfumed dogs.

'*Jou ma se moer!*' he bellowed at her and she screamed back: '*Fok off!*' The two voices, bound by hate and need, interleaved in a peculiarly South African harmony. A gay couple minced past, moustaches bristling in amused distaste, as if despairing at the drop in standards in this bright new Third World country.

There was no security door to protect Elmarie's block of flats. A rubber plant, placed in the foyer to give the impression of luxuriance, had been bleached yellow by the afternoon sun drilling through the glass façade and revealed neglect and decay instead. It reminded Jeremy of the faded Sea Point widows, whom no amount of perfume and dressing up could rejuvenate.

Elmarie answered the door in her red dressing gown, shaking drops of water from her long brown hair. Her green eyes glittered defiantly into his; they were set wide apart, giving an impression of child-like innocence that was dispelled immediately by the tone of her greeting.

'Come in,' she said, inflecting the last word, pronouncing it sharply like a challenge. She had fine blonde hairs on her top lip and one of her front teeth was slightly skew. A scar flashed like a streak of lightning down the centre of her pale forehead. These were perhaps the only flaws in an otherwise perfect face – full lips, round cheeks flushed from the heat of her bath, small upturned nose that was obviously not Jewish.

She presented her mouth to be kissed – she was only just shorter than Jeremy – but he touched his lips on one of her high cheekbones instead. She closed her eyes for a moment at the pleasure of the intimacy as he wrapped his arms around her back and drew her close to him. But then she shook herself out of the trance and pulled away abruptly. The sweet smell of her soap lingered in the air between them. He followed her across the threshold into the flat.

The thick carpet, on which Persian rugs were scattered, helped give the lounge a richness that contrasted with the austerity of his cottage. The small peach-coloured room was cluttered with furniture: a white sofa, two brown armchairs, a coffee table, television set and a bookcase which contained literary titles and some cassette tapes. On one wall hung three Greek plates; on another a tapestry showing Noah's Ark, with pairs of animals leaning against the rails, being washed away to isolation by the floodwaters.

On top of the bookcase stood a photograph of her father: a young man with short dark hair and a fifties-style pencil moustache. His eyes were laughing at the photographer and the expression brought warmth and humanity to a face that could have been forbidding because it was so clinically handsome – a male version of his daughter.

A small dining-room table with three chairs took up a corner; it was covered with files, magazines, paper and pens – Elmarie did not own a word processor – accounts and a key-ring with her name on it. They had to step around the table as she led him into her bedroom. She had a large antique double bed of dark wood; its oppressiveness was offset by a cheerful white and pink duvet. A fluffy white rug lay on the floor where her foot would touch when she got up.

'I didn't expect you so early,' she said.

'I missed you,' he confessed, then teased: 'I thought I'd catch you in a compromising position with one of those journalists from your office.'

'No such luck,' she shot back, 'but you'll have to wait until I'm ready.'

He sat on the very edge of the bed as if he were on the point of flight; the roar of the hair-dryer drowned out any possibility of conversation. A novel – *Under the Volcano* by Malcolm Lowry – lay on her bedside table. He picked it up, attracted by the cover showing two children wearing skull masks trying to buy a drink in a crowded taverna on the Mexican Day of the Dead, but its impenetrable prose defeated him. His mind was tuned to reading law, not literature; he had no patience with novels.

Outside, a bell was tolling: '*Dolente . . . dolente!*' as in his dream. He heard it in the sudden stillness when Elmarie switched off the noisy machine, and he went to the window, but could not see a church, only the darkening blocks of flats and, between them, the oily swell of the sea.

'What was that?' he asked.

She was brushing her hair back, her mouth hung slightly open.

'What was what?' she asked abstractedly, watching herself in the mirror.

'Nothing.'

She took off her dressing gown and his eyes fastened with fascination on her slim naked figure with its small firm breasts and triangle of light brown hair that flared up from between her legs. He could never look at her enough; he was immeasurably grateful that he had access to such a beautiful body. He walked towards her in anticipation, but she was already putting on her jeans. He laid his hands on her brown shoulders and bent his head so that his lips could brush the warm skin on her back; she had soft, golden hair running down her spine. Then he pulled aside her curtain of shoulder-length dark hair and buried his mouth in the nape of her neck. She turned to face him and he kissed her while she snuggled closer, purring like a cat.

The sour-sweet smell of wine entered his mouth from hers, stale and erotic. A crystal glass, half-full of the pale yellow liquid, stood on her dresser beside an open packet of cigarettes.

'Come, let's go for that walk!' she exclaimed, pushing him away.

He blinked from the dizziness of their embrace, and, holding her fingertips in his, looked into her marble eyes. 'Have you eaten?'

She picked up her red T-shirt from the bed and slipped it over her head without putting on a bra. Her nipples were erect from their lovemaking and showed through the thin cotton.

'I had lunch in the canteen at work,' she said. 'I'm not hungry. Let's go.'

Reluctantly, he arranged his trousers so as to try and conceal the obvious swelling and they left the flat together. They crossed Main Road, lit and throbbing with shops and traffic and diners entering restaurants while beggars sat on the pavements outside. The air was rich with the smell of charcoal-grilled meat. He took her strong hand in his; he hated fat-fingered, pampered hands like his mother's.

'So how was the march?' She had understood the code-word 'function' which he had used on the phone. 'I was worried about you. Your secretary didn't know where you were but I guessed.'

'It was peaceful,' he replied. 'Were you watching?'

She bit her lip and said: 'Yes.'

'I could feel you up there, looking down.' He grinned. 'Like God.'

'Could you see me frowning?'

He laughed uneasily, but said nothing. The swelling in his groin had died down as they walked and as the threat of confrontation grew between them.

'I hate these marches,' she declared. 'They can get out of hand so easily.'

'Not if they're well controlled,' he said, 'and if the police stay out of it.'

'So it's all the police's fault?'

'You're a journalist. You cover these things. What do you think?'

'I'm not that sort of journalist,' she declared and pulled a face. 'I write about the lifestyles of the rich and famous and how to have the best orgasm.' Then she frowned. 'But you can't blame the police for everything. They're also under stress. I know. My mother's husband, Gert, used to be a policeman . . .'

'You've told me,' he said, trying to defuse a line of conversation that was potentially explosive.

'And whose side are you on?' she asked in a mocking tone. 'Did you toyi-toyi?'

'Like I was born in the townships,' he answered, rising to the bait in spite of his resolve. 'I shouted "Viva ANC" and waved my fist in the air.'

'You've got a lot of time,' she said cuttingly. 'I wonder how many other lawyers were there.'

'I didn't count,' he answered sullenly.

'You must be in heaven now that your organisation has been unbanned.'

'I'm pleased the lid is off the pot. The political situation can start to normalise.'

'Be careful what comes out of that pot.'

'At least there's hope now. There wasn't before.'

'What sort of hope do you see when a group of terrorists is allowed to run around freely?' she jibed.

He dropped her hand as if it had started dripping acid. 'They only turned to terrorism when peaceful ways failed to change anything,' he protested. 'You know that. They couldn't vote, their marches were banned, their leaders were arrested . . .' His defence of the ANC began to sound like the list of clichés he read in the newspapers. 'What would you have done if you were black?'

'I would have crossed the border and gone for military training in Russia,' she said vehemently, 'then I would have come back to fight. And that's what the Afrikaners will do if the blacks come to power.'

Their arguments were like familiar trains, suddenly out of control, racing towards each other down an old track. He said nothing, hoping by his silence to avoid the inevitable collision. But she was in full cry.

'What about the Jews?' she demanded. 'You people stirred all this up. But when things get too hot, you'll run off to Israel. The Afrikaners have nowhere else to go.'

'That's rubbish and you know it,' he retorted. 'The few Jews in the struggle could never have made millions of blacks rebel. Don't you think the blacks are clever enough to recognise their own suffering? Anyway I'm not going to run away. I'm a South African. This is my country.'

'All your Jewish friends said that before they emigrated.'

'That's what *they* decided, not me. And most of those who left went to America or Australia, not Israel. There's nothing to stop the Afrikaners from going as well. I hear some Afrikaners are buying farms in South America . . .'

'The Jews have got their homeland, the English have got theirs. Why can't we also have a country? That's all we want – a piece of land for ourselves.'

They had reached the beachfront and Jeremy looked about self-consciously, hoping no one was listening, but Elmarie's mood switched suddenly. 'Let's get an ice-cream,' she cried, her eyes bright as a child's. 'Come, don't let's fight.' She snuggled against him. 'Love me.'

But he could not turn off his anger. It sat in his chest like heartburn; it fogged his mind. Maybe his mother was right. Maybe he should find a 'nice Jewish girl' and settle down and make Jewish grandchildren.

'You know that I love you,' she said softly, melting into his side. 'I just get so cross sometimes.'

'I just can't stand racist talk,' he answered in a choked voice. 'It goes against everything I believe in . . .'

'Then why won't you marry me?' she burst out. 'Is it because I'm not Jewish?'

He did not answer; a darkness fell as if a bag had been dropped over his head and he could not see the light.

'Isn't that racist?' she asked. 'I get the feeling that you're just waiting for the right moment to leave. I mean why should you hang around here – all your friends have gone. And you aren't married, you've got no responsibilities. You can just pack your rucksack.'

The darkness opened a crack and the bloated face of the dying tramp leered at him from the depths of his dream. Then Elmarie was pulling his hand, tugging him towards the soft-serve counter. The trains that were their arguments had glanced off each other without serious damage. He allowed himself to be led, the bag of guilt dimming his sight. Maybe this was what bound him to the beautiful *shiksa* – guilt, in which his mother had schooled him well. Or maybe it was the perverse excitement of her mood swings: he never knew where he stood with her; she kept him guessing.

He dug into his pocket and produced a note which she exchanged for two cones. She kept the change and he did not ask for it. Across the road, the building in which his mother had her flat loomed over them like a tombstone. If Esta looked out of her tenth-floor window, she would see them, small as ants, as the darkness began to fall over Sea Point and the sun squeezed like an orange melon into the sea, leaking red juice across the horizon.

Jeremy bit blindly into the hard chocolate skin covering the vanilla ice-cream that she had put into his hand; Elmarie nibbled at the nuts which studded hers.

'Sometimes I want to leave here as well,' she said sadly. 'We've really turned into a Third World country.' Jeremy's stomach tightened, but he remained silent, grimly sucking the soft sweetness from within the brittle chocolate shell. 'Look at that mess down there.' On the beach below, black seaweed snakes curled around empty plastic cold drink containers.

'Do you know how those bottles get there?'

'Sailors drop them overboard?' he ventured, wondering what the point was.

'No,' she said scornfully. 'We had a story on it last week. It's the blacks. They use sea-water for medicine. But they're so stupid. They carry armfuls of empty bottles down to the sea, but when the bottles are full they're too heavy. So most get left behind.' And then she smiled. 'You're so involved with the blacks. Didn't you know that?'

He shook his head and continued to walk, making her hurry to catch up. She brushed the hair away from her forehead with the backs of·her fingers and her scar was as angry as blood. As beautiful as she was to him when they made love, as other men walking on the promenade might view her, flushed with the heat of anger, he could only see her as a monster, sexless, the cause of his upset.

A long, low mesmeric chant escaped from the background noise of the lapping sea as if someone were consulting his ancestors. Jeremy stopped and Elmarie joined him, silent, knowing she had gone too far. They stood side by side at the railings overlooking a tidal pool whose walls – painted white – had been carved out of the black rock. A spotlight, watching over the beach with its baleful orange eye, picked out a black man dancing on the flat top of one of the walls. He wore a white suit, white shoes and a white open-necked shirt; he could have stepped out of a night-club. The sea had left a wet sheen on the surface where his shuffling feet landed; he was dancing on water.

A few passers-by stopped to look at this enigmatic figure, his sharp clothes so much at odds with the primitive impulse that had him singing and clapping his hands in time to each measured step. Jeremy found that he had put his hand on Elmarie's shoulder and was stroking her neck, his exasperation dissipated; she was once again a soft human being, no longer a monster, but now a potential object of love.

Behind them, a few meths-drinkers were having a party of their own, parodying the dignified steps of the man on the wall. They fell and sucked in breath through toothless mouths and waved wine bottles, arms swinging like windmills as they heaved themselves from the sides of the public toilets where they seemed to cling like flies.

The sides of the tidal pool wall bulged into the dark sea, as wrinkled as elephant hide. The dancer's white reflection shot down, pencil-thin, into the black depths. Flecks of spume lay like candy floss on the water.

'Let's go,' Elmarie said, pulling away from Jeremy, slightly subdued by the haunting refrain of the man's song.

A procession of cars with black, yellow and green ANC flags draped over their bonnets hooted along Beach Road. Black fists punched out of windows and excited throats roared: '*Amandla!*' Elmarie tapped her jeans pocket, looking for her cigarettes and, realising she had left them at home, asked irritably: 'So, when are they going to let Mandela go?'

Jeremy thought for a long time before he answered. 'They'll have to do it soon or they'll lose all the goodwill they've created.'

'So why didn't they release him today?'

'Because he would have stolen de Klerk's thunder. F.W. is a very clever politician.'

'So clever that he's sold out his own people,' she said bitterly, unable to contain her temper. 'It doesn't matter to you. You don't intend to get married and have children in this country. When things get too bad here, you'll go to Israel or America or wherever . . .' .

Jeremy could not dredge up the emotion to argue; he did not have her energy to keep coming back for more. His arm was at his side, dropped from her shoulder. They walked in silence back to her flat. When they met, he had been dazzled by her beauty, she had nursed him back to health after his father died, they had attended political meetings together. He had had no reason to suspect the huge gulf in world views between them. She had hidden her standpoint well – or he had been too blind to see it.

'Do you want something to eat?' she asked after she had unlocked the door and they stood in the lounge. 'I've got some stew in the fridge. I can heat it up.'

'It's not kosher,' he said meanly, and immediately regretted the remark; her comments drove him to be nasty, she goaded him until he reacted.

'Stop making fun of everything I say,' she lashed out.

'I'm sorry.'

'You don't let up,' she accused him. 'Any chance to get at me. We can't go on like this. We just bicker all the time.'

He could have replied: 'You start it, don't you see? Your insecurity that I'll run away will one day make me go. You will create what you most want to avoid.' But instead he said: 'We can't break up. I won't give my mother the satisfaction.'

She gaped for words and finally came up with: 'You want to keep our affair going just to spite your mother? You *are* mad.'

He shook his head as if he were trying to dislodge a heavy weight that had settled there. 'No,' he conceded and the word had to be dragged out of his mouth. 'Because I love you.' He put his arms round her shoulders and squeezed her until her face, hard with anger, was forced to wrinkle into a smile. 'Can't we try and be nice to each

52

other?' he pleaded. 'It used to be so good between us.' Her lips were moist when he found them, but then she pulled away. She stretched for her pack of Camels on the coffee table and her hand trembled as she took one out. She turned her head while she lit it so she would not blow smoke into his face.

The doorbell rang and Elmarie started, fearful, Jeremy thought suddenly, that it was another man coming to visit; perhaps one of the Afrikaner reporters from her magazine with the same conservative outlook, someone with whom she had more in common. She reached the door with quick steps and opened it. Almost with relief she blurted out: 'Hello, Ma.'

The woman Elmarie let in wore a yellow tracksuit and white running shoes although her stocky figure had not known much exercise. Her weatherbeaten face, pounded by years of smoking and drinking, betrayed traces of the beauty she had bequeathed to her daughter. Her bleached blonde permed hair did not make her look any younger; instead it added to her decrepitude. She came in with a cigarette dangling from her mouth.

'Hello, Jeremy,' she said in a guttural accent. They always spoke English for his benefit, even though he was fluent in Afrikaans, as an advocate had to be.

'Hello,' he replied. He did not address her by name; not Mrs Coetzee, nor Marie. If he married Elmarie, would he be able to call this woman from a foreign culture 'Mother'? It would be very difficult. 'How are you?'

'Well,' she stressed. 'I'm fine.'

'Come in, Ma. Do you want a cup of coffee?'

'I'll have some tea.' She sat down, putting her handbag on the table. 'You know, Jeremy,' she confided, 'I took a chance coming here on the freeway tonight.' She gnawed on the nail of her right index finger. 'I didn't know if it would be safe.'

'I'm glad you made it,' he said, a little too solicitously. 'You never know what could happen on a day like this.'

But his touch of sarcasm was lost on her. 'Just let them try and throw me with a stone,' she replied defiantly. She stubbed out her cigarette in an ashtray and unzipped her bag: a revolver lay heavily in a nest of tissues and cosmetics. 'They'll get what for.'

Cautiously, so as not to betray his alarm, Jeremy moved well out of the line of fire. Marie took a packet of Lucky Strikes from her bag, tapped it so that one slid out, and flicked her lighter.

'*Ag*, I don't know what the Government is doing,' she said, inhaling deeply. She shook her head and looked down into the carpet. 'When we voted them in last time, they didn't say anything about all this.'

Elmarie returned with a laden tray. 'Is anything wrong?' she asked, seeing her mother's expression.

'I was just telling Jeremy I can look after myself. I've lived with the blacks and the coloureds long enough.' Marie moved her bag to the floor to clear a space for the cups and Jeremy surreptitiously ducked out of the way of the gun again. 'When we were children, before all this apartheid, we lived next to the blacks.' She pulled on her cigarette, then exhaled and was lost for a moment in a cloud of smoke. When she reappeared, she looked Jeremy in the eye for the first time since she came in. Her thick eyebrows were brown, which gave away the real colour of her hair. 'You seem surprised? They lived with us in the same street. Then they had to move out. You know why?' She uttered a gravelly laugh when he shook his head. 'Because our husbands sometimes used to take a black woman to the back room and sleep with her.' She jabbed out her cigarette and lit another. 'The Nats were scared the Afrikaner men were going to become tramps and live with the *kaffirs* and have coloured children.' She licked her lips as if her mouth had suddenly become dry and then continued: 'You know when this apartheid law goes, there'll be real trouble here.'

Elmarie handed Jeremy a cup of tea, and, as he took it, he realised his fists had balled so tightly that his fingers were stiff.

'It's not just one law,' he explained. 'There are lots of laws, dealing with every part of life in South Africa. The Group Areas Act stopped different races living in the same suburbs. The Immorality Act made it illegal for blacks and whites to sleep together. There are many others as well. But they don't work any more: it's become impossible to force people apart. Some of the laws have already been scrapped; the others will go soon . . .'

'No, I don't know about that,' Marie Coetzee replied, 'but the rich people can buy their apartheid. The rest of us just have to accept.' She shrugged and stirred her tea. 'Well, my boy. It's all over now. My first husband was a stoker on the railways. When he died, Elmarie was still a child. I brought up my daughter the best I could by myself. Nobody helped me. Now it's up to her.'

'Ma, how do you like these cups?' Elmarie asked, obviously changing the subject. 'They're new.'

'*Ja*. Very nice.' Marie picked up her cup and absently examined the intricate design of multicoloured butterflies rising from garlands of pink and blue flowers. 'Where did you get them?'

'At an antique shop. They only had three. I bought them all. I love them.' The cups were fluted and awkward to drink from. You had to put your lips in one of the indentations and there they remained, unable to slide around the rim. Beautiful traps. Jeremy murmured that he also liked them.

'And how's Gert?' Elmarie asked, using her questions to keep the conversation off politics: the events of the day had cast a long shadow. Her hands gripped her cup as if she were trying to warm herself against some hidden source of coldness. Her face had frozen into a brittle smile when Marie mentioned the death of her father; the scar was an icy fault in her smooth brow.

'I last saw him on the weekend.' Marie sipped her tea, looked at the cup closely as her mouth got caught and suspiciously put it back in the saucer. 'He was drunk again. He passed out on the bed and I took my housekeeping money out of his pocket.' Her laugh sounded like someone trying to start a car with a flat battery. 'It was pay-day. He'll never know it's gone. He'll think he spent it in the bar.'

She smiled at Jeremy warmly as if she had accepted him as part of the family; she had forgotten their political differences. It was hard to be angry with her even though he detested her racist attitudes. She blew smoke into the room and her possible son-in-law did not flinch as the cloud wafted over him. When she smiled, her face softened like rain falling on parched earth.

'I live off his police pension,' she said, leaning forward, taking Jeremy into her confidence. 'He gives me his cheque every month and then I give him a little bit back, like pocket money. Otherwise he'd drink it all away.' She coughed and put her hand in front of her mouth, her cigarette trailing smoke in the shape of a question mark. Then she recovered and continued: 'He's got a job as a security guard and I also help him spend his salary.'

'Someone's got to keep the household going,' Elmarie apologised for her mother.

'Why haven't you seen him since the weekend?' Jeremy asked. 'It's Friday today.'

'He works night duty and sleeps in the day. When he wakes up, I go out.'

'They're like two little mice,' Elmarie said. 'They've both got their own rooms and they hide from each other.'

'I'm all alone at night,' Marie went on stoutly. 'But I don't get scared. I leave the *stoep* light on.' She swallowed the last of her tea and made to get up. 'All right,' she said. 'I just popped in to see you. I was visting some friends in town.' She cast a hooded glance at Jeremy from under her bushy eyebrows. 'I've got lots of friends, you know.'

'Of course,' Jeremy said sympathetically.

'Well I'd better go before it's too late.' She smeared the butt of her cigarette into the pan of the ashtray, already grey from the detritus of all that she had smoked during her short visit. The coughing returned and gripped her in a series of convulsions as if she were being punched in the stomach. She drew in a deep breath, sucking in the air through her mouth before exhaling roughly. 'You know,' she boasted when she could speak again, 'I've got five ashtrays in my lounge.'

'Ma, you smoke too much,' Elmarie said anxiously.

'*Ja*, well I'm too old to change my habits now.' Marie picked up her bag, stood, and said as she walked to the door: 'I bought some sago at the Hyperama today. I'll make you a pudding.'

'Thanks, Ma.'

'OK, bye Jeremy,' Marie called. 'Nice to see you again. Bye Elmarie.'

'Drive carefully,' the lawyer said. 'I'm sure you'll be fine.'

'Give me a ring when you get home,' Elmarie added. She showed her mother out but the women did not kiss; they had not touched at all.

'Mothers!' Jeremy exclaimed after the door had closed. 'The cause of all our troubles.'

'Don't blame them,' Elmarie rebuked him. 'You've got to take responsiblility for yourself. My mother was a shit but I don't blame her. She didn't give me anything like your parents gave you. I didn't have a wonderful education. I had to leave school in standard eight and go to work in a bank. I did my matric through a correspondence college.' She looked around for a cigarette, did not find one, and instead took a sip of wine from a half-empty glass. 'So I don't know why you're blaming your mother. I wish I had a mother like yours.' She put the glass down too hard and some wine spilled on her fingers; she licked it off. 'My father was killed when I was seven and my mother stopped caring for me. Despite what she says. We travelled up and down the country wherever she could get a job. I went to five different schools. She used to have men in her room and she didn't even care if the door was open. I used to hear them . . .' Elmarie turned her head away so that he could not see her expression, but her breath was shallow. 'At least your father gave you security. Everything I have I made for myself. But I don't blame anyone.'

It was no use pointing out that she was indeed laying blame. What a boil his comment had lanced for so much venom to pour out!

'Listen,' he said quietly. 'I've had a heavy day. I'd better be going too. I'll see you tomorrow.'

'What have you done today?' She wouldn't let him escape; he usually slept over on Friday nights. 'You've been *toyi-toying* with the blacks while I've been working.'

'My case was postponed. It was no use me sitting in the office drinking tea, especially when the march was on. What did you expect me to do?'

She sighed. 'I don't know. Our relationship doesn't seem to be working, Jeremy.'

'I'm really tired,' he grunted. 'I don't want to discuss it now.'

She put her hand to the scar on her forehead as if she were stroking a lucky charm for reassurance. 'You're always running away.'

He was too drained to argue or to feel guilt at leaving her. 'I'll call you,' he said, closing the door behind him. He walked down the stairs rather than take the lift. His shoulders slumped and he dragged his feet on the yellow tiles. He glared venomously at the rubber plant and went out into the hot summer air. The bell was tolling again as if someone had died, but it seemed to be tolling in his head; he could still not see a church.

A group of black women jostled past, talking loudly at one another. Jeremy looked for his mother's maid, Vivian, but she was not among them. One of the women broke into the first shuffling steps of a *toyi-*

toyi and she thrust her fist heavenward, her fat buttocks heaving beneath her print skirt. Giggling, the others, all probably domestic workers, followed her example, punching the air. The leader ululated and roared her support for the ANC and her comrades began to echo her cry of triumph. The band turned down the next street, solid as a tank, while windows burst open and freshly-woken white faces popped out, yelling abuse at the disturbers of sleep. 'Give them the vote!' shouted a man with a walrus moustache, but the comment bounced uselessly off the baying, armour-plated beast.

A scene of beautiful destruction met Jeremy as he entered the City Bowl – the great black horn of Devil's Peak sparkled and glowed with jewels of fire. Loneliness began to eat at the numbing fatigue that had shielded his emotions, exposing a raw nerve of panic. He drove too fast through the sleeping streets, desperate for the safety of his cottage.

His hydrangeas, which had ripened into swollen pink globes over Christmas, were now looking rusty and jaded. But the house embraced him with the smell of himself as, thankfully, he turned the key in the lock and opened the door.

One of the pleasures of living alone was that nothing was out of place when he returned; everything was as he had left it. Nor did he have to talk to anyone, to placate wounded feelings, to get into bed with someone he felt like throttling. How would he cope with marriage? Immediately he went into the kitchen and switched on the kettle. While drinking his coffee he decided that when he made some money, he'd replace that hideous green carpet in the lounge. He was too tired to think of Elmarie.

◆

Jeremy was wrestling with sleep. He heard the floorboards creak and soft steps pattering towards him. He lay on his back, his throat exposed. He tried to roll over but his limbs were paralysed and would not obey. As the nightmare's hot breath ruffled his face and its crazed fingers curved around the knife, he woke and sat up, sodden in the shroud of his sheets. He glimpsed a mournful face with matted hair and snot dripping from its nose on to its wiry moustache, and goose-bumps rose with the cold on his skin.

4

Australia

Jeremy Spielman entered his office holding the brief that Fatiema had given him at reception. With a flicker of despair he tossed the bundle of documents on to his desk, then took off his jacket and hung it in the cupboard. Another *pro deo*. It was set down for three days – if it lasted that long, at two hundred rand a day it would cover his office rent for the month. But not much more.

The south-easter was assaulting the city with the pent-up breath of all its demons. If you left a window open, the glass would explode and the wind would suck the papers from the maelstrom of your room. The trees in the Botanical Gardens below strained to hold on to their limbs as the gusts contorted them to snapping point.

Jeremy settled behind his desk and flipped through the papers of his new brief. The accused was Themba Tshabalala, charged with murdering Gloria Kekana and attempting to murder Edward Kekana. He was out on bail of two hundred and fifty rand. The list of witnesses included the investigating officer, Detective Sergeant Cupido, the state pathologist, Dr H. Frisch, five names of people who lived in the black township Nyanga, and Edward Kekana. There was no magistrate, so it was unlikely that a confession had been made.

The lawyer rang an extension at the Supreme Court and got through to the prosecutor.

'Hello, is that Jan Botma?' he asked in Afrikaans. 'It's Jeremy Spielman here. I'm acting for . . .' he looked again at the Xhosa name on the charge sheet '. . . Themba Tshabalala. I've just picked up the brief. Have you got some documents for me?'

'*Ja*,' Botma answered. 'There's the post-mortem report and let's see what else . . .' His voice trailed away and there was a sound of papers being shuffled.

'*Ag*, don't worry,' Jeremy said. 'I'll pop down to your office this afternoon and collect it all. By the way, can you give me the number of the investigating officer? I must get hold of my accused.' He jotted the reply on the brief cover. 'OK, thanks. I'll see you later. Bye.' He depressed the receiver and dialled again.

'Nyanga police station good afternoon,' an Afrikaans voice reeled off without pausing, fluid as a burst from an automatic rifle.

'Hello, can I speak to Detective Sergeant Cupido please?'

'Hold on.'

While the lawyer waited, he marked the trial dates in his diary, then paged back, looking for a convenient time to hold the consultation. The blank spaces far outnumbered those marked in.

'Cupido,' said a voice that Jeremy recognised by the accent as belonging to a coloured. 'Can I help you?'

'Hello, this is Advocate Spielman. I'm acting *pro deo* for an accused in a case of yours. His name is Tshabalala. I'd like to see him in my office on Monday at 11 o'clock if that's all right.'

'*Ja meneer*,' said the policeman. 'He'll be there.'

'Thank you. It's on the tenth floor, Huguenot Chambers . . .'

Jeremy put the phone down, struck by the frightening thought that, apart from his trip to the attorney general's office to fetch the documents from the prosecutor, and, unless the unexpected happened and something came in, work was over for the day. He positioned the brief neatly on top of the few others on the corner of his desk. This little action of instilling an unnecessary order on that which already existed took up another minute of the hundreds that now stretched endlessly before him. Fighting down a sudden panic that rushed like nausea from his stomach, he pushed back his chair, stood up and walked to reception, concentrating on keeping his footsteps steady. He needed someone calm, like Fatiema, to talk to.

Lewis Singer was seeing off clients. He dabbed his handkerchief to his nose with fleshy fingers: the air conditioning gave him hayfever. He turned as the lift doors closed and Jeremy was too late to get out of the way.

'Hi. How about a cup of coffee?' he suggested. 'I've got a few minutes before my next appointment.'

'Why not?' Jeremy answered through clenched teeth, taken by surprise. 'In my office.'

Zubeida, one of Fatiema's assistants was leaning against the frame of the open kitchen door; a hubbub of secretaries was taking morning tea in the kitchen. 'Two coffees please,' Jeremy requested, and

Zubeida scowled at him for a minute before disengaging herself reluctantly from the wall. Pigeons, sliced into thin sections by the blinds, were preening themselves on the window-sill, huddled out of the wind.

'So, how's business?' Lewis asked, settling back in one of Jeremy's new chairs, bought from the proceeds of his last case, a prison murder: the old rickety seats with which he had opened his practice might not have withstood Lewis's weight.

'It's great,' Jeremy lied, wishing now he had put the meagre pile of briefs, especially the *pro deo*, into a drawer. 'Work has really picked up.' His panic had subsided and remained only as a mild case of heartburn.

'Are you pleased you've joined us? It's a big step coming from an attorney's office to the Bar.'

'I've been here nearly two years,' Jeremy replied with a touch of impatience. 'I've adjusted.'

'Already two years? Hell, time flies.' Lewis's tie, green with red stripes, followed the contour of his chest, rising up the hillock of his paunch. He lifted his arm to scratch the back of his head and there was a yellow stain under his armpit. 'I seem to recall that you came to the Bar after your father died. That was quite brave.'

'It seemed right at the time,' Jeremy said unhelpfully. 'You know how things turn out.'

Lewis shrugged, suggesting that he did not, but he was not going to pursue the matter. It was just as well that Zubeida came in then, clattering with the coffee cups, because their conversation had exhausted itself. She let the silver tray drop on the table and spun around wordlessly, showing her displeasure at having been asked to do anything. She had a mole on the outside of her right hand.

'A particularly graceless woman,' Lewis commented when she had disappeared down the corridor. 'Maybe she hates Jews.'

'She's like that with everyone,' Jeremy answered shortly. 'Milk?'

'And two sugars.' Lewis dug in his shirt pocket and came out with a cigarette; he found a box of matches somewhere in his trousers. 'Mind if I smoke?' he asked, lighting up.

'Go ahead.' Jeremy pushed an ashtray closer. His old desk top had its share of burn marks; another one would not make any difference.

But the coffee had thawed him and he asked: 'Are your wife and kids well?'

'The kids are growing up. The older they get, the more they cost,' Lewis chuckled. 'Especially these days. Let's hope de Klerk can pull it off . . .' He blew smoke out of the corner of his mouth.

'Pull what off?'

'Get sanctions lifted.'

Jeremy looked out of the window to the left of his desk. The top of the mountain was covered by a dirty thick wad of cloud that dashed down its face, driven by the demented wind. 'He'll have to free Mandela first.'

'Any day now,' Lewis prophesied. 'It must be. Doesn't your girlfriend know when? She's a journalist . . .'

'Elmarie. No, she's on women's magazines, not newspapers.'

'Beautiful girl,' Lewis said, changing tack, a strategy he had developed to throw his opponents off balance. 'I met her at a Bar dinner. Last year was it? You must marry her.'

'We don't have any plans yet,' Jeremy replied, taken aback.

'What are you waiting for?' Lewis said with the air of one who has mastered human nature through his legal practice. 'She's not going to hang around for ever. Commit yourself, my boy.'

'Well, we're just seeing how it goes,' Jeremy hedged, resenting the intrusion. But with the bludgeoning insensitivity that had prevented Jeremy from ever getting too close to him, even when they were at school together, Lewis asked: 'Is it because of your mother?'

'What do you mean?'

'I know Esta Spielman. She wouldn't want you to marry a non-Jew.'

'Maybe,' Jeremy conceded, on the defensive as if he were being cross-examined.

'You're not going to spend the rest of your life with your mother!' Lewis exclaimed with a cunning smile that was almost lost in the flesh of his cheeks, pleased that his interrogation had produced the results he had suspected. 'You can't live for her.'

'I suppose not,' Jeremy said, wondering how to get Singer out of his office; he remembered how, at school, he used to avoid the pale, fat boy. Things had not changed.

'How is your mother?' Lewis asked with a slow smile. 'I've always had a soft spot for her. I'll never forget in the lift club, she used to stop and buy us suckers on the way home. Not like some of the other mothers.' Lewis shifted his weight and the chair creaked. 'With all their money it was amazing how stingy some of them were.'

It was the first time that Lewis had shown even a hint of bitterness about his childhood; the bland face screened his emotions completely. Jeremy said nothing, wondering suddenly what grudges Singer harboured against him from those days. He flipped back into the files of his memory, seeking out cruelties he may have inflicted on the fat boy, but he drew a blank.

And then Lewis had skipped on to a new subject, perhaps one that was at the heart of his concerns, for now his eyes were intense black pools at the bottom of the well of his spectacles. 'Talking about Jewish mothers, what future do you think the Jews have in this country?'

'The same as anybody else.' Jeremy was non-committal; it was the only way to handle Lewis. 'Why, what do you think?'

'I don't know. I have a family. I worry about my children . . .'

'Must the Jews be more concerned than anyone else?' Jeremy asked disingenuously. 'I worked in the townships with Jews for Justice. We had no problems.'

Lewis stubbed out his cigarette. 'We're the scapegoats, just like we've always been. The right-wing Afrikaners believe the economy's in a mess because the Jews have exploited the country for money and power.' He took off his spectacles and dangled them between his thumb and forefinger as if he were trying to hypnotise a witness. 'I've spoken to them. They think we're only loyal to Israel and that we side with the blacks.' He blinked and put his glasses back on his nose. 'And, on the other hand, the blacks accuse Israel of supplying arms to the Government.' He licked his very pink lips and shook his head. 'I don't know, Jeremy. We fall between the two stools of black and Afrikaner nationalism. Neither wants us and both are suspicious of our motives.'

'So when are you going to Australia?'

'What do you mean?' Singer asked, a little too quickly.

'Well, word has it that you've been admitted to the Bar in Sydney.'

Lewis patted his pockets, searching for another cigarette. 'Who said that?'

'General gossip on the floor. You know, nothing is secret in this place for long. I'm surprised you hadn't heard before.'

Singer did not reply, but sat very still, his round cheeks and thick glasses masking his discomfort. Jeremy enjoyed watching him squirm, as he had been made to earlier.

'I don't blame you,' he added mischievously. 'As you've said, a man with a family has to make plans.'

Lewis found another crumpled cigarette and popped it in his mouth like a cork in a bottle. His fingers were steady as he lit it. He blew smoke across the desk as he asked: 'What are *you* going to do?' He had neither confirmed nor denied Jeremy's allegation.

'I'm staying here, of course,' Spielman said stoutly. 'I'm a South African. I might not be very active politically any more, but I love the country.' He allowed hismelf a crooked smile. 'I love the mountain even if I hardly ever walk on it and I love the sea even if I seldom go to the beach. I also like some of the people although most of my friends,' he said pointedly, 'have taken the chicken run.'

'I wish I could share your enthusiasm,' Singer responded grimly. 'But this morning I saw a black fellow who owns a taxi company. The thugs in the township keep on burning his taxis because they hate anyone who has anything. He's decided to go back to the Transkei, where it's quieter, and open a shop. We've got a lost generation of black kids who only know violence as a way to solve problems. They want to drag everyone down to their own vicious level. What future do you see for this country?'

'I'd rather die here than in a foreign field.'

'And there is more likelihood of dying here,' Lewis answered, adding: 'For a Jew this is a foreign field.'

'If you believe that, then maybe those black and Afrikaner nationalists are right about the Jews,' Jeremy argued. 'Besides, Australia is just as foreign.'

Singer had recovered his composure, if in fact he had ever lost it. 'In Australia they respect the right to life, and the right not to be raped. They have standards there; it's civilised,' he said. 'You might want to stay here under an ANC-Communist government. I don't.'

'So you are going?'

Lewis squashed his half-smoked cigarette in the ashtray and drained the last of his coffee but gave no answer. Jeremy looked at the remains of the cold liquid covered with a white film in his own cup.

'Do you want some more?' he offered, suddenly sorry at the antagonism between them; it seemed based largely on his resentment that the class nerd had done so well, while he was still struggling.

Lewis held out his hand, palm forward. 'No thanks. I've got work to do.'

'Yes,' Jeremy lied. 'So have I. Busy day ahead.'

As Singer stood to go, he looked at the Magritte print. 'That's a bit bloody,' he said with a hint of criticism. 'Must make some of your clients feel a little uneasy.'

'State of the nation,' Jeremy said, trying to be light-hearted. 'Thanks for popping in.' He could not resist adding: 'Come and say goodbye before you emigrate.'

Lewis winked and commented: 'Remember what I said about Elmarie. Even if she was Golda Meir's daughter you'd have to make it work. If the two of you get on, then marry her.'

Jeremy shrugged. 'We've all got our crosses to bear,' he said, closing the door behind his colleague.

The phone was bawling at him and he lunged across the desk to catch the receiver before its promise of work evaporated. 'Hello, Mom,' he snapped in exasperation when he recognised her voice.

'I can't go on like this!' she screamed, her breath hammering down the line in agitated gasps. Jeremy unhooked the phone cord from the corner of the table-top where it had snagged and he flopped into his chair. 'What's wrong?'

'It's all these *schwartzes*,' she panted. 'You can't even go shopping any more. You know old Mrs Feitelstein? I play bridge with her . . .'

'Yes, Mom, calm down. Tell me what happened.'

'She was walking back from the OK Bazaars. They pushed her on to the pavement. In broad daylight, mind you! And they pinched her bag.' Esta paused accusingly as if it were his fault, as if, by sticking up for the oppressed for so long, he had unleashed this black wave that was flooding the streets of Sea Point and sweeping away frail old Jewish ladies. 'They took her to hospital in an ambulance,' Esta sobbed. 'Her hip is fractured, they think. She's an old lady – hips never heal properly. It's not safe anywhere!'

Guiltily – she always managed to make him feel guilty – he said: 'I'm sorry, Mom.'

'They're taking over now,' Esta said mournfully, slightly mollified by his conciliatory tone. In the past, he might have lashed out at her, excusing the actions of the criminals because apartheid had wrecked the societies from which they came. But since the ANC had been unbanned, he could allow himself to be more critical: the blacks could now defend themselves; they didn't need him to speak for them. Guilt at being white was deferring to guilt arising from being the son of a Jewish mother.

'It's dangerous here, Jeremy,' she said, and he could imagine her stubby fingers, which could fly so wonderfully across a keyboard, dabbing a tissue to her sweating chest. 'I don't know when they'll come for me next. Every day there are break-ins and old people are getting murdered. And now Mrs Feitelstein. I get short of breath when I just think of it.'

Marie Coetzee was also scared. For a moment, Jeremy longed for the two mothers to get together, to become friends, share their fears over a cup of tea at the Wimpy Bar. But he knew it would never happen: they were worlds apart; not only did they fear the blacks, but each other.

'Just keep your door locked, Mom,' he offered lamely, 'and don't go out after dark.' He could not suggest that Esta carry a gun in her bag like Elmarie's mother; Marie was an alley cat, Esta a pampered tabby.

'What sort of life is that for me?' his mother complained. 'Thank God your father isn't alive to see the way this country has gone.'

He would have coped with it better than you, Jeremy thought, playing with the idea of putting down the receiver and pretending they had been cut off.

'Mom, I'm sorry,' he said. 'There's nothing else you can do.'

'I don't want to live like this,' she moaned, her voice breaking again, 'like an animal in a cage.'

'Then you'll have to emigrate,' he said wearily. 'Lots of white South Africans are living in Australia. I hear Australians play bridge, and there are old people who need to be entertained, so you'll have plenty to do.'

'Don't make fun!' she scolded. Leaving the security of her home for another country was even more terrifying than staying to face the black onslaught. 'We'll have to find another lady for bridge. Mrs Feitelstein won't be able to play again.'

'Hopefully she's not all that badly hurt, Mom,' he soothed her. 'And I'm sure you'll find someone. All the ladies in Sea Point will want to join you.'

'Do you think so?' she asked in a small voice, like a child needing encouragement.

'Of course.' She was beginning to sound calmer, and he thought it safe to wind down their conversation. 'Mom, I've got to go now. A client is waiting to see me.' It was at least the third lie he had told this morning. His capacity to deviate from the truth had increased dramatically since a judge had pronounced him a fit and proper person to practice as an advocate of the Supreme Court of South Africa.

'When are you coming to see me?' she persisted, not wanting to let go. 'You didn't come for supper last Friday night. You didn't even phone.'

'Oh Jesus, I'm sorry.' Despite the air conditioning, a wave of heat flushed through him.

'It's that *shiksa* you're going out with. She makes you forget your Judaism.'

He wiped his face with a piece of toilet paper he found in his pocket and loosened his tie and top button. 'It had nothing to do with her. I was working on Friday.' How could he say he'd been to an ANC march and then had a fight with Elmarie? His mother would not possibly have understood.

'On Friday night?' She probed his story with rare perspicacity. 'You were working on Friday night?' But she was not a skilled cross-examiner, and instead of drilling him on his inadequate answer she let him off the hook. 'Uncle Hymie was very upset,' she said. 'He was expecting you.'

Did they even know what had happened on Friday? 'I've got to go,' he said desperately and slammed down the phone, cutting her goodbye in half.

He stood up, poisoned by the thought that he was neglecting his mother who had given him everything, and went out to wash his face. On his way, he asked the women at reception to bring him more coffee. Just as well he did not smoke, he thought, or he'd have finished a packet of cigarettes by now. He dashed water over his burning skin; he would never purge the blood that stained his brow.

◆

The wind was rocking his house like a ship at sea – the walls and the ceiling moved independently of one another: cracks opened where they joined and grit fell on his desk. The roof timbers squalled ominously as gusts of wind walloped the house. Soot from the burned mountain turned surfaces black, driven into the cottage through invisible apertures.

In the newspaper he read that a hurricane-force 'black' south-easter had rampaged through Cape Town, ripping off roofs, plunging its fists through display windows, roughing up pedestrians who had to cling to poles to stay on their feet. The wind had even toppled a bus – the first time this had happened in one hundred and thirty years. Passengers escaped seconds before the double-decker crashed on its side, and no one was hurt. 'Black' was an unfortunate adjective, he thought.

First the fire, now the wind; the forces of nature were echoing the extraordinary upheavals in the affairs of men. When the National Party Government set out on its bulldozer ride of social engineering called apartheid, it crushed every stone on which the country's social structures were built. Since 1948, all South Africans – black and white – had been living in the distorted landscape produced by that juggernaut's mad progress. But then, forty years later, the same Party produced the enigma named F. W. de Klerk. No one could have guessed what lay behind his smile, hardly even a smile, in fact just a slight raising of the left side of his mouth. Like a conjurer he produced the key to switch off the Government's monster machine, and to allow the ruptured country to heal. A week ago he announced that the season of violence was over and that Mandela would be freed unconditionally. Now the country waited anxiously to hear when.

In the meantime, the gale drove a waterfall of cloud over the edge of the mountain with such ferocity that Jeremy pictured the blast lifting his house from its foundations and dropping it into the sea. A huge cloud, resembling a toddling baby, straddled Kloof Nek between

Lion's Head and Table Mountain. It was black at the core but glowed like gold as the sun caught its edges. The lumbering infant menaced the city, threatening to stomp down Kloof Nek Road, crushing everything in its unco-ordinated path. Clouds, like mirrors, however, did not necessarily reflect the truth, but rather the prejudices of the observer. It was all a matter of perspective. Tiring of this shape, the wind transformed the giant child into a winged horse, rearing up on its hind legs, ready to gallop up the sheer face of the mountain.

Jeremy put down his magazine with weary hands and switched off the light. Elmarie was already asleep beside him.

◆

Elmarie lay on the settee, her feet over the arm-rest. She had not yet taken off her walking shoes. Jeremy's eyes played hungrily on her bare legs, lingering at the soft places where they entered her white shorts. There was no fat on her legs, although, like her mother, she hardly ever exercised. 'I was enjoying our walk,' she complained, now clearly pleased to be lying down. 'I hope it was worth coming back to watch this. We so seldom do anything together.'

'Here.' Jeremy handed her a glass of orange juice and their fingers became entangled. He downed his drink in a few gulps.

'What a big mouth you've got,' she laughed, sipping gently.

'I should be a good lawyer, then.' The face of another lawyer, F. W. de Klerk, had appeared on the screen, the television lights crackling like electricity on his gold spectacle frames. Jeremy was throttling his empty glass as a growing excitement spread fire into his chest. Magically, he flicked the sound on with the remote control wand. If Elmarie was moved at all, she did not show it. The scar on her forehead was colourless.

'Of course you'll be good,' she smirked. 'You have to support me. I can't work forever.'

Her words echoed something his mother had once said. 'Sh,' he answered impatiently. 'He's speaking.'

'I'm sorry,' she said, pretending to be miffed. She lifted her hand for him to take, or stroke, or kiss, but he ignored it and she directed all her attention to the screen with a grunt of displeasure at him.

De Klerk's face was as bland as an egg, except for the politician's twitch that masqueraded as a smile. His wedding ring showed that he was to be trusted, a family man. In his Afrikaans-accented English, rolling his 'r's' very slightly, he told the world: '. . . I am now in a position to announce that Mr Nelson Mandela will be released at the Victor Verster Prison on Sunday, the 11th of February, 1990 at 3 o'clock. Yesterday evening, I met with Mr Mandela in Cape Town . . . During the meeting, Mr Mandela was informed of the Government's decision regarding his release . . .'

Jeremy's fingers were white around his glass. A tingling sensation rushed from the middle of his back up his neck and into the base of his skull, circling his forehead like a crown of Christmas lights.

'He's coming out!' he whooped. 'Tomorrow he's coming out!'

Elmarie forced a smile and said quietly: 'I'm happy for you. I know this is important.'

'After twenty-seven years in jail, he's coming out,' Jeremy exulted. 'And in my lifetime! This is history. What a wonderful fucking country.' Leaning over, he planted his lips firmly on hers, but she pulled her head aside.

'I've been smoking,' she said by way of excuse. She had on a tight T-shirt which fitted like a second skin. He covered her breasts with his hands – his glass had vanished – and sought her lips again.

'I don't care about the smoking,' he persisted, and she accepted his mouth. They clung together, locked like a statue, until she pulled back, her green eyes sparkling.

'You took my breath away,' she gasped. 'What a lover! They should release Mandela more often.'

His hands moved down her body to the tops of her thighs which he had coveted earlier, and, while de Klerk answered questions from journalists, Jeremy made love to her on the carpet.

5

Freedom

The phone was calling from the lounge. It drove out the dirty, pleading face that peered through the cracked mirror which separated this world from a deeper one. Who would wake him so early on a Sunday? He found Elmarie's hand and squeezed it for reassurance in the tangle of the bedding. Even though he had only one sheet and a duvet, the bed got into an insoluble puzzle when they slept together. During the week, when he was alone, there was so little disturbance it seemed that only a ghost had spent the night there.

Jeremy forced himself up and plodded down the passage, groping for the noise. He fumbled the receiver to his ear and a woman's voice said: 'Hello, is that Jeremy Spielman?'

'Yes.' He realised the curtains were open and that he stood naked in full view of the eyes of the flats overlooking his lounge, although he had done it so often before that the tenants must have been bored at seeing him. He retreated to the bedroom, taking the phone with him, jerking the extension cord when it got stuck behind the leg of a chair.

'This is Paula Evans of the Cape Democrats,' the voice said briskly. 'As you know, Nelson Mandela is being released today. There'll be a welcoming rally on the Parade. We need volunteers to act as marshals. Can you help us?'

'I'm not sure,' he demurred, glancing at Elmarie as he dropped into the nest of bedclothes. 'I've got to consult with clients today,' he lied, 'and I don't know how long my appointment's going to run.'

'If you can, will you meet on the Parade at 12 o'clock? Try to wear khaki and a red headband or scarf. We'll tell you what to do.'

'OK,' he said, aware that his voice, thick with sleep, must have sounded very reluctant to her. 'Bye.'

She put down the phone without a greeting although she would not be angry. Businesslike, she would strike a line through his name, just one of the many on a list compiled over years of struggle, and go on to make the next call.

Talking so openly on the phone still left him feeling uneasy; an army of security policemen with their tape recorders, or whatever they used, were probably transcribing the conversation and filing it away. They would not have stopped their surveillance just because de Klerk was liberalising South African politics: they had their own rules and agendas. His file must have been fairly thick by now, filled with details of activities which, in a Western democracy, would have been considered quite normal, but in South Africa were usually illegal.

Why had he refused to help Paula Evans and her Cape Democrats? Before he became involved with Elmarie, he would have jumped at the invitation. But she was so negative about his politics that, over the years he had known her, a subtle shift seemed to have taken place in his own approach: he had become more conservative – and it was only when he was put to the test, as with the phone call, that he realised just how much of an influence she had had on him. To appease Elmarie, he had chosen not to help the oppressed; it was an extension of his decision to leave Jews for Justice. Perhaps he no longer belonged to the country in spite of what he had told Singer; perhaps it made no difference if he lived in South Africa or Australia.

'Who was that?' Elmarie asked. The shadows under her eyes made her face look bruised in the mornings. He tried to imagine her as an old woman and wondered if, after waking up beside her for thirty years, he would still find her as achingly beautiful. But his imagination failed: he could not see beyond today. He pulled back the duvet, took the nipple of her right breast between his lips and started to caress it with his tongue.

'Who was it?' she insisted, her eyes beginning to mist over.

'A woman from some political group. She wants me to become a marshal at the Mandela rally today.'

'I thought you'd quit all that,' Elmarie said with a trace of accusation.

'I once filled out a Cape Democrats membership form,' he said, drawing back. 'I get their newsletter. But I've never attended any of their meetings.'

'So you are going?'

'I'm not sure,' he said, aware that he was on the retreat. 'She told me to wear khaki and that sounds like an army. I don't want to belong to any army, whether backing the Government or the ANC. Anyway, now that the ANC is legal, they don't need me.' He heard himself try to justify his submission to her will.

'If you go, our relationship is over,' she threatened. 'I'm not going out with someone from the ANC.'

'Fine,' he bristled. 'Then we'll have to break up.' How could he love someone with whom he disagreed so fundamentally? How could she love him? Obviously their relationship was based on needs that were much stronger than their differences; they were still together despite some appalling arguments.

'I don't want the police coming for you again,' she said softly, using her concern to try to appease him.

Jeremy decided not to get involved in a fruitless discussion. 'I'll watch the release on TV,' he answered. 'Then I'll go down to the Parade as a spectator only. It'll take at least an hour for them to drive through from the prison. Will you come with me?'

'Yes,' she said slowly, drawing out the word as if she were agreeing only under severe protest. Yet, at the concession she was making, love for her flooded through him again.

'Good,' he replied, bending down to kiss her other breast.

She groaned in pleasure, a languid smile turning her lips up like a cat's. She lay back, her hands behind her head, her eyes closed, surrendering herself to him, allowing him to do whatever he wished.

He licked the tip of his finger and traced it across her nipple so that she twitched with the pleasurable shock of it, then he kissed her on the mouth. He entered her gently while brushing back the hair from her face, and moved slowly inside her. Her orgasm sent groans into the street where the neighbours were packing their picnic baskets into their cars, preparing for the beach on this hot Sunday morning. Her nails carved flaming furrows into his back.

Jeremy came after her, quietly, with an electric burst that rocked his eyes back in his head and filled him with a rush of inexplicable guilt.

'Kiss me between my eyes,' she asked dreamily. Wanting now only to extricate himself and be on his own, he pressed his lips on the crack that divided her forehead into two equal parts.

'Thanks, my darling,' she said, aware of his need to escape, but enjoying having him in her for those few extra moments, even taking a malicious pleasure in keeping him trapped. 'I'm in love with your mind,' she added wistfully. 'I want to make love to your mind.'

'I'll get us some coffee,' he responded, reaching for his bedside tissues and wincing as he withdrew from her.

'You do that,' she answered, drawing the duvet up to her chin and closing her eyes. Jeremy pulled on a pair of shorts before again exposing himself to the eyes of the flat-dwellers, but no one seemed to be watching; in fact he had never seen anyone on the walkways that extended across the face of the building. For all he knew, the apartments were empty. He drew the lounge blinds, cutting out the pool of sun on the carpet, and the room lost its smile.

In the bathroom, the mirrors presented him with a sullen early-morning picture, his unwashed hair revealing the gaps on his scalp which, as much as his house, were part of his father's legacy. Every day he lost more hair; perhaps he should answer one of those adverts on the sports pages of the newspapers. But if there were a genuine cure for baldness, would prominent people like F. W. de Klerk, with all the wealth and resources of the State at their disposal, not have found it? It was terrible how your body, which was all you had, should start to undermine you from the inside, self-destructing. In the mornings, unmade-up, Elmarie was still beautiful. What beauty did she see in him? Perhaps that was why she said she loved his mind: his body was not attractive enough. If he and Elmarie had a son, he would leave the poor child with a genetic time-bomb of all sorts of retrogressive hereditary ills. Did other parents not see this before they launched their defective seed into the world?

One of the mirrors was cracked, thanks to the efforts of an over-zealous charring woman; he had not bothered to have it fixed. If he looked into that crazy glass, he saw two halves of himself which overlapped, a distorted picture of an incomplete person. Sometimes that mirror showed him the tramp within, the down-and-out who lived in his dreams. He dipped his eyes as he switched on the taps.

While the kitchen thundered with the sound of the geyser, he watched the coffee drip through the filter into the pot. Why should he have hair on his chest where he didn't need it, but lose that which was most important – on the crown of his head?

Elmarie was dozing when he returned to the bedroom and he left the steaming cup on the bedside table. He kissed her on the shoulder;

maybe he should marry her before he went completely bald. Who else would want him?

As he eased into the bath, he noticed that one of his pubic hairs had turned white. He pulled, but it would not come out and he closed his eyes in disgust at the signs of age. He reached for the soap as if by purging the outside he would eliminate the worm within. When he let out the water, a harvest of hair remained behind, ringing the tub. He washed it out thoroughly, making certain the last strand disappeared down the plug hole.

The Sunday paper was jammed into his post-box and he twisted it out, screwing up his eyes against the sunlight that hit him with a hammer blow. The street was empty – the neighbours must have already left for the beach – and he retreated into the security of his cottage, relieved that he did not have to face anyone. The mountain was an immense white-hot slab of rock looming over the terrace of houses opposite.

Elmarie had woken at the sound of the door and she was smiling as her sleepy fingers found the cup of coffee. She grimaced as she put it to her lips and tasted that it was cold, but she swallowed nevertheless. Jeremy sat at the foot of the bed and dropped the paper between them.

FREE! the headline screamed in letters five centimetres high, and then told the story: 'Nelson Mandela walks out of prison a free man today . . . At 3pm the world will have its first sight of the 71-year-old ANC leader. During twenty-seven years in prison he has been elevated into a legend . . .'

The photograph was in black and white; the first picture of Mandela since he went to jail. Both he and de Klerk stood stiffly, awkwardly, in the State President's office, each man taking stature from the presence of, yet straining away from, the other. Mandela was taller than his rival for the soul of the country, but de Klerk, in his dark suit, was as stocky as a rugby player. Mandela's dark hands were clasped before him as if protecting himself from the world's eyes after nearly three decades in the darkness. De Klerk's white hands hung at his sides, palms turning outwards, showing off a studied confidence and openness. Both leaders were forcing themselves to smile: de Klerk had the usual supercilious twist to the corner of his thin mouth; Mandela's full lips were wreathed in wrinkles. A South African flag dropped limply behind the President's left shoulder; the grey head of the pretender to the throne was cosseted by books. Mandela had burst out of the belly of the beast, and already had one foot on its neck.

'He looks Chinese!' Elmarie exclaimed, on her elbows, her small firm breasts hanging like pendulums, one over each man.

'I wonder how they're going to stop some maniac from taking a pot-shot at him,' Jeremy said. 'The Parade could be a dangerous place today.'

'Maybe it's just as well that you aren't a marshal,' Elmarie said, then announced: 'I'm going to bath. I hope you haven't used all the hot water.'

'This has really driven the white racists crazy,' Jeremy continued, speaking to her slender back as she slipped off the bed and stepped lightly out of the room. Even though he had just made love to her, the sight of her graceful naked figure stirred new spasms of lust in him. But she was gone and he returned to the news item which had sparked his last comment.

Thousands of white right-wingers belonging to the neo-nazi Afrikaner Resistance Movement had held a rally in Pretoria's Church Square the previous day. Chanting 'Kill Mandela!', they marched through the city carrying a child's coffin which contained 'thirty pieces of silver' in two-rand coins. They wanted to hand it to police at the Union Buildings for delivery to de Klerk. They carried swastikas. Before they set out on their mini-trek, they burned a Star of David. An Israeli flag, held aloft during the march, had on it the words: 'Hitler was right. Jews are communists.'

For a moment, Jeremy felt light-headed. 'In the past,' he murmured, 'the Afrikaners only went after the Jews for what we did. But now it's for what we are. There's no choice any more.' He rubbed his forehead on the heel of his hand, a wave of tiredness making him shut his eyes; his thighs began to ache as if he had suddenly developed a fever. He sat on the bed, his head in his hands, fighting off the dizziness that threatened to lay him flat until Elmarie returned, rubbing her hair dry with a towel. A few drops of water spilled on the paper.

'It's such a lovely day,' she said brightly. 'It would be a pity to waste it. Let's go out for lunch. I'd like to sit in the sun somewhere. We can come back and watch TV.'

But a lethargy had fallen on him: suddenly the excitement of Mandela's release had been squeezed out. He wanted only to crawl back into bed, cover his head with his duvet and sleep. He was unwanted in his own country, like the Jews in Hitler's Germany, like the blacks in South Africa since then. He did not mention the article to Elmarie, but allowed himself to fall back while he watched her dress.

'I had a dream last night,' she said, speaking not to Jeremy, but to the mirror as she brushed her hair away from her forehead. 'I dreamed that I was sitting at an outside table at a café in the *Karoo*, drinking coffee and eating a hamburger. A group of *Voortrekkers* rode up on horseback to warn me that the blacks were coming.' She did not sit on the pine chair which was at the level of the mirror, but bent forward at the waist to see herself; her set of fine silver bangles tinkled on her wrist. He did not respond and she continued as if she were speaking to herself, as if she did not care whether he was listening or not. 'The *Voortrekker* leader sat on an enormous white horse. He had strong shoulders and a full square beard down to his chest. He carried a muzzle-loader in one hand and held the horse's reins in the other, just like you see in the pictures. Behind him, teams of oxen were pulling wagons on the N1 past my car.' Her lips were cocked in a smile at the strangeness of the image; Jeremy saw her face in the mirror. 'He told me to be careful. The black warriors were on the other side of the hill. Then a little Afrikaner girl jumped off the back of one of the wagons and ran across the veld to where the blacks were . . .' Elmarie stood up straight and turned to face Jeremy. Her scar was like a dark fault in the rock face of her forehead, separating two plates. Her lips were pursed pensively. 'I wonder what it all means?'

Jeremy recalled the blond boy on the back of a flatbed truck in the shadow of fierce black orators who hurled words as angry as rocks at the Government. Was this symbol of a white child finding a place among blacks entering the collective unconscious of South Africans? Was Elmarie the little girl in her dream? Was this, perhaps, another side of her that she concealed, the flipside of the xenophobic Afrikaner which she showed him?

At the thought that she might be more liberated than she let on, energy began to flow back into his body. 'Did she reach them?' he asked, and when Elmarie looked mystified, explained: 'The girl. Did she reach the blacks?'

'I don't remember,' she said. 'I woke up, the dream petered out, there wasn't an ending . . . who knows?' She stood at the foot of the bed. Her head fell back on her shoulders and she seemed to be looking into the distance beyond the walls. 'The *Voortrekker* leader . . . he was my father,' she said quietly. Then suddenly irritation flickered on her face. 'Get up. Come. Get dressed.'

He dragged himself reluctantly to his feet under the lash of her nagging. He did not tell her of the vagrant who lived within him, who hobbled through his dreams.

◆

The eyes of the cottage across the road were shuttered. Jeremy realised that he had no inkling of the political convictions of anyone else in the street. But then he was no longer sure of his own political convictions either. As a white in South Africa who had rejected the Government's oppression for so long, the events of the last week had knocked everything inside out: alliances had to be re-examined as the political situation normalised in the months, or years, to come.

He opened the car door for Elmarie; the hot air that escaped punched him in the face, taking his breath away. She got in gingerly as if she were putting her toe into the water of a scalding tub.

'When I make some money I'll buy a house with a garage,' he said defensively, in reply to her unspoken protest, letting the car roll downhill. He could not hold the steering-wheel and had to bounce his palms lightly on its ring of fire until it cooled sufficiently for him to take a firm grip.

'This heat . . . it's God punishing us,' she said darkly. 'We've broken our vow to Him.'

'Rubbish,' he snapped.

'Why are we driving into town?' she asked in a voice edged with concern. 'I thought we were going to have lunch.'

'I want to see the Parade.'

She fell silent and stared straight ahead, bottling up her anger. The heat undermined the smooth sculptured planes of her face, drawing out bobbles of sweat which marred its otherwise flawless surface; the effect of her bath was undone.

Road blocks across Darling Street prevented Jeremy from driving directly to the City Hall and he had to circle the Parade to get a view. An ANC flag was draped over the balcony where Mandela was going to speak; the grand old orange building was dressed subversively for the day. Photographers perched on a platform in the cage of a scaffold, erected opposite the balcony: they would wait for hours, trapped under the white-hot African sun, for a shot of the returned messiah; Jeremy hoped these were the only kinds of shots fired. Buses and taxis bored into the terminus, crammed to bursting with worshippers who had come to greet their saviour. And wave after wave of blacks *toyi-toyied* like a mighty sweating army on the square which once used to be a parade ground for white soldiers. The row of palm trees between the Parade and the City Hall made the scene even more exotic, as if Cape Town had been transformed into one of those North African cities forbidden for so long to the children of apartheid.

An intense black face with wild, excited eyes and flaring nostrils jammed suddenly against Elmarie's window and she yelped in fright. Jeremy had a glimpse of a scar riveted to the man's forehead by crude stitchmarks. He slammed his foot on the accelerator and the car lurched forward, leaving the face open-mouthed behind.

'OK. Let's go into the country for lunch,' Jeremy said. Elmarie sat rigidly beside him.

◆

Groot Constantia's vineyards rolled gently into the green distance in the valleys between the soft Cape mountains. The white gabled Cape Dutch building was guarded by two puny cannons which could no longer protect Elmarie's Afrikaner heritage from the black enemy within.

They sat in the courtyard of the restaurant and ordered a lunch of traditional Cape food from a fresh-faced student while the hot summer air hummed around the tables and the waiters fussed over the patrons – mostly elderly whites and as far removed from the events in the city as if they were on the moon.

'It's going to be a long, hot afternoon for those people on the

Parade,' Jeremy said. 'If Mandela is released at three, he'll only get to the City Hall at four.

'It's a wonderful day and I don't care about Mandela or anyone else,' she answered, brushing her fringe away from her eyes with impatient fingers.

He felt the gulf between them widen just another fraction, but smiled when the waitress brought his braised *snoek*, Elmarie's curried mince and two glasses of dry white wine. He found his eyes drawn to the waitress's breasts as she bent over to put the dishes down, and he quickly looked away as if he had been caught, like a naughty schoolboy, doing something wrong. Her hands had freckles; her nails were short and unpainted. He wondered if she were happy that Mandela was to be set free, if she even knew. She was young enough to be a student: the campus must have been buzzing today; she could hardly have been unaware.

'It must be a special occasion for you to order wine,' Elmarie said, wriggling her shoulders, her green eyes glittering mischievously. She raised her glass. 'To Nelson,' she added sardonically, and he tilted his drink, meeting her eye, but not touching his glass to hers.

'I keep off booze during the week because I need a clear head,' he said, realising as he spoke that he had no need to defend himself. He cut into his food, carefully parting the small flakes of fish, and put the fork to his mouth, chewing mechanically, not concentrating on the savoury taste which usually delighted him but today had no flavour at all. He added: 'And I have a beer when I finish a case.'

The waitress returned to ask if they were enjoying their meals and Jeremy grunted his assent: they always ask you when your mouth is full, he thought irritably.

'Very nice. Excellent,' Elmarie declared, too loudly, as if she had seen his wandering glance earlier and was now reclaiming her territory. The waitress smiled and withdrew. She had soft, brown eyes, unlike Elmarie's which were challenging, aggressive. She had a cheerful mouth, as if she came from a stable, happy background, unlike the traumatic childhood from which Elmarie had fled, heavy with defensive baggage.

Jeremy hurried down his food, which sat in his chest, but he left the wine. As soon as Elmarie had finished, he called the waitress and asked for the bill. She had written her name, 'Lara', on the bottom.

Sweet Lara, he thought, our lives have crossed briefly and we'll never meet again. I'll go on with Elmarie, you with a bold young man from one of your classes, who shares your interest in scuba diving and going to clubs. As pretty as you are, it would not have worked between us: the age difference is too great. He paid by credit card and gave her a tip that had her smiling broadly and saying: 'Thank you very much.' Her long eyelashes fluttered and Elmarie stood up, pushing her chair back so firmly that it grated on the ground.

Jeremy put his arm around her shoulders, remembering how it used to be between them: the thrill to see each other, the comfort in each other's presence, the way she had sat with him night after night when his father died, and, emotionally naked, he had allowed her through his defences; he let her in when he was at his weakest. At what point had the slide begun? When had antagonism replaced mutual support? Perhaps when they realised they had widely differing political sympathies and their first love could no longer paper over the cracks. As whites they were no less victims of apartheid than were the blacks.

Elmarie was smoking a cigarette which she balanced between the index and middle fingers of her left hand. She turned her face to blow the smoke away from him and he squeezed her as they walked past other couples and parties of tourists with cameras slung around their necks and families who had stopped under the oak trees to feed the squirrels.

The white homestead was built in 1685, soon after the Dutch colonised the Cape. It had existed in a violent hiatus for three hundred years, together with the country's whites, in fearful anticipation of this moment when the conquered people, gnawing and agitating from within, finally gained their freedom.

'We'd better go,' Jeremy said.

Elmarie blew out a cloud of smoke and let herself reluctantly be guided towards the car. 'What a pity to waste the day in front of a TV set,' she complained.

'We'll be outside soon afterwards,' he said. 'Mandela's speaking on the Parade. Remember?'

'I'm not going!' she exclaimed. The person who wore Elmarie's hard face at that moment was not the same one to whom he had made love in the morning.

'Why, what's wrong?' he asked as gently as his disappointment would allow.

'It's a celebration for blacks, not whites,' she retorted.

'It's a moment of history, no matter what colour you are.'

'Well it's not my history,' she replied. 'They're not my people.'

'Why do you hate blacks so much?' he asked, dropping his arm and inevitably separating from her.

'I don't!' she flared. Then she brushed aside her hair, revealing her scar. 'You see this? A black driver did this to me and killed my father. He was drunk. He swerved across the road and hit us. He wasn't even hurt. He walked away. I was seven years old. It happened on Christmas Eve . . . we were going to the café to buy a cold drink.'

'I know the story,' he said tiredly. 'I'm sorry, I really am. It was terrible. But it's no reason to hate all blacks.'

'I don't,' she snapped. 'He was punished. He went to jail. Although it didn't help me. It didn't bring my father back. Now can we drop the subject?' They had reached his car and he opened the door for her. Silence bruised the air between them all the way past the university.

'I'd better take you home,' he said at last, 'because I'm going to the Parade.'

'Whatever you want,' she said sullenly, and they continued on the Western Boulevard flyover past the city to Sea Point without talking any further, each wrapped in a coat of sombre colours. He stopped outside her flat, with the engine running, waiting for her to get out.

'Are you coming up?' she asked as if they were strangers on their first date. She was biting her bottom lip; her hand hesitated over the door handle.

'What's the point?' he asked. 'What will it achieve? More fighting?'

'We'll watch Mandela together.' A smile started to play on her mouth as she tested his reaction. 'You know I love you. You're wonderful.' Her eyes dipped. 'I just get carried away sometimes.'

Shaking his head at the way she manipulated him, wondering what weakness in him allowed him to be led, he manoeuvred his car into a parking bay on the steep slope of the driveway and locked the steering-wheel. They took the lift up and walked along the balcony past the giant palm tree which rose up to the fourth floor.

Mandela's release was late. Jeremy and Elmarie sat on the sofa, drinking coffee and wine, while the television announcer, bred to serve a capricious master, padded through an inane, inoffensive commentary, filling up the time it took for the final touches to be put, in a prison warder's house, to Nelson Mandela. The cameras showed to the world a back road outside Paarl, where thousands had crushed to welcome the mythic prisoner. The circle, which had begun with his arrest twenty-seven years before, was about to be closed. Wholeness was at hand, the doctor who was, single-handedly, to cure the country's problems was about to be produced: Mandela.

'Rub my foot,' Elmarie begged, taking off her shoes. 'It's clean.' She put her legs across his knees and stretched out luxuriously, her back on the arm-rest, holding her wine glass on her chest between her breasts. Her lips were open as if she were ready to be kissed. He took her toes in his short fingers, massaging them to their bases, one by one, then ran his fingertips along the soft skin between them, rubbing the palm of his hand over the high arch of her foot.

'I love it when you do this,' she purred. 'People forget to be intimate with each other.'

'If you want love, you must generate it,' he said. 'You must make me want to love you. Too often you don't.'

Her jaws tightened as if she were about to protest, but then she thought better of it, and lay back, allowing him to knead her foot while they waited.

Mandela walked out at 4.20, an elderly grandfather and statesman from the Eastern Cape, hand-in-hand with his wife, Winnie. As he neared the cameras, he thrust both fists in the air, a heavyweight boxer who has just won the championship, while the crowd surged towards the ring, greeting him with triumphant ANC banners.

'There's your Messiah,' Elmarie sneered as the tall, thin man stooped to enter a car, festooned with ANC flags and posters, which then forced its way through the solid ranks of his supporters.

'At least he doesn't look Chinese,' Jeremy said, trying to strike a flippant note, but the joke fell flat. 'So now he's out,' he added. 'It's a new chapter. Nothing will ever be the same again. For better or worse, everything we have known is going to change.'

'Are you going to join the ANC?' she asked tartly. The switch had been flicked; her loving half had been swallowed by the dark side.

'I don't think so,' he said after a pause. 'Not yet.' He had become an outsider in the struggle. Could he blame Elmarie? She had told him not to blame and she was correct. But he had definitely taken a step back because of her: that was a matter of fact. And the tramp in the fractured mirror within him tipped a cocky hand to a weatherbeaten face and grinned slyly. Under Jeremy's thumb a pulse beat in Elmarie's foot.

'Why not?' she needled. 'You're so obsessed with them.'

'Because,' he searched for an answer, 'because I don't feel that I deserve to join. I haven't suffered for the struggle. I haven't been detained or tortured or had limbs blown off in car bombs. What right have I got to hop on to the bandwagon of the struggle?'

Elmarie stared at him in disbelief. 'I didn't know you had to suffer before you joined a group of terrorists! I'd have thought they'd welcome you with open arms. You're an advocate. Have pride in yourself. You don't have to stand back for anyone.'

He let go of her foot, slid from under the weight of her legs and got up.

'I'm going to the rally,' he said. 'Are you coming?'

'No,' she answered determinedly. 'I don't like hot crowds. And it's not my cause.' She swung herself off the couch and stood before him, arms folded like a policeman, blocking his way. Then she turned and walked to the window, still clutching the wine glass to her breast. Forlorn as a lost little girl, she stared past the wind-chimes which dangled in the listless air at the oak tree that filled the space between her flats and the block across the way. The sun spattered dollops of gold on the surface of the leaves. She looked wistfully at the great fairytale tree as if she wished that its spirits could rescue her from this grim reality.

'You go,' she said at last, while he hovered uncertainly in the centre of the room. She had bitten the skin at the side of her thumbnail, drawing out a pearl of blood.

'Will you be OK?' he asked, putting his hand tentatively on her shoulder.

She twisted around, her face pale, her eyes suddenly sad and marked by fine lines that were the beginnings of the stamp of age. 'I'll be fine,' she said in a tone of voice that made it clear how much she was suffering. 'Don't worry about me.'

He swallowed his guilt and said: 'I'll see you afterwards.' He made for the door as the sun illuminated the red wine clasped in a crystal goblet in her strong white hands, making it shine with a holy light.

'Whatever you like. I may not be here.'

'I'll take my chances,' he answered with a confusion of anger and pity at her. He almost flung himself down the stairs, two or three at a time. He was always leaving under a cloud. He yearned for her when they were apart, but they were pitiless with each other when they were together.

The mountain lay like a lion across the city, the proud dome of Lion's Head falling away to a dramatic sweep of neck then flattening out into a long stretch of back before rising again in the swollen rump that was Signal Hill. The late afternoon sunlight drew the colour from the beast, leaving it drab and lethargic, sprawled lazily across the city.

Jeremy was dressed in cool cotton trousers and a loose-fitting white shirt, but still the heat had soaked him by the time he got to his office. At times he feared the heat; it was a reminder of how frail all life was on the planet. The gentle sustaining sun of mild spring days was really a fireball that could punch through the disappearing ozone layer and scorch the green lands into deserts. You lived under an illusion that all would be well whereas in fact chaos waited for you to drop your guard.

He parked in his bay on the second floor and took the mercifully cool lift to the ground. He walked down the well of St George's Street which was now in shadow from the tall buildings and cut across Adderley Street to the Parade.

What had been a largely empty area in the morning, when they drove past on their way to lunch, was now filled with human flesh. The square was a dam of people, compressed into a space which was, by the minute, less able to accommodate them, while more flowed in and none left. Every tree was ripe with spectator fruit; the statue of King Edward VII was crawling with human lice; the scaffold for the press was so infested that only a miracle kept it from collapsing.

Jeremy squeezed past traffic cops with two-way radios and motor-bikes tethered to crowd-control barriers in Corporation Street and pushed through corridors between rows of spectators, stepping on toes and apologising, but no one seemed to mind – pain was dulled in the heat of the throng. Young and old, fathers with children on their shoulders and wives tucked under their arms, had left the townships en masse to see Mandela. Elmarie would have hated the heat and the sweat and the smell. The crowd blanketed the whole open area, from the post office across to the Castle, from the City Hall down to the bus terminus.

Jeremy could not see any part of the Parade beside the immediate elbows and necks and backs of heads. But he had a more or less clear view of the City Hall balcony where the world's most famous just-freed political prisoner would appear, until a tall sour-smelling man with a back like a barn door moved right in front of him and he had to sidle to the left, and focus again between a new set of heads.

His back began to ache as he stretched to get a glimpse of the balcony which was pulsating with officials nursing microphones and he reflected ruefully that his short Jewish ancestors had not made it easier for him to attend mass rallies in Africa. He recognised a few city councillors and the American politician, Jesse Jackson, leaning out of the ground floor windows of the City Hall – privilege bought front-row seats.

A chain of enterprising youngsters had attached themselves like lizards on the knobbled stone wall from the pavement up to a window next to the balcony. Cool plastic containers flowed along this chain, quenching inflamed thirsts from the city council's bathrooms. By 5 o'clock the crowd still kept the midday heat trapped in the Parade, although a few umbrellas in ANC colours and the dizzy fronds of the palm trees lining Darling Street gave some relief.

If Jeremy had lifted his feet from the ground, he would have been suspended in the python grip of the heaving, sweating mass of humanity; every surge forward had him toppling over on to the broad back of the man in front whose T-shirt said: WORKERS OF THE WORLD UNITE.

Anti-apartheid cleric and patron of the United Democratic Front, the Reverend Allan Boesak had the microphone and was pleading from the balcony: 'Comrades keep back. Nelson Mandela will be with you soon. He has waited twenty-seven years to see you, so you too must be patient . . .'

A tiny woman with a face fashioned from rawhide yelled back from somewhere near Jeremy's right elbow: 'Tell him to come now! We're hot and hungry and thirsty. We just want to say hello and then go home!'

'We've had enough of politicians!' a shrill voice echoed. 'If you was part of the struggle, you'd be down here with us!'

'Comrades, please have patience!' Boesak cried. '*Amandla! Amandla!* Please be quiet . . .'

It was just across the square, in a little coffee bar in St George's Street, that Jeremy used to meet Elmarie, secretly, because she had a boyfriend. They would huddle over their cups exploring the virgin territory of each other while she stole glances at the steamed-over window, expecting François to walk past and find them. Thrilled by her beauty, Jeremy was drawn into her world of mystery, also hiding, although he was not sure why. It was not from François – if that was his name; he could not remember. Perhaps it was from his mother. Mesmerised by the curve of Elmarie's throat, frustrated by the neckline of her blouse as she leaned forward on her elbows, longing to cup his gentle lawyer's fingers under her breasts, his mother's voice poisoned his mind.

'We can do business with them, we can take money from them, but we can't marry them,' Esta hissed. 'They're different. They don't understand us. They'll take what they can from us but in the end, to them, we're always bloody Jews.'

'It's not like that with Elmarie and me,' Jeremy fought back. 'We understand each other. We've got a lot in common. When we get together we just talk and talk . . . We go to movies . . .'

'My boy, a marriage isn't based on the movies. You've got to come from the same place. Your values must be the same.'

Elmarie was covering the trial of a rich businessman who was accused, and later convicted, of killing his wife in a jealous rage because she had a lover. One of the partners in Jeremy's firm was acting for the accused. Elmarie came to interview the lawyer in the firm's offices when she first saw Jeremy; he was hurrying, head down, deep in thought, he was hurrying on his way to the photostat machine and she fell in love with him. At least that's what she said. He had reminded her of a character in a novel, or she had dreamed about meeting him, or he had made her think of François but a more sensitive version; it was some reason as whimsical as that. After she had fought down her first rush of infatuation, she pursued him and said she needed to interview him in the coffee shop. Who would not agree to be questioned by a beautiful woman? He went.

In the weeks that followed, they would steal moments, he from his attorney's office, she from her magazine, and they would stare into each other's eyes as if a deeper meaning were to be found there than they could get from words alone. The air between them was charged as they hid on hot days in that poky coffee shop with its green railway-carriage seats and tear-jerking tang of onions that knocked out the smell of her perfume. Sometimes their hands brushed while reaching for the sugar or the milk and, embarrassed, she would pull away surreptitiously, pretending they had not touched or that the incident was meaningless. But his skin tingled afterwards and he pressed his fingers to his lips, trying to seal in the contact. It was as if she would fulfil him, make him happy for ever, flow like red wine into the empty places in his soul to bring him the peace that he craved.

She told him afterwards that she used to comb her hair, study her face in the cloakroom mirror for spots and touch up her make-up (she wore very little) each time before they met. She was not able to concentrate on her work in the hours before, and felt an incurable emptiness when they parted. He, meanwhile, did not have time between clients and court to spruce himself up and he was amused to think how vile and worn he must have looked. Perhaps she was attracted to his jaded air because it created the impression of someone who worked hard enough to look after her.

And then, after he paid the waitress and gave her a tip for her knowing smile and wink, Elmarie would return to her relationship – unhappy because François was insensitive to her needs, even though he 'came from the same place' as she.

'So you see, Mom, that's not the overriding factor. One can transcend backgrounds,' he said. 'Not even coming from the same background provides security.'

'Well it helps,' she said, adding in a moment of rare humour: 'Just don't come home with a black,' and her laugh bubbled from the side of her mouth.

He only found out about Elmarie's fear of blacks and her dark side after enough meetings in the coffee shop had led her to his cottage and bed and the foundation of their relationship had been laid; by then it was too late to escape the consequences of their different value systems. She would have been better off with François . . .

Jeremy's father was struck by weariness and snow entered his cheeks; a blood test confirmed that he had leukaemia – the worst form. In one blurred week, he was admitted to Groote Schuur's cancer unit, had a hole drilled into his chest through which they pumped poison that was supposed to cure him, and then on Saturday night turned purple as blood exploded through a weakened artery and flooded his brain. His wedding ring, which he no longer needed, slipped off his monkey fingers as his enemy killed him.

And Jeremy was introduced to the City of the Ill and the Dying; its slippered citizens robed in white, connected still to this world through tubes and bottles, emitting blood through natural or manufactured orifices. There was a terrible inevitability about this place: every free person outside its walls was a potential resident in its wards. No matter how young and healthy you may be now, this grim ante-chamber to a more permanent abode waits to take you in. Only the lucky escape from its stiff beds. Selwyn Spielman was not one of them. Elmarie stepped into the breach and sat with his son, night after night, while Jeremy learned how to face life without the security of a father. From then on he owed her a debt of gratitude, just as he owed one to his mother: both women had nurtured him when he was at his most vulnerable.

The sound of shots from across the Parade riveted him back to the present. Heads were turning anxiously, shoulders swivelled against the weight of the crowd. Jeremy stood on someone's foot, but no one cried out. He felt a rush of pain at his helplessness, trapped like a ship in pack-ice. The crowd was surging away from the noise and young men were sliding like bandits in a Western off the green roofs of the stalls on the Parade. Had rogues in the police begun to fire into the crowd, trying to stampede it and turn the day into a disaster, to prove that the brave new South Africa could not work? But it was impossible to see what was happening on the far side of the square and after a while the shooting stopped, the fear cooled, the people forgot about the incident and returned from this distraction to the long vigil for Mandela.

In a shrill voice, Boesak was still cajoling: 'Please, Comrades, have patience. Where is your discipline? Take my word for it, he is coming. We will see Mandela. Please listen to me! Just take my word for it, he is coming. We are bringing him out. When I appear on this platform again, it will be with Mandela. I am not kidding. It will not be long now ... Please Comrades, don't push ... The tower is going to fall over ... No, no, no, please don't hurt anyone ...'

'*Ag*, just let him come!' someone piped up.

Jeremy was battered and exhausted as the sun began to dip behind the skyscrapers in the city centre. How long should he wait? Would the great man still make it? The seething mass remained, despite its misgivings, ever hopeful that the Messiah would arrive on that balcony, take the microphone and deliver the message that everyone wanted to hear: 'Apartheid is dead!'

But then a hard crack had the adrenalin pumping again: this time the disturbance was very close. Heads popped out of the scrum, eyes spun again, searching for the new danger, Boesak's microphone was stung into silence. But it was not police gunfire, nor a bomb, nor the crowd rioting. The journalists' scaffold, worn down by the weight of the day's spectators, buffeted by tired shoulders, had finally given up the unequal struggle. It sank slowly to its knees, like an elephant with a hunter's bullet in its brain, and those with privileged positions dripped off like insects from their dying host. The long poles caved in gently, allowing everyone to descend gracefully to rejoin the mass from which they had risen up. And, swallowing them, the crowd settled down again to wait.

Jeremy's skin was sticky from dried sweat; the tacky hair under his armpits glued his arms to his torso – he wanted to go home and bath. Nearby, a woman stood proudly, Mama ANC, unbowed by the vigil under a white-hot sun – a rock of Africa. She wore a flowing, traditional tribal dress of black, yellow and green stripes – ANC colours – voluminous as a tent over her full figure. A red turban capped a noble face with a high forehead and bright, intelligent eyes.

Perhaps Elmarie was right: this was not his fight; he was not one of the oppressed masses, but a soft, white lawyer unused to township dust, filled with romantic notions of the black struggle. He should leave this arena to the real adversaries who had waited centuries for liberation.

The sun was gone when the roar came. Jeremy forced his wrist up against the wall of flesh around him to look at his watch: it was 7.40; the great man was almost four hours late. The hail of noise entered his body through his skin and he found himself roaring too, as if every soul on that vast square were linked, when Mandela descended to stand in the semi-darkness between the pillars on the balcony of the City Hall. Then the pain in his limbs, the stiff joints and aching back were forgotten as the man of myth emerged, waved, and hoisted his arms in salute.

Jeremy's feet were swept away and he almost fell as the crowd washed forward remorselessly. But the woman in the ANC caftan turned into clay and stood firm, entrenched in the earth while the mob swirled around her as it sought to unite with the fountain of power.

Bowing only very slightly to the years, the grey-haired old man in the shadows threaded the handles of his gold-rimmed spectacles around his ears with a watchmaker's fingers. He pointed his fist over the heads of the masses as if he were bestowing a blessing, and then launched a single missile to explode in the South African sky: '*Amandla!*'

As if the wind were applauding, the ANC flag hanging limply above him rippled to life. '*Awethu!*' erupted from half a million throats and bounced off satellite dishes, driving into homes around the world the message of a people declaring themselves to be free.

And a second missile: '*Amandla!*' on a higher trajectory than the first.

'*iAfrika! Mayibuye!*'

Surrounded by his ANC family, his wife Winnie to the left and colleague Walter Sisulu to the right, Nelson Mandela, known by his clan name 'Madiba', spoke to the world for the first time in twenty-seven years.

'Friends, comrades and fellow South Africans,' he said in a voice that wavered at first, but which grew stronger as he went on. 'I greet you all in the name of peace, democracy and freedom for all. I stand here before you not as a prophet, but as a humble servant of you, the people . . .' The platitudes did not matter; the occasion did.

Was Elmarie watching this? Was she, a journalist, able to transcend her prejudices and find some interest in an historic moment? A few weeks ago, such scenes would have been unthinkable on South African television – how quickly the fate of nations changes – for then the ANC was public enemy number one. How could incredulous whites make the sudden leap to see the former terrorist organisation as the

Government's main negotiating partner and the most likely force to drag the country out of its international isolation?

'Our resort to the armed struggle in 1960 with the formation of the military wing of the ANC, Umkhonto we Sizwe, was a purely defensive action against the violence of apartheid,' Mandela was saying with a wooden delivery. 'The factors which necessitated the armed struggle still exist today. We have no option but to continue . . .'

This must be going down well in those conservative white households which still have their television sets switched on, Jeremy thought wryly, and the frightened liberal homes where anxious parents once again turn their thoughts to emigrating 'for the sake of the kids'. Elmarie's words drove out Mandela's: 'Your liberal friends *toyi-toyied* with the blacks, but when the ANC was unbanned they were the first to run. Why didn't they stay in this new South Africa they wanted so badly? They helped stir up the blacks and made it unbearable for the rest of us.'

'I can't answer for those who left,' Jeremy had responded with an anger that was directed as much at them as at her.

Darkness was falling suddenly and comprehensively. The poor liberals! They were despised by the conservative whites as sell-outs, '*kaffir-boeties*', and hated by the blacks for getting in the way by mouthing sweet democratic nothings without forcing the racist regime to accept majority rule.

A Canadian news team had popped up next to him. The video operator was standing on a three-rung aluminium ladder which had a Cape Town baggage ticket still tied to its frame – a well-travelled ladder, tool of the modern journalist who has to get above the crowd, who can't let genetic shortcomings prevent him from taking the pictures. The team were probably refugees from the collapsed scaffold, forlorn and skeletal in the dusk.

Mandela was reading his speech, less a politician than an elderly schoolteacher, rusty after decades in prison, yet aloof, without the fluid movements of a practised orator, still stiff as a robot-man. 'I am a loyal and disciplined member of the African National Congress,' he said slowly and deliberately. 'I am therefore in full agreement with all of its objectives, strategies and tactics.'

To the rest of the world Cape Town must look like the cities of

Eastern Europe in late 1989 when massive protests in the streets brought down the Communist dictatorships, Jeremy thought; and I'm in the middle of it, squashed, reeking, hot, a lawyer no superior to a common labouring man. It was those triumphant nightly parades on the television screens of the capitalist West that gave de Klerk the courage to allow the liberation movements to go free, knowing that their mentors in the East had lost their teeth.

'The future of our country can only be determined by a body which is democratically elected on a non-racial basis,' Mandela said and the crowd hummed its approval. 'There must be an end to white monopoly on political power . . .' He looked up briefly, then went back to his notes. 'It must be added that Mr de Klerk himself is a man of integrity who is acutely aware of the danger of a public figure not honouring his undertakings. But as an organisation we base our policy and strategies on the harsh reality we are faced with and this reality is that we are still suffering under a policy of the Nationalist Government.'

Could Elmarie see her lover there, sandwiched close to the front near the Canadian television team, identifiable by his thinning hair and Jewish nose and restless eyes, set too close together, descended from shopkeepers who had to keep a lookout for marauders? Was she worried for his safety after the shooting earlier – the threat of bandits of a more modern kind? Or was she sticking pins into his photograph as Mandela pulled the rug from under the comfortable delusions of the whites, protected so long from the flip-side of apartheid?

'In conclusion,' Mandela said, 'I wish to quote my own words during my trial in 1964.' He adjusted his spectacles and raised his hand in emphasis. 'I quote: "I have fought against white domination and I have fought against black domination. I have carried the ideal of a democratic and free society in which all persons live together in harmony and with equal opportunities. It is an ideal which I hope to live for and to achieve. But, if needs be, it is an ideal for which I am prepared to die." '

The tall, impeccably dressed, frail man on the balcony was such an easy target for a madman wanting to plunge the country into chaos – the marshals had long since given up trying to keep order. It could have been a white or a black extremist, edging through the crush across Darling Street, keeping his pistol hidden under a jersey or in a bag – even elderly white women carried guns in their handbags. He could have pumped a volley of bullets into the elegant orator before the crowd swamped him and tore him apart. But the soldier would have been prepared to die for his cause.

Helicopters throbbed in the night sky as Mandela finished speaking. He turned his back on the crowd but then swivelled around. 'I hope you will disperse with dignity and not a single one of you should do anything which will make other people say that we can't control our own people.'

A dying octopus, the crowd seemed to lose its power. Jeremy could stand again, flex his arms without hitting anyone, kick some life into his stiff knees, as he had seen meths drinkers do on cold winter mornings after a night spent in a doorway, and begin the journey home.

While coach-loads of people huffed to the station and foreign television crews packed up their equipment, knots of onlookers remained amongst the litter and the torn branches and the steel bones of the press tower, draining the dregs of the great occasion. In the street, opposite the City Hall balcony, was the wreck of a car that had tried to get a dignatory through the crowd: its windscreen was smashed, its body dented as if revellers had danced on the bonnet and roof, unable to contain their joy.

Jeremy walked back alone past a row of broken shop fronts, glass crunching underfoot. A wall of khaki-clad marshals protected the cavern of a looted department store, having taken over that responsibility from the police who stood on the opposite corner with their dogs. If he had accepted the invitation of Paula Evans, he would have been a member of that alternative security force. As it was, he remained on the outside; he had turned his back on the struggle for the sake of his relationship with Elmarie. The crowd control barriers were twisted as if a giant hand had picked them up, wrenched them and tossed them aside. It was better that Elmarie had not come with him, although she was far tougher than the fragile image she liked to project; in fact, at times, he was sure that she was tougher than he.

His car also stood alone in the grey concrete parking area at Huguenot Chambers. It did not seem as if any of his fellow lawyers had gone to the rally. They were even more conservative than he. As much as he was cut off from the Comrades in the anti-apartheid struggle, so was he alienated from his colleagues.

Tomorrow he was meeting Themba Tshabalala, his next *pro deo* accused. Would this black man have gone to the Parade to welcome Mandela? Or did his impending case weigh on him so heavily that he would have missed the moment in history crucial to all South Africans? Mandela's freedom came at a time when Tshabalala was about to lose his. Mandela was stepping into the light of the new South Africa while Tshabalala, a product of apartheid's turmoil, was heading for the darkness. There was a bitter irony in that: what should have been a dawn of hope was, for countless blacks, no more than a long, drawn out sunset.

Against a fiery evening sky, the mountain was a gaping black void which swallowed light in the shape of a lion. Trees stood like hackles on its neck and across its rump; one stuck out on its forehead, an eyebrow that needed plucking. Diamonds glittered on the body of the illusory beast as if holes had been pricked in its dark fabric, letting through the light. Over Sea Point, cascades of flaming clouds reflected the sun sinking into the Atlantic Ocean as if signalling Apocalypse.

Jeremy did not call Elmarie when he got home because he still did not feel comfortable about speaking on the phone, even though the ANC was unbanned, Mandela was free and the security police could not possibly have been interested in a liberal lawyer. Paranoia died hard. He noticed irritably that he had forgotten to switch on the answering machine.

The phone screamed at him as he slid into the bath, images of the enormous crowd imprinted on his mind and his bruised muscles. Wearily, he pulled himself up and dripped his way across the lounge, leaving wet footprints on the carpet; if you want the phone to ring, have a bath, he thought.

'Jeremy!' Elmarie barked. 'Are you all right? I've been calling all afternoon.'

'Yes,' he said, turning his naked back on the flats across the way. 'Look, I'm sopping wet. Let me finish here and then I'll come and see you.'

'OK.' The relief in her voice washed away all the acrimony of the arguments between them earlier. She still loved him, even though they sat in opposite corners of the political ring. 'The party got a bit rough,' she said, lapsing into code language. 'I was worried . . .' Who were they fooling? If the police were listening, would they not understand that 'party' meant 'rally on the Parade'?

'I'm fine,' he reassured her. 'I'll see you later.'

◆

Elmarie had on her red towelling dressing gown, tied loosely at the waist, giving her a false, comfortable, almost middle-aged bulkiness. She slammed the door, pulled Jeremy against her and held him tightly, so that he was smothered in her warm smell of bath soap and shampoo. Her scar, that hid the worm inside her head, blazed red beneath her fringe.

'They said on the TV that there was looting,' she exclaimed breathlessly, looking into his eyes, touching her fingers to his hot cheeks, brushing his hair with her nails. 'Someone was shot dead . . . I didn't know if anything had happened to you . . . there were so many people . . . I felt so helpless.' She kept squeezing him as if to make sure that this warm body in her grip was indeed alive, to let him absorb her anxiety.

'This feels like what I went through on the Parade,' he joked, but she did not let go. 'I'm fine, really,' he said. 'We heard shots but no one knew what they were: there were too many people in the way. I'm pleased you didn't come. It was quite scary.'

'The police said it was gangsters . . . They shot a boy in the window of a shop he was looting . . . They used birdshot . . .' Elmarie was babbling in relief. She kissed Jeremy on the mouth and he tasted sweetness on her lips and smelled drink on her breath, the reek of parties. Her flesh trembled against him, her hair got into his face and he had to arch his neck back to breathe. There was no sign of her drinking in the lounge; she had disposed of the evidence, but she could not get rid of the smell. It excited him, the feeling of abandon that the drink gave. Her gown fell open and he put his lips to her throat and inched, with small kissing movements, down the front of her body, between her breasts until he could reach no further. He had his hands on her shoulders and was easing her arms out of the sleeves of her dressing gown while he kissed her mouth and she dug her nails into his back. He was not sure if it was he or she who pulled the other down on to the carpet, but he gave a quick glance to the window to establish that the curtains were closed before he surrendered to her warmth.

While he moved inside her, he remembered how, as a teenager, he had lusted after photographs of naked women in the pages of banned magazines with a hunger that was only satisfied many years later. Now he tried to look at Elmarie through the eyes of that adolescent, with that same hunger, only this time having under his fingers the curves of her living flesh and not *Playboy*'s cold glossy pages. Her eyes were closed, but when she felt him staring at her, she looked back with such love that he knew how badly the professional eyes of the enticing models had betrayed genuine intimacy.

PART TWO

PART TWO

6

All That Shines

In the grounds of St George's Cathedral, a vagrant lay out for the count, his legs bent at the knees, imitating an athlete, except that he had done his running and had nowhere further to go. His eyes were screwed closed in a lettuce face, his puffy red hands reached for dreams that he had no chance of grasping in this life. A wet patch stained the tarmac of the parking bay in which he lay. Someone was going to have to move him as the traffic started to settle in for the day. Jeremy wrinkled his nose at the stench of old seaweed that escaped from the man who might have been dead but for the shudder that rippled through his rag-clad body.

The lawyer strolled down St George's Street into the mall – past vociferous pockets of rand-a-bag fruit-sellers, past vendors crouching behind the sandbag fortifications of their newspapers, past a man charming a flute before an upturned hat that served as a begging-bowl, the sunlight glancing off the flat faces of the coins that passers-by had tossed in with a wish and a prayer.

'Shoeshine,' said a timorous voice as if unconvinced that anyone would take up the offer. Two black entrepreneurs had set up their business on a pink cloth in the mall – a row of brushes, about fifty tins of polish and a blue plastic bucket seat.

Jeremy glanced at his dusty black shoes – they had not been polished since last week – and, on impulse, sat down on the seat which rested, without the frame of a chair, directly on the brick paving. Immediately, one of the men, wearing a white overall with the word SHINE printed on the back, knelt to his task, frowning in concentration. His companion continued tentatively to suggest 'Shoe-shine' to those walking by. His black and white checked trousers had slid down over his buttocks, adding to his air of disreputability, but his face was round and friendly; an impish smile suggested that he shared a secret with you.

'How much?' Jeremy asked, suddenly concerned that he was in the clutches of rogues and about to be fleeced, but it was too late as the first dab of polish was already on and he sat so close to the ground that to get up against their wishes might have entailed a struggle.

'Eight rand,' checked pants said after a slight hesitation, his smile growing wider as if he realised that the balance of power had swung in his favour. A cap kept the bright morning sun out of his eyes, but pearls of sweat cluttered his forehead and he wiped them away with his sleeve.

'That's too much,' the lawyer protested. The salesman shrugged as if the matter of the price was beyond his control: it had been ordained by God and he was simply the bearer of the bad tidings. Emboldened by his attempt to bargain, he turned to offer his services to a coloured security guard who was striding past, carrying a tog-bag, his hair slightly rumpled as if he had just come off night duty.

'What's the price?' the man challenged in a hard voice: the release of Mandela had not put rosy blinkers on *his* eyes; he did not believe that the miraculous conversion by the country's leadership had filtered down to the rascals at street level.

Again the slight uncertainty, as if the salesman knew that his bluff had been called but he could not deviate from the price he had quoted his naive captive in the blue bucket seat. The smile flickered as he ventured again: 'Eight rand.'

'*Ag* no.' The security guard dismissed him with a curl of his moustachioed lip. 'I can *buy* a pair of shoes for that.'

'You see,' said Jeremy, enjoying the fledgling struggle for economic supremacy, 'you charge too much.'

'He's just a *skollie*,' checked pants retorted. His smile had gone out altogether. 'You know how much this costs me?' His arm swept over the row of flat tins.

'But you need business to pay for them,' the lawyer pointed out. 'It's no good pricing yourself out of the market.'

The man stared back at Jeremy without blinking: he gave no sign that he understood. His companion was buffing the lawyer's shoes with a balled sock covered by a nylon stocking. Mechanically he stabbed it this way and that, then stopped suddenly as if his meter had expired. He stood up. The shine was over. Jeremy studied his shoes; he could see very little improvement.

'All right, give me four rand,' checked pants conceded. The lawyer fished in his pocket and found a ten-rand note which he handed over.

The salesman turned on his heel without a word and vanished around the corner. His bottom was round and his arms hung at his sides without swinging: it was an effeminate walk.

'Where's he gone?' Jeremy asked, glancing at the tins and the brushes as though the shady pair would make the whole lot vanish with a flick of the pink cloth.

'He's coming,' white overalls said, frowning as if he doubted the truth of what he was saying. But as the minutes ticked by and there was no sign of his partner, Jeremy started feeling anxious: he had to get back for his consultation.

'If he doesn't bring my change, I'll have to take one of your tins,' the lawyer warned, looking at his watch.

'What kind of people do you think we are?' the man said, aggrieved. 'You think we steal from you because we are black?' But before Jeremy could reply, the salesman returned, grinning, and with a triumphant swivel of the hips thrust out his fists. Unclenching his fingers, he revealed notes curled like dried leaves on his calloused palms. Jeremy picked six rand from the offering, not sure whether to feel guilty or angry. He nodded his wry thanks, keeping his eyes down, watching the sunlight glint off his shoes.

There was still time to walk down the mall to Woolworths where Jeremy browsed through the clothing section until it was time to return to the office: he might have tried on a pair of slacks had he not been delayed by the shoeshiners.

On his way back he saw that a gang of five men had gathered around the shoeshine chair, chatting to the uneasy pair with an intimacy that put them all in the same camp. One of the newcomers slipped over to a tourist and showed her something surreptitiously in a cupped hand, probably offering a stolen watch or ring at a bargain-basement price. Jeremy was disappointed: he had wanted to believe that these men were not crooks.

The lawyer bought a newspaper from a vendor opposite the coffee shop with the green seats where he used to meet Elmarie. FREE AT LAST the headline declared, but was qualified by the subhead: LOOTING MARS HIS RETURN. The news seemed to be devoted almost entirely to Mandela's release. Jeremy folded the paper under his arm as he headed back to Huguenot Chambers.

In the lift were two attorneys. One carried a briefcase; the other had several brown folders containing legal documents. Jeremy's eyes fixed on the hypnotic lights indicating the changing floor numbers as if he were staring towards heaven. One of the lawyers in the lift was saying: 'Do you know enough Hebrew to understand? The Angel of Death is called *Malach Hamavet* . . .' His breath was sour. Then the doors opened at Jeremy's floor and, stepping out, he did not hear the answer.

A black man was sitting on one of the soft chairs in the reception room, his elbows on his knees, staring at the pot plants and the pigeons on either side of the window. He wore running shoes, jeans and a brown plastic lumber-jacket. He had close-cropped hair and there was a mark on his forehead which looked like an old wound. His fingers were squeezing a cloth cap as if it might yield drops of comfort if he wrenched it furiously enough. The photostat machine hummed as someone made copies; a cluster of advocates walked away from the reception desk in the company of their attorneys, but the solitary figure did not seem to notice; he was enveloped in his own world, trapped by the nightmares behind his eyes.

'Your client,' Fatiema said and Jeremy stepped over to the man, who snapped out of his trance and stood up. His shoulders were broad, his chest like a bear's; he dwarfed the lawyer.

'Hello, I'm Jeremy Spielman, your advocate. How do you do?' The cultured tone was an attempt to instil awe, to conquer strength with sophistication.

'Fine,' the man said. 'My name is David Tshabalala.' His voice was surprisingly gentle, even feminine. The ragged smile on his lips seemed to have been torn out of his face by his private ache; it revealed a missing tooth. His hand was dry and rough to shake.

'This way please.' The lawyer led the man down the corridor to his office, past the photographs of former prominent members of the floor, now dead or raised to the Bench. He indicated a chair opposite his and the alleged murderer lowered himself gingerly into it, clearing his throat nervously. Jeremy took off his jacket, hung it over the back of his chair, and loosened his tie before sitting. He positioned the brief with the tips of his fingers so that its edges were level with the sides of his desk, and scrutinised the face before him. It was not obviously violent, twisted by rage or scarred by gangsters' battles except for that flaw on his forehead. The face was so ordinary that you would not look twice at it in the street. The smile, which had been more of a snarl, was gone, and in its place was an anxious wrinkling of the forehead above eyes that hid no evil. Was this the man on the Parade who had pushed against the windscreen, frightening Elmarie? Jeremy had only fleetingly glimpsed that distorted face: so many blacks were scarred.

'Would you like some tea or coffee?' Jeremy asked and the frown was displaced by an expression of astonishment; white men in suits were obviously not usually polite to him.

'Coffee,' he said.

'Will you bring me two coffees, please,' Jeremy told Fatiema on the intercom, then turned to his client. 'It says here your name is Themba?'

'People call me David. The whites can't remember our Xhosa names.'

'All right, David. You are charged with murder and attempted murder.' Tshabalala nodded, but did not speak. 'These are very serious charges, and I'll say it bluntly. If the judge finds that you are guilty of murder, he can sentence you to death.'

The man's eyes flared wide with fear, then narrowed as if he were calculating his next move. His neck muscles were so taut that Jeremy would not have been surprised if he had jumped up and run out of the office. Then his shoulders softened slightly and he asked: 'Will the judge sentence me to death?'

'If he finds you guilty of murder without extenuating circumstances, that is anything which makes you less to blame. But these are difficult words. It all depends on what happened. You must tell me your story. I will argue in court for you.'

'How much will it cost?'

'It won't cost you anything. The State pays my fee. I'm appearing for you *pro deo.*'

'Why should the Government pay for me?' David asked suspiciously.

'Because there's a chance you might get the death sentence: that's how it works.'

A knock on the door had David's eyes darting in search of the police who were coming to take him away for execution, but it was only Fatiema bringing in the coffee. This place was full of traps: there were secrets in the books, in the woodwork of the bookshelves, in the soft voices and polite smiles, in the way the lawyer rested his elbows on his desk and nuzzled his chin into the pyramid formed by his fingers while his relentless eyes explored the territory of your face.

Smiling, Fatiema put down the tray and closed the door behind her, leaving the slightest trace of perfume in the air. A curl of grey hair had escaped from the custody of her scarf below her ear.

'And how do I get off this death sentence?' David said aggressively, then watched in amazement while the white man poured milk into his coffee and passed the cup to him. The cup clinked cheerfully; it sounded so civilised in this panelled office – this dead place – away from the heat and the dust of the townships.

'It depends . . . let's hear your story,' Jeremy said, taking a pen and writing paper from his drawer. 'Your full name is Themba Tshabalala?'

'Yes.'

'How old are you?'

'Twenty-six.'

'Are you married?'

'Gloria was my wife.'

The lawyer referred to the charge sheet. 'Gloria is the person who was killed?'

'Yes.'

'All right, we'll get back to that. Do you have a job?'

'I work for Mr John Wilson at Llewellyn Construction.'

'What do you do there?'

'I'm a bricklayer.'

Jeremy glanced at his client's knobbled hands. 'What do you earn?'

'A hundred rand a week.'

'OK. Now let me know what happened. Just bear in mind that I can't lie.' There was a look of bewilderment in David's eyes which were bloodshot from concentration. 'What I mean is, if you tell me that you killed her, I can't say to the judge that you did not.'

David nodded. He heaped four spoons of sugar into his coffee and stirred it vigorously, pondering how to answer. His cap crouched on the table, beaten but defiant.

'So did you murder Gloria Kekana and try to murder Edward?'

106

David swallowed his coffee in two or three hurried gulps. He wiped his mouth with the back of his hand. 'Did anyone see me?'

'These are the witnesses. Do you recognise any of them?'

David glanced down the list, tracing a blunt finger over the names; then he snapped his head up and his wide nostrils flared as he exclaimed angrily: 'Yes, I did it! I killed her!' He covered his face with his large hand and his anguished voice came from behind his palm. 'They were making me mad!'

'Tell me how.'

David blinked at the question as if he had just woken and was unsure where he was. He picked up his cap, a nervous tic, wrung it and almost put it down on the sugar bowl. He contorted his face as if he were reaching into his mind to pull his memories out by the roots. 'Gloria was living with her father,' he said slowly. 'She had left me. One day our baby got sick and we took her to the witchdoctor . . .' He stopped, overcome by the effort of putting names to the images in his head. He did not continue.

'Why did you go together?' Jeremy asked, picking any question to get the dumbstruck man across the table talking again. 'If she left you, I mean?'

'So that I would pay!' David declared, as if the answer were obvious to any father.

'Go on.'

'When we left the witchdoctor, Gloria was carrying the baby. I grabbed the child out of her arms . . . I thought she'd follow me home. But she ran away.' His workman's hands trembled, rocked by small quakes from within, as he was forced to confront the events that had led to him sitting in this white lawyer's office, fighting for his life. 'I heard a car behind me and then Gloria and her father jumped out. He said he was going to report me to the People's Court again and I lost my mind. I stabbed him and before I knew what I was doing, I stabbed Gloria, too. That's what happened.' David sat back, his story told, his role in this ordeal complete. Now let the white man save him. He screwed up his eyes in pain as if a hammer had struck him on the head.

'Are you OK?' Jeremy asked. 'Can I get you an aspirin?'

'I'm fine,' David said through clenched teeth. 'I don't want anything.'

'Well . . . then let's go on. Is Edward Kekana the father?'

'Yes.'

The lawyer jotted down the answer and scanned his notes. He would have to fill out the details with appropriate questions, establish a motive, try to sort out the lies from the truth: and all for eighty-five rand. It was going to be a long session for little reward. His mother was right: he should try to play golf – anything to build up a better practice.

'You said they were making you mad?' he asked. 'You mean Gloria and her father?'

'Yes.'

'What did they do?'

'Kekana never wanted me to marry Gloria,' David said tiredly, as though he were reluctant to re-enter the city of his memory. 'I didn't have enough money. He wanted her to marry the priest's son in his church – a rich man. But she loved me so she came to live with me at my mother's house . . .' David's eyes closed again briefly as if the pain attack were not yet over.

'Are you sure I can't get you something?' Jeremy insisted and when David shook his head he asked: 'How did Kekana react to that?' His curiosity went beyond the case: Jewish mothers were not the only parents who interfered in their children's relationships.

'He tried to turn Gloria against me. He sent me a letter saying that if I wanted to marry her, I must pay him fifteen hundred rand.'

'That's a bit of a cheek!'

David gave him a quick glance. 'Not really. It's our custom to pay *lobola* to the father of the bride when we get married.'

'Yes, of course,' Jeremy said, then added to cover his mistake: 'I mean it's a lot of money.'

'Too much,' David admitted. 'I could only pay a thousand rand.'

'Was Kekana satisfied?' Jeremy asked, wondering if this line of questioning was leading anywhere: he did not yet know what he was looking for; he would have to probe until he hit the nerve.

'I think so.' David rubbed his chin pensively. 'He told Gloria to wear old clothes to show she was engaged to me.' A brief smile alighted on the springboard of David's tight lips, then leaped off again. 'After that, things were fine between us for a few months . . .' He was staring at the wall behind Jeremy's head as if it were a screen on which he could monitor the deterioration that followed '. . . I used to visit my friends on weekends and we used to drink a little. Gloria did not like it and she told her father. He said I must be a good Christian and I must not drink or smoke.'

Jeremy nodded and watched the fine hairs on the back of his hand in the sunlight that filtered through the window. It was not bright enough to draw the blinds. The great rock face of Table Mountain cupped the city centre protectively; it had no power to save the far-off black township from which this man came. Its cracks and crevices frowned at the whites who had committed such terrible wrongs against their black fellow-citizens over the centuries. It brooded over those in its care who claimed: 'We did not know.' It warned of the wrath of the oppressed who would rise up and smite their tormentors.

'You said Gloria left you. Why?'

'Her father poisoned her mind. After she had the baby, she wanted all my money. She even used to complain if I gave pocket money to my mother . . .'

Jeremy wrote: 'Call the mother as a witness.'

'And she was jealous,' David continued. 'She said I had other girlfriends.'

'Did you?'

'No,' David laughed, but only as far as his throat where the sound turned into a rattle. 'One woman was enough trouble . . . Every time we had a fight, she ran to her parents. One day she did not come back.' He stopped as if he did not know what more the lawyer wanted. What was important? What could save his life? He settled back and Jeremy looked at his meaty hands: it was a wonder that Kekana had survived the attack. Self-defence wasn't going to be an issue here and there was not much more to go on besides a history of quarrelling – but which couple did not have that?

'You mentioned that Kekana had threatened you with the People's Court. What was that about?'

David scratched the back of his head before answering. 'Kekana sent me a letter. He said he wanted the rest of his money. I told him I did not have it.'

'Go on,' Jeremy urged. Money was a good avenue to explore; establish extenuation – that's what the case was going to be about. A domestic squabble over money was an easily identifiable factor in reducing the moral blameworthiness of a murderer: the judge would have no option but to take it into account.

'Kekana called us to a meeting, my mother and me. He said the thousand rand I'd paid him wasn't *lobola* at all; it wasn't money to buy Gloria as my wife. He said I owed it to him for making her pregnant.'

'You must have been upset,' Jeremy prompted. 'Gloria had left you and her father still wanted more money.'

'I was so cross!' David's eyes blazed. 'I called him a thief. I told him Gloria and I were married and he knew it. How could he say the money was not *lobola*?' David was crushing his cap as if it were Kekana's skull. 'He said I was rude and had no manners. He said I must not speak to an elder like this. So I left the meeting and walked away.'

'Walked away,' Jeremy wrote. He wondered if Elmarie was at work, 'licking arses' as she put it, and if he would ever earn enough to support her and their children. Certainly not by doing *pro deos*. He could not give her babies if no money was coming in. And the competition was intensifying; the Bar was filling up with young advocates and there were not enough cases to go around. He realised that his client was talking and he had not been listening. It was bad form to allow his personal problems to interfere with his work; that was no way to build up a practice.

'Sorry, please repeat that,' he said. Some of his colleagues used tape recorders, but if he were to pay a typist to transcribe the consultation, it would have rendered the whole exercise economically pointless.

'I said that Kekana went to the Comrades in Nyanga and complained that I was rude to him. The next day they dropped off a letter with my mother. It said I must go to the People's Court . . .'

And a rough deal he would have got too, the lawyer thought. The township youths' understanding of justice, after their experiences in white men's courts, was so warped that it was often expressed in terms of brutality.

'Did Gloria know what her father had done?' Jeremy asked, forcing himself back to the present.

'Yes. I met her when I was walking to court. I told her that the Comrades would beat me. She said she would try to help me.'

We'd better not emphasise that, Jeremy thought. 'What happened at the court?'

'Kekana told his story to the Comrades and then I told mine. They said I was wrong to be rude to an elder and I must learn discipline. So they sentenced me to sixty strokes.'

'It seems that you'll get a much fairer trial at our court than you had in Nyanga,' the lawyer was moved to say.

'Maybe,' his client replied. He lifted his head proudly and showed Jeremy the face of one of the *toyi-toying* warriors on the Parade. 'The People's Court can be cruel, but it's ours. The Comrades know what's going on in our community and this is how they try to keep everything under control. That time Nyanga and Crossroads were very tense.'

'I'm sorry,' Jeremy said, wiping the back of his hand across his mouth. He had been out of the townships for too long; he was seeing things from a white perspective which was perhaps unavoidable. In the days when he worked with Jews for Justice in Crossroads, he would have anticipated that the black man would be loyal to his own structures. 'Did they give you your strokes?'

David nodded. 'They said I must take off my clothes. They let me keep on my underpants. I asked them not to beat me on my head because I've been injured already on my head and they agreed. They made me bend over a table.' He pulled his lips back in an expression of pain. 'Then they started to hit me with *sjamboks. Aau!*'

'Sixty lashes?'

'No. Gloria stopped them after about thirty. She jumped between them and me. She said it was enough. She told them to stop before they killed me. Someone told me afterwards; I was almost unconscious by that time and I didn't know what was going on.'

For the sake of your case, that's a pity, the lawyer thought. She saved your life and then you stabbed her to death: what an irony – if she had allowed them to murder you, she would not have died. In fact, I might have been representing somebody else, accused of killing you. We must play down Gloria's intervention. 'Did they listen to her?'

'Yes. They said I must never insult Kekana again and I must not see Gloria. They told Kekana if I made any more trouble for him, he must report me to the court again.'

'You must have been badly injured?'

'I was. My back and my legs were bleeding for a few days and I could not walk. My mother wanted to go to the police and lay a

111

charge, but I told her to leave it alone. It was not a matter for the police. It was just between us in the community.'

'Do you have scars?'

'Here. Look.' David unfolded himself and stood. He took off his lumber-jacket and unbuttoned his white shirt, hanging both over the back of the chair. The air conditioning could not extinguish the sharp smell of sweat that escaped. David had a barrel of a torso, but it was not muscular; his chest was puffy and his stomach was giving way to fat: it looked soft; the beer was beginning to mould him. 'This is what Kekana did to me,' he said bitterly. 'My father-in-law!' His back was criss-crossed with angry weals, healed, but evidence that would sway any white court.

Jeremy nodded in satisfaction. That lattice-work alone should get him off a death sentence. No judge would remain unmoved by the sight of such mutilated flesh. The attack must have been ferocious. To what levels of depravity had the township youth been forced that they could treat one of their own like this? How had the suppression of his countrymen for the sake of racial purity stripped them of their humanity? Or was it wrong to blame apartheid? Perhaps this was just a version of tribal justice come to town. Elmarie would argue that they had chosen to behave like this and should be condemned, not excused.

'OK,' the lawyer said, and David eased back into his shirt.

'Afterwards, a Comrade came to tell my mother he was sorry they'd hit me, but they had to because that was my punishment.' David was sitting now, doing up the last of his buttons. 'I stayed in bed until I got better, but I was lucky – I didn't lose my job.'

'And did you stop seeing Gloria as the Comrades told you?'

'I only saw her to give her money. She came to my mother's house every Friday night after I got paid and I gave her twenty rand for the baby. But she always met me at the gate. She never came inside. She said she was scared her father would complain to the People's Court again. But I know the real reason: she didn't love me and she was going out with the priest's son.'

'And on the night of the killing,' the lawyer said, putting the final piece into one of the puzzles, 'you snatched the baby in a desperate attempt to get your wife to return to you. But Kekana, your nemesis,' David frowned at the word he did not understand but Jeremy did not explain it, 'threatened you with similar punishment and you lost control. All your anger and frustration boiled over and you stabbed him?'

'Yes!' David exclaimed. This white man could put labels to the thoughts in his head; he would paint word-pictures that the white judge would understand.

'All right,' Jeremy said, tipping the pieces of the other puzzle on to the table. 'That explains why you attacked Kekana. But I still don't understand why you killed Gloria.'

'I just lost my mind,' David said uncomfortably. He wiped his eyes with the back of a hand that was balled into a fist and shrugged his shoulders.

'Were you getting revenge on her because she'd left you for another man?'

'No!'

'That's what the prosecutor will say. He'll try to show that you planned to murder her because you were jealous.'

'I said "no"!' David glared at this little white sorcerer who was sticking hooks into his flesh.

'Then why?'

'I don't know,' the black man said sullenly.

'Did she threaten you?'

'She might have.'

'That's no answer. Did she or not? You were there.'

'Yes,' David Tshabalala said desperately. 'Yes, she threatened me, like her father. They both said they'd report me.'

'Are you sure? You don't seem to be.'

'I'm sure.'

'Is that a reason to kill her?'

David glared at his tormentor. 'I was drunk.'

'How drunk?'

'At lunchtime there was a party. Three of us shared some beers and a half-jack of brandy. In the afternoon, I had a few more beers. And at the witchdoctor I bought a bottle of Gordon's gin, so I was quite drunk.'

Jeremy shook his head. He had heard all this before: killers and rapists trying to use drunkenness to excuse their behaviour. Where had the image of law as a glamorous profession originated? Probably

113

from the movies and books. In reality it was all so sordid. The Bar was an interface between the elite and the low-life.

'And do you think the judge is going to believe that?'

David put on his blank face and the lawyer waved his hand dismissively.

'You were saying that you have a head injury. Is that the scar on your forehead?'

'Yes.'

'How did you get it?'

'My uncle hit me with a hammer one day when I told him his music was too loud.'

'That's an extreme reaction.'

'My drinking started then,' David offered. 'And my headaches.'

'Headaches?'

'When I get excited or cross, my head hurts a lot.'

'Was your head hurting when you stabbed Gloria and her father?'

'Yes.'

The lawyer looked at the Magritte print on the wall behind his client. The eyes of the statue were closed as if she were at peace. But the anger of the wound on her forehead showed that her death had been violent. A startling image of Elmarie's scar blazed before Jeremy's eyes: the drinking and the temper. She too had received a head wound. For a dizzy moment, the link made him put his fingers to his face to block out sight.

'You'll have to see a psychologist,' he said. 'I've worked with a Dr Higgins at Valkenberg: he's a very good man. He'll tell us whether the blow affected your behaviour. I'll also have to see your mother. Is there anyone else you want to call as a witness?'

David shook his head.

'What about your uncle?'

'He's dead.'

'Anyone else? Your employer? Teachers? Priests? Someone to say you're normally a very solid citizen and that you don't usually go round stabbing people?' He could hear what sounded like facetiousness in his voice although he did not intend it.

David did not answer; he just stared at the lawyer as if he were mad. Would Mr John Wilson come to court for one of his bricklayers?

Jeremy put his pen to his lips. 'Well then, we seem to have covered

114

everything,' he said. 'How can I get hold of you? Do you have a telephone at home?'

'There's a phone at the house on the corner. You can leave a message for me there. Or at my work.'

The lawyer wrote down the numbers. He wanted to ask if David had been one of the warriors heaving and sweating on the Parade: in speaking out for the People's Courts, the black man had shown a glimmer of political consciousness. But this case was not connected to politics and Jeremy decided that it was inappropriate to intrude into that territory. He sat back and put his pen down, indicating that the consultation was over.

'I'll be in touch with you about Dr Higgins.'

David flexed his fingers and looked at his watch, as if checking which train he could catch next, then stood up and Jeremy walked after him to the door.

The next batch of supplicants sat uncomfortably in the lobby, waiting for their gurus to dispense legal salvation. Jeremy pressed the lift button for David who stood awkwardly, shuffling from one foot to the other. When the lift came he threw a quick nervous glance at the lawyer, like a swimmer whose life-line has been cut, and Jeremy smiled reassuringly to give him the courage to get in.

'Hello, Mr Spielman!'

Out of the lift stepped a tiny advocate with thin grey hair and red eyes. He swatted Jeremy on the arm with a square, stubby hand. In the other, he carried a battered old leather satchel. His suit was crumpled as if he had fallen asleep in his armchair during lunchtime.

'How are you, Alistair?'

'At my age, you don't ask!' he trumpeted.

In a Spitfire, Alistair Redford had helped defend England against the German Air Force during the Battle of Britain. After the war, when he returned to Cape Town and rejoined the Bar, he expected that the big English firms of attorneys would support him out of gratitude for his heroism. But strangely enough what little work he got came from Jews. He grew increasingly embittered and his crusty eccentricity alienated all but the most patient. His wife had died and he lived in a small flat in the suburbs. He was the young advocates' bogeyman – they all feared ending up like him.

'Fatiema!' he greeted with a lonely, lecherous old man's smile. He strode up to the desk with a wide gait like a fighting cock. 'And how are my girls?'

Spielman turned away in embarrassment as the clients in the waiting room stopped their low conversation to see who was breaching the decorum of the sanctuary. But a small white flutter on Redford's dark sleeve caught Jeremy's eye and held him back before he could flee. Clinging like a flag of peace in a stiff breeze, wings quivering ever so slightly, was a butterfly. Fatiema's gaze followed Spielman's and she smiled when she saw the delicate, magical creature which had chosen to guide the peevish old pilot from a position on his crinkled elbow.

'I'll have a coffee please!' Redford bellowed, oblivious to that charm on his jacket. 'I've got to be in court at 2 o'clock,' he said loudly for the benefit of the hushed, startled congregation on the white settees. He turned and winked at them then bustled off down the passage, fumbling in his pocket for his keys.

Jeremy let his breath out slowly. He shook his head at Fatiema and she said in Afrikaans: 'The man is enchanted.'

Spielman returned to his office, on the run from the spectre of Alistair Redford. He opened the top right-hand drawer of his desk, took out his phone index book and flipped through it until he found the number he wanted under 'H'. He dialled and tapped his pen impatiently on the side of the phone as he waited for the switchboard operator to transfer the call.

The south-easter, roaring in from False Bay, had laid a tablecloth of clouds on the flat summit of the mountain. They swept over the cliffs in great white folds, their shimmering fabric covering the flaws in the rock face.

'Hello,' said an erudite voice with the hint of an English accent.

'Dr Higgins? Advocate Jeremy Spielman here. Hello. How are you? I'm defending a chap on a murder charge. He's got a head injury that might have influenced his behaviour. Can you look at him?' Jeremy waited while the psychologist checked in his appointment book. 'Next Tuesday at 3 o'clock? I'm sure that'll be fine. I'll tell him to be there. His name is Themba Tshabalala. Thanks.'

The lawyer made a note in his diary to call David and his mother, then started to pack up. There was no point sitting here; nothing more would happen today. He stuffed into his briefcase the pages on which he had transcribed the consultation, put on his jacket, and hitched up his tie. Suddenly the office felt drab and tatty. Alistair Redford, the face of failure, leered at him from the painted whorls in the imitation wood which covered the walls: the fear within the sanctuary of the elite. Jeremy straightened one or two loose law reports on the shelf where they loitered but that did not help. His pot plant, a nondescript monster, needed water yet again; the soil was yellow and parched – a reflection of the mood of its owner. But no matter how many jugs he emptied into that lugubrious bowl, the poor sand, barren as township soil, could not retain the moisture. He locked his office door, not that he had much worth stealing, and walked head down to the cloakroom, fortunately not bumping into any of his colleagues. He put his case on the floor and dashed some water on his clammy face.

What a way to earn a living! He made his money out of the misery of others. Lewis Singer would say that lawyers, like doctors, were only helping people who were in trouble already. But Jeremy Spielman felt that he was being as exploitative as his father and his Uncle Hymie: a poor black needed the white lawyer's skill to save his life; Jeremy used the client to pay his rent. The irony was that the apartheid state, which had created the problem, was paying.

Held up at a red robot in the steaming traffic, Jeremy bought the afternoon paper from a sweating vendor even though he would have a later edition delivered to his house. He did not know what he had done with the morning paper; he'd probably left it in the office. He glanced at the lead story: Mandela had told a news conference that there was no conflict between the ANC's 'total commitment to peace' and its continuation of the armed struggle, which was 'merely a defensive act against the violence of apartheid'. That logic recalled the graffito on a toilet wall in the law faculty on campus: 'Fighting for peace is like fucking for virginity'. The comparison was crude, but so was the death of the innocents caught in the maelstrom.

A cold-eyed gull had hooked its cruel yellow beak between the feathers of a pigeon which had been knocked down in Long Street and was pulling off red strips of meat. How like seagulls we are, Jeremy thought, tearing flesh from those who are closest to us. Then the lights changed and he drove home.

The late afternoon sun baked down on the City Bowl. Mr Pretorius was walking laboriously up the slope of Ivy Street, past the scrawny oak tree on the corner, staggering under the weight of his illness. As always he wore his hat and jacket, even in the heat. He stopped beside Jeremy who was taking his briefcase from the passenger side of the scalding car.

'Hello,' he said, touching his fingers to the brim of his old white hat. Purple veins bulged dangerously close to the surface of the skin on the backs of his hands. White prickles sprouted on his paper-thin cheeks where his razor had forgotten to reach. He hesitated as if he wanted to talk but the lawyer had no polite words to exchange. Jeremy's thoughts were clogged with the mud of the political earthquake rocking the country, with the fears of whites like Elmarie and the hopes of millions from the ghettos like David Tshabalala.

'When I was your age, I could run up the mountain,' Mr Pretorius said. 'I used to take my pupils for cross-countries. But,' he added in disgust, 'now look at me.' Bitter lines grew from the corners of his lips as he contemplated the decay wrought by age.

'You're very brave,' Jeremy ventured, 'to live alone.'

But the old man did not hear. 'I got sick after my wife died,' he said in his thick Afrikaans accent. 'But you know, life must go on.' He shrugged phlegmatically. 'At least I've got my dogs. When she died, I felt as if I'd been cut in half. I suppose that's why I got sick.' He dabbed his knuckles to his cheeks which were glistening with sweat or tears.

Recalling the strange comment of the other day, Jeremy asked: 'How is your eye?' as he slammed the car door closed.

'Goodbye,' Mr Pretorius said abruptly and set off again, leaving the lawyer shaking his head at the frustration of talking to an old man whose hearing ebbed and flowed.

The cottage smelled musty; Jeremy had closed all the windows in the morning when he left for work. He undressed and paged through his newspaper, which, like the morning paper, was dominated by the Messiah's return. In one of the articles, the rally organisers condemned the looting and the violence and blamed a 'criminal element'. An ANC spokesman said the crowd had become uncontrollable after a series of delays in getting Mandela to the Parade. The hold-ups began when Winnie arrived late to fetch her husband from the prison and then stayed inside too long. 'It would have made sense for the family and the reception committee to talk to Mr Mandela for only a short while before leaving the prison,' the spokesman said. 'It's not like walking out of the house to go to the movies.'

Jeremy sat on his bed in the cool dark shuttered room to remove his newly-polished shoes, but he did not have the energy to get up.

The tramp of his dreams sauntered past his eyes. A half-inflated balloon, attached by a piece of grubby string to the hobo's belt, defied gravity as it stuck to the air above his head. He turned and grinned, exposing his canines that were fangs, for he had no other teeth, mocking the man who observed him through the cracked glass which separated the two halves of consciousness. In that moment, a knife jabbed upwards, seeking out the vagrant's belly: it was welded to the hand of a fanatical assassin who had devoted his whole life to this moment. It found its target with a satisfying thump and, as the tramp inhaled his first breath of death, the balloon deflated.

Jeremy was woken by the insistence of a *muezzin*, calling the faithful to prayer. But when he opened his eyes, the sound was gone and he wondered whether it too was part of his dream. Night had crept in through the slats in the shutters and filled the room. With a shock he realised that he had not spoken to Elmarie all day; maybe she's found someone else who can give her everything she wants, he thought resignedly, someone who will support her and cocoon her from the harsh new South Africa, an Afrikaner who will both be sensitive to her needs and agree with her politically.

Before he fell asleep again, Jeremy reflected on the irony of the boy killed during the rally: he had lived through a lifetime of oppression only long enough to see Mandela get his freedom, but not to secure his own. How many more like him would there be?

A bell was tolling for all the sadness in the world.

7

Inspection

There were no roadblocks at the entrance to Nyanga as there had been in 1986 during the squatter war. Jeremy Spielman drove into the black township from Borcherds Quarry Road which ran under the freeway and next to the airport. To his left, a squatter camp cringed in early morning squalor, dwellings of black plastic wrapped over wattle frames like bandages over lame feet. To his right were the little box houses of the settled community, neat and poor. People meandered from the pavement into the street, unconcerned at the cars and taxis that wove dangerously between them; Jeremy drove slowly, attracting some smiles and a few hollow stares. One or two fists were waved – in welcome or in anger – at this white man who was audacious enough to drive alone in the township.

Trestle tables and stalls were set up in the squares; free enterprise was flourishing despite the unbanning of the Communist Party whose ideas did not seem to have taken hold here. Pyramids of fruit and vegetables, painstakingly constructed, threatened to topple if customers got too clumsily close, entrails hung from trees and posts, sometimes covered by flies, and the sweet smell of cooking meat had the saliva clogging his mouth. The richness of these markets was incongruous in that wasteland of sand under bluegum trees and black wattle which, instead of making the place friendlier, left it even more desolate.

In the distance, the outline of the mountain reminded him that he was still in Cape Town, although far from the spots where the tourists visited. Ironically, this blemish was right next to the airport and was the first sight that tourists had of the city. The mountain, which gave the city its tourist-brochure charm, had little impact on the black suburbs, tucked far away on the Cape Flats by the planners of apartheid. These social engineers had turned the townships into the enemy, ticking away relentlessly inside the cosy white land.

In May 1986, war parties of conservative squatters from Crossroads, widely believed to have been helped by the army and the police, turned on their ANC-supporting neighbours with a violence not seen before in liberal Cape Town. Teargas lay heavy as fog in the alleys of the squatter cities as the vigilantes burned down the shacks of the militant Comrades, raising skyscrapers of black smoke which were visible in the centre of Cape Town. Desperate people, dirt-poor already, were stripped of their last possessions and, in at least thirteen cases, their lives. Retaining only their pathetic dignity, the survivors fled to refugee centres set up by relief agencies under the cloak of the Red Cross, in churches, schools and community halls.

For months, Jews for Justice looked after four hundred squatters in a church hall in Nyanga East, and volunteers collected food and clothes daily from the white community, which they ferried, dangerously at times, to their charges.

At first, Cape Town, appalled by the violence, gave generously. But as the crisis dragged on and there seemed to be no end to the squatters' predicament, the benefactors lost interest and shrank back into their insularity.

Jeremy's group disbanded, the problem far from solved. The displaced squatters refused to accept the Government's offer to resettle them in Khayelitsha, a new township even further away from the city. They wanted their own land back and in the meantime they built homes even more impermanent than before, on any scrap of open ground they could find. Jeremy had heard reports that they were embittered and angry at their former supporters who had abandoned them. But most of the volunteers had to return to jobs and families which they had neglected during the long chaotic Cape winter. Besides, the immediate panic had been dealt with and the new problems were different: Jews for Justice had been the firemen; someone else had to be the social workers to help reconstruct the community.

Jeremy punched his foot on the brakes as a young man bolted into the road. The youth, for that moment a cartoon character made of lines from an animator's pencil, skipped around the bumper, stretching out of the way of the still-moving car, and hurtled down a sidestreet. No one was chasing him and the reason for his hurry was not obvious. The car lurched to a stop and Jeremy sat frozen, dumbfounded at the near miss. A minibus taxi screeched past in the opposite direction; if the runner had come by a minute later, the taxi would have got him. Or maybe not. Perhaps there were laws here regulating survival that whites knew nothing of. The young man knew, when he set out on his apparently suicidal run, that he was charmed; the spirits of his ancestors would protect him.

Which ancestors had intervened to save Jeremy one day during the ferocity of the Crossroads war when, innocently carrying loaves of bread and sacks of meal in the back of his car, he blundered into an army of vigilantes not far from the place where he had now stalled? The warriors, armed with a scrapyard's worth of sharp metal objects, were grimly bearing down on one of the refugee centres; their white armbands identifying them as *witdoeke* (he always wondered where they got those neat strips of material). They must have known that he, together with most whites in the townships at that time, was bringing aid to the Comrades. Their eyes raked his car as he crawled through their ranks; one wrong move, one sign of fear, and the axes and spears would have pierced his windows and transfixed him to his seat. But he forced a cool smile to his lips and fought the temptation to slam his foot on the gas. He was their guest, totally at their mercy. What wild thoughts pulsed through their minds as they saw a helpless pale white man crushed in their midst? What murderous impulses did they have to suppress? But they let him through, hardly scathing the paintwork of his car, perfect hosts, and he arrived at the relative safety of the church, shocked and throbbing with elation at his escape. As he bumped into the sandy courtyard and was mobbed by excited children, a Casspir armoured troop carrier rumbled past in the direction of the impending battle and an evening of teargas descended, drilled through by gunshots.

Now the issue and the leaders had changed and Jeremy, fed only by sketchy newspaper reports, did not know who was fighting whom, and about what: a lot of the squabbling seemed to be over claims to land and allegiances to rival warlords. That made entry into the townships even more dangerous: he did not have defined enemies, but neither had he friends.

Why had he come back? No one did inspections in loco for *pro deos*; the fees did not justify the waste of time and petrol. Photographs of the death scene were usually more than adequate. Only in very complicated cases, or where the client was paying, would the advocate take a look himself. Fatiema raised her eyebrows when he told her

122

where he was going but she did not say anything. She knew he was returning to the townships to try and bury some of the fears that the whites had built up over the new South Africa. As if the sight of the lost generation of black youth, whose only schooling had been in revolution, was calculated to soothe Jeremy's anxiety. They lounged in motley brigades under the ubiquitous Coke signs on the sides of the *spaza* shops, eyes as dull as flint in dead faces. Unease scratched its nails across the windows of his car.

Jeremy had the Tshabalalas' address on the cover of the file which contained his consultation notes, the charge sheet and the psychologist's report. The unpainted brick house was one of a row of similar coops in the street. A fence of diamond-mesh chicken wire caged in a bare, sandy plot, separating it from its neighbours and the pavement. A single window blinded by a curtain and a closed front door kept the world at bay, although the garden gate was off its hinges and hung awkwardly like a broken wing.

Jeremy stopped the car and could not prevent himself from looking over his shoulder as he opened the door. A group of children had collected from nowhere and shuffled up to him; a small boy with Bambi-brown eyes took the lead and smiled shyly, revealing teeth as white as those in a toothpaste advert. The lawyer smiled back. Elmarie would say he was being patronising, that he would not smile at a white child: perhaps she was right; it did not matter. He held his briefcase tightly under his arm and hoped he would not be mistaken for a Government official. In a suit, slightly plumper and without as much hair, he certainly looked nothing like the activist who had been accepted so easily by the anti-apartheid Comrades in 1986; then he was at least recognised as being a friend to an influential section of the angry youth. Now he was just a white doing business in the townships.

He pushed open the gate which squealed plaintively as it grated against its frame, setting off a chain of yelps from a dog that was out of sight. In response, the front door of the house flew open as the lawyer walked up the path, followed by the children – why weren't they in school? – and David's head peered out, eyes blinking in the brightness, as if he had just woken.

'Come in,' he said.

Jeremy stood uncomfortably on the doorstep for a moment, then followed his client into the lounge. Two very big women sat on a floral settee and a cluster of children played on the floor with tins and a broken pink doll, making the cramped room look even smaller. Some of the youngsters who had met him in the street entered as well; when the room got too full, the others jostled at the door. He nodded at the adults, eliciting shy giggles and a series of clicks.

'This is my mother, Thelma Tshabalala,' David said. A thin woman raised herself from a narrow chair and extended a limp hand in response to Jeremy's. The skin was lizard dry and horny. She had on an austere black dress, as if she were going to a funeral, for the visit of this lawyer who was going to fight for the life of her son. Her slow smile of welcome exposed a gap between her front teeth. Her hand strayed for the comfort of the crucifix that hung on her chest.

'How do you do?' the lawyer said, not flinching before the scrutiny of those who had assembled to gape and standing firm against the children underfoot who threatened to knock him off balance.

'Fine,' she mumbled, clearly overawed.

'Could we have a word in private?'

She turned and led him, wading through the floorful of children, to the kitchen from which there emerged the sickly smell of cooking bones. Her son, David or Themba, depending on whether you were white or black, remained in the lounge with the fat women and the menagerie of children who were all talking at the same time. Jeremy could not understand what they were saying. At school he had studied Latin, a dead language necessary for law. They did not teach Xhosa or the other languages of his countrymen, because official policy was to class all blacks as aliens, citizens of sham countries created by the Government, and there was no need to talk to them in their own tongues.

The kitchen was gloomy: light strained to enter through a small window high up. The pot emitting the vile smell was bubbling on a primus stove and a pile of clean dishes, ready for the meal, was stacked on the dresser. Four old, mismatched, wooden chairs stood round the kitchen table and Thelma pointed the lawyer to one before she took her place at another.

Jeremy had not told his mother that he was going to see his client in Nyanga: she would have been beside herself with worry. To Esta, the townships were an extension of Beirut. Here he was, sitting at a table opposite a mother, just as he sat at Esta's table, except that this mother was simple and humble whereas his mother was a bombastic racist. But, he reflected, this mother's son had killed his girlfriend whereas his mother's son, despite extreme provocation at times, had not.

'I'm sorry about your trouble,' he began, and her pinched face seemed to shrivel even more. She searched for a handkerchief in the pocket of her jersey and buried her eyes in it. Then she looked up at him with an animal craftiness; cornered, she was compelled to overcome her fear and to speak.

'What will happen to my son?' she asked in a tone so low that he could barely make out the words.

'Mrs Tshabalala,' Jeremy's voice echoed like a bell inside his head. 'I'll do my best to save his life, although he may well go to jail.' He was like a surgeon, speaking to the family of a cancer patient, encouraging them to be optimistic while they waited for the outcome of the operation, but preparing them for the worst. 'I will need you to come and talk to the court,' he said and her eyes snatched at the door, trying to open it so she could flee this terrifying suggestion. 'You must tell the judge about your son,' he persisted, 'if you want to help him. You *do* want to help him, don't you?'

She stared at the lawyer as if she had no idea what he was talking about, as if the shock of his prognosis was still sinking in.

'Do you know what I'm saying?' Jeremy asked, struggling for air in that stuffy, stinking room, wondering what ghosts he was trying to lay to rest by being here, or what hope for the future he was seeking. He undid his top button and loosened the tight knot of his tie.

'Yes,' she said slowly. 'You want I must go to the court.'

'Your son needs you in court,' he replied patiently. 'You must tell them what sort of person he is, and about Gloria.' He lifted his briefcase on to one of the empty chairs, clicked it open and removed the file marked STATE v TSHABALALA which he put on the small table. 'You're the only one he has.' He took a pen from his inside jacket pocket with the gravity of a warrior unsheathing his sword. He placed his pad neatly before him and squared the edges with the sides of the table as he would have done in his office. Thelma averted her eyes from the paper as if she feared it was waiting as a trap to incriminate her. Jeremy realised he was breathing shallowly to stop himself from gagging at the rich cloying cooking smell; he noticed that a ring of white foam had seeped out between the rim and the lid of the pot.

A movement at the kitchen door caught his eye. A small boy, barefoot and in short trousers, had sneaked in. There was such an earnest expression on his young face, as if he had seen things that should have been reserved for adults. He said nothing, just gazed blankly at the white man. Did he blame Jeremy for the horrors he had lived through? Was he now sizing up the oppressor, smelling him, calculating how to avenge himself, his family, his community? Or did he aspire to learning and the allure of the suit, the car and the status of the lawyer? The need for blood or learning: South Africa's future depended on which pan of the scale was more heavily weighted.

'One of your children?' Jeremy asked.

Thelma jerked out of her trance and turned on the boy, letting out an explosion of invective in Xhosa that had him skipping smartly out of the room. Jeremy flinched at the ferocity of her response; the tension of the murder charge was very close to the surface in this soft, slow woman.

'My daughter's son,' she said apologetically.

Jeremy flipped over the cover of the notepad and scribbled on the top page to get the ink flowing then folded that sheet over as well so he could get a clean start.

'Mrs Tshabalala, how many children have you got besides David?'

'Two,' she said. 'Two girls.'

'Do they have the same father as David?'

'Yes.' She coughed and sneaked a glance at the lawyer making notes, but when he looked up she shifted her eyes away quickly, not wanting to be caught.

'Are they married? Where do they live?'

'One lives in this house with her child and the other with her husband in the shacks. There's no place for them in Nyanga. They cannot find a place.'

'And your husband?' Jeremy asked, gesturing to the photograph on the sideboard. 'Is that him?'

She put her handkerchief over her eyes again and touched her crucifix. 'He was killed by a gang of *tsotsis*. I brought up my children alone.'

And what a hard life you must have had, Jeremy thought with

sympathy. Black women are the rocks on which Africa is built. The men are snatched by the predators, leaving the women to bring up the next generation. How would his mother have coped here? Perhaps the comparison was unfair. Her character had been shaped by an insular, cosseted life. She had never had to live in a hovel with rough, unpainted walls; the food Thelma ate, Esta would have fed to her dogs. She had never had to struggle to get what she wanted, only to hold on to it.

'David told me that his uncle hit him on the head.'

The woman stared at Jeremy before nodding; she lived in a world of her own; she re-entered the real world only briefly and when absolutely necessary, to answer questions.

'Was that your brother?'

'Yes.'

'How did your son behave before the attack?'

'Before, he was very quiet. He didn't lose his temper. If something troubled him, he used to try and think what the answer should be.' The light returned to her eyes for a moment then flickered out.

'And afterwards?'

She answered in a flat voice: 'Afterwards he used to fight with everyone . . .'

'With you and his sisters?'

'Yes.' She stopped as if she had been switched off.

'Go on,' Jeremy urged.

'David, my son, he was not quite right afterwards. When he put things down, he could never remember where. He forgot everything. He could not keep things properly in his mind. Then he fought with his boss at the power station and he lost his job. He did not work for a long time.'

'Now he is a builder?'

'Yes.' She was sitting up straight as a broom, as if she had been propped into place. A sudden coughing spell bent her over and she stuffed the handkerchief to her mouth to try to smother it. When the paroxysm was done, she reverted to her upright position, waiting for him to reactivate her with the next question.

'And he started drinking a lot?'

She nodded. 'He used to drink on the weekends. Sometimes it was with the people who stay in the shack in the backyard and sometimes at the hostels. When he came back, he was cross and he used to swear at us or chase us or even hit us.'

'And your brother? David told me he's dead.'

'He was a gangster. They killed him in a *shebeen*.' Her forehead was wrinkled and she wiped her hand over her eyes as she contemplated the misfortune that had travelled with her throughout her life. 'He only made trouble for me.'

Jeremy turned the page. 'David told me he brought Gloria to live here.'

'Yes. They paid me rent.'

'Where did they sleep? It's a small house.'

'Sometimes in the lounge, sometimes in the shack at the back.'

'Did they fight?' he asked, wondering as he did so how they could have avoided fighting. He and Elmarie fought and they did not even live together. Imagine sharing a room, and not even the same room every day.

A sob rippled through Thelma's stooped shoulders. She used the crumpled handkerchief to mop up the tears which welled up in her eyes.

'I know this is a difficult time for you,' the lawyer said sympathetically, 'but we have to do it for your son.'

A sudden smile flashed through the forest of her misery. 'Thank you, sir.'

'Will you tell me about one of the fights?'

For a while she kneaded her hands in silence. Jeremy became aware of people talking and laughing outside; their lives went on even though hers had stopped like a shattered clock on the night of the killing. And the killing will go on, Jeremy thought, born in squalor and poverty, marauding gangs, drunken squabbles, domestic disputes sorted out with knives. Friday night carnage resulting in hacked and broken flesh at Groote Schuur's casualty department. This was the mess that Mandela had inherited, the perhaps reluctant Messiah come from prison to save the souls of his flock in the townships. What expressions of bitterness and disillusionment would greet his inevitable failure? The prospect was chilling.

'Well,' Thelma began, her sad brown eyes pleading with the past to release her memories. 'One night David's friend, he sent him a message. The *tsotsis* were throwing stones at his house. He asked

David to come and help him. But Gloria thought he was going to see another woman and they had a very big fight. Even the neighbours could hear them shouting. My son only came back the next day and then Gloria and the baby were gone. David was so worried. He looked all over for them. He thought they were dead. But then, Mr Kekana, he sent a letter. It said that Gloria was staying in his house and she was not going to come back. Some men came to fetch her clothes. My son was so upset . . . he started to drink a lot, even more than before. He would not speak to anyone. I think his heart,' and she pointed to her own chest, 'his heart died then.'

'Was that the last time Gloria lived here?'

'Yes. She used to visit him sometimes, to fetch money for the baby, but she did not sleep here any more. David found out that she had joined a church choir and he was afraid she would get another boyfriend.'

'And then Kekana called you to a meeting about money that David owed him?'

She smiled wanly in recollection. 'Yes. There was a meeting. Mr Kekana said the money David had paid him was not *lobola* and my son called him a crook. Then Mr Kekana reported David to the People's Court. They gave him many shots with the *sjambok*.' Her head was now bowed as if her thin neck could no longer support its weight. 'He had to stay in bed until he could walk again. His sheets were full of blood and I could not get them clean again. He never went to Mr Kekana's house after that. He was too scared of that man.'

So Thelma corroborated this crucial part of her son's story. 'Did Gloria ever bring the baby here?'

'Once or twice,' the old woman replied, sniffing as if the odour from the cooking pot had finally got in her nose. 'But if the child was sick she never forgot to tell my son to pay.'

'And that's how they came to be at the witchdoctor the night that Gloria was killed,' Jeremy declared, tying the final knot into the tapestry.

'That's right.'

'What was your son like after that night when Gloria died?' Jeremy asked, almost as an afterthought. 'I mean, did he behave calmly, or was he aggressive?'

'*Yu!*' she exclaimed. 'He was completely mad. He used to drink a whole case of beer all by himself. I could see he did not care if he was alive or dead. He went out late at night. On the weekends, he drank even more.'

'He must have built some interesting houses,' Jeremy muttered under his breath, then asked: 'Did he ever talk to you about his problems?'

'No, he did not tell me his feelings, but I know he felt bad about what he had done. Only his work took his mind off his troubles. I told him he must live for his child.'

'Where were you when David killed Gloria?'

'Here,' Thelma said, her chin held high. 'In my house.'

'So you didn't see what happened?'

'I only know what my son told me.'

Jeremy wished he could bring his mother and even Elmarie's mother to hear the heartache and torment of this suffering black woman. Would Esta find sympathy in her neurotic heart for this mother from the townships? And Marie Coetzee? 'Savages!' she would snarl. 'What do you expect from them?'

He pushed his chair back and Thelma followed his example. He was taking the lead in her house. She was numbed by his presence and by the gravity of the situation in which her son had landed. As he was putting the file and notebook back in his briefcase, she cleared her throat and, holding the back of the chair like a walking aid, said: 'I ask you, sir?'

'Yes?' He noticed that her cheeks were blacker than the rest of her face, probably the destructive legacy of so-called skin lightening creams which ironically burned the skin and made it darker.

'What will happen to my son?' she pleaded, struggling with a question which she had already asked and to which she had received no adequate reply. 'He gives me money every week – sometimes thirty rand and sometimes fifty rand. If he goes to jail . . .' She paused, as if uneasy that he might think she was more concerned for herself than for David.

'Is that your only money?' he asked. He felt a desperate sorrow for this woman who was about to lose not only her son but also her breadwinner.

She hung her head, her eyelids drooping. 'I used to work for Mrs Anderson in Rondebosch,' she said in a flat voice, 'but then I got sick and I had to stop working. Mrs Anderson, she helped me, but she doesn't help me any more.'

'Don't you get a pension?'

She shook her head. 'The doctor said I'm not so sick to get a pension . . . and Mrs Anderson, she got someone else. And there are no other jobs for me.'

'You must tell that to the judge,' the lawyer said. 'Will you do that?' The cooking smell in the matchbox-sized room was beginning to overwhelm him. This was the Third World that Elmarie was so scared of; she feared the drop in standards as much as the violence, the masses descending on Sea Point with their goats and chickens, four families to a flat.

'Yes,' said Thelma Tshabalala hopelessly. 'Thank you, sir. I will tell the judge.'

He suddenly wondered if she had ever been inside a court, if she even knew what a judge was. 'Good,' he said. Should he offer to support her? But he couldn't even support Elmarie; how could he spend money on a stranger? Without her son how would Thelma afford even to buy the bones she ate? How would she stay alive? Was this, ultimately, why Jeremy had gone into the township? On a crusade to save David and his mother as he had tried to save the squatters all those years before? Or was it because he sympathised with a husband so disturbed by domestic turmoil he'd been pushed over the edge?

'I'll see you in court next Monday,' he said. 'You must be there at 10 o'clock. If I have to speak to you before then, I'll leave a message at your neighbours'.'

She nodded and stuffed her handkerchief into her jersey pocket. Jeremy opened the door and pushed into the lounge ahead of her, anxious to breathe in fresh air. The room was even more crowded than when he had entered, as if the word had spread and the multitude had gathered to greet the healer. There was a mother with an infant tied in a blanket to her back, a wrinkled grandmother wearing a fierce bullfrog expression and a scarf on her head, a teenage girl with a shy smile whose hands were folded in the lap of her neat pink skirt. Thelma did not seem to have control over the neighbours and their children who had invaded her house to see the lawyer.

How easily a personality cult can develop in these poor situations,

Jeremy thought. More than ever the people now needed strong leaders with whom to identify who could take up issues on their behalf; urbanised versions of tribal chiefs. But what dangers might such allegiances hold, as warlords, often flying the banners of political groups, competed with one another, sometimes bloodily, for territory and resources? In these conflicts the losers are the Davids and the Thelmas, Jeremy thought, who are sacrificed on the altars of their leaders' ambition and greed. This was the kingdom that Mandela had inherited.

David was waiting nervously, his big body too large for the small room. He turned to Jeremy with eyes hungry to know how the consultation had gone.

'Will you take me to the scene?' Jeremy asked as the hubbub died and a path to the front door opened for him.

'Scene?' David asked blankly.

'Where it happened,' Jeremy said, trying to be cryptic, not wanting to be too explicit before the hordes in the lounge.

'Oh yes,' David answered. 'There.' His slumped shoulders reflected his hopelessness. 'Come.'

Little fingers clutched the lawyer's trouser legs; some of these children were still young enough to grow up as part of an enlightened generation in a free country. They were untouched by the dark days that had produced the illiterate 'lost generation' whose slogan had been 'Liberation before Education' and who were now finding that the former was meaningless without the latter. Could these children drag South Africa out of the mire into which she was sinking, or would it be too late by the time they were adult?

Jeremy squeezed his eyes shut against the piercing daylight assaulting them after the semi-darkness of the house. He dropped his briefcase on the back seat, reached over to unlock the passenger door for his client then turned the key in the ignition, a machine-gun roll of engine. 'Which way?'

'Go straight there,' David pointed, 'then turn over there . . .' He directed with hard jabs of his flat hand that just stopped short of penetrating the glass.

A young man wearing a jacket with a torn sleeve was dribbling an empty milk carton in the street with the skill of one of his heroes from the soccer team, Kaizer Chiefs, aiming at an imaginary goal. He swivelled to the left, then to the right, dodging defenders, then lashed the 'ball' across the road in front of the car. Jeremy flinched but did not disgrace himself by ducking as the carton arced over the bonnet, spraying a volley of milk drops across the windscreen. The footballer grinned at the startled lawyer and gave him the thumbs up. David did not seem to have noticed, or, if he had, did not find the exhibition extraordinary enough to comment.

The road separated a squatter settlement from a row of brick houses. Because of the streetlights, visibility would not be an issue unless the witnesses had been far from the action. There were no kerbs; the pavement was on the same level as the road, divided from it by the gutters which were punctured at intervals by storm-water drains. One or two yards boasted moth-eaten trees.

'OK,' said the lawyer, 'how did it happen?'

David was sitting on the edge of his seat, head against the windscreen as Gloria's may have been in her father's car as she cast about urgently for David and her child.

'I was walking down the street here, with the baby in my arms, and they were driving after me, like so.' He made a steady movement with his hand, emulating the car following him. 'I slipped there because of the pain in my head, otherwise I would have got away and Gloria would still be alive.' He shut his eyes for a moment as if struck by the malevolence of those ancestors who had conspired to bring about the sequence of events leading to the tragedy. 'Kekana tried to make a turn here, but the road was too narrow. So he stopped the car there,' David pointed to a spot in the dust almost under a streetlight, 'and they jumped out and chased me. Kekana started to shout and threaten me and I got so scared that I stabbed him, just to keep him quiet. Then Gloria ran away from me, and she fell, over there I think.' The words dropped like lead sinkers from his mouth. 'I stabbed her on the ground.'

Jeremy stopped the car and leaned out of the window. He looked at the tarmac where Gloria's body had lain, sucking in its final breath, limbs thrashing in a frantic last bid to claw back the life that was inexorably leaking out. But on the hot black pockmarked surface there were no signs of her dying: no blood remained, not even a rusty stain, no scraps of cloth, no additional grooves gouged out of the tar by David's flailing knife. The road was as unremarkable as some of the battlefields in Natal that Jeremy had visited, where only a signboard indicated that this patch of veld had borne the weight of slaughter while the surrounding areas had not. Only the vapours, rising from the ground on a full-moon night, showed where the dead had lain.

'What happened to the baby?' Jeremy asked at last.

'Somebody took her. I don't know who it was.'

'There's one thing you did not explain to me properly when you came into my office. I said I understood why you attacked Kekana, but not why you killed Gloria. Can you tell me now?'

David shrugged his shoulders, as if the events of that night had happened to someone else, younger, more impulsive, and he was now reluctant to take responsibility for that person's actions.

'You told me you were drunk,' Jeremy said. 'You also told me you thought she threatened you. But if you don't come up with a better answer, the judge might decide that you planned to kill her out of revenge or because you were jealous. The prosecutor will be going all out for the death sentence . . .'

David's body seemed to have caved in and he stared gloomily back at the squatters who were watching him point out something to a white man. In this time of suspicion, might they not think that Jeremy was a policeman and David an informer? Might they not attack the Tshabalalas' house with rocks and petrol bombs one night to drive out the collaborator?

'It was the pain in my head that made me kill Gloria,' David said at last. 'I told the doctor . . .'

'Dr Higgins, the psychologist?'

'Yes. He asked me lots of questions about my head.'

'I've got his report,' Jeremy said. 'We'll call him as a witness. It's a good point to raise but is that all you can think of? Can't you tell me anything else?' If he pumped in enough questions, he felt he might dislodge something. He had to; he had almost nothing at present to go on.

'Yes.' The word squeezed out as if the hangman's noose was already biting into David's throat, choking the breath out of him. 'I had to free her,' he gasped. 'I had to free her from her father's evil which lived inside her.'

He fell silent, resting his big head on his fists like a child. Out of a sudden frustration, Jeremy pressed his foot down hard on the accelerator so that the car jerked forward before speeding off. He could not tell David that an answer like that, painful as it was to drag into the open, would mean nothing to a white judge. It seemed ironic that an explosion of anger at his wife had thrust David into Jeremy's life at the very time that Mandela, freed from prison, was symbolising the liberation of the black people in South Africa. Why had fate thrown down to Jeremy the challenge of finding the key to keep this artless, basically good, confused man out of jail?

The corrugated iron shacks and black plastic structures of the squatter camp stretched away on the left, vulnerable to wind and heat and rain. People he had helped during the Crossroads war were probably living in some of them; he had failed them too. While David hid under the blanket of his distress, Jeremy remembered Iris Dyantyi.

Iris was one of the stalwarts in the group of squatters that Jews for Justice looked after. Her open, childlike face gave no hint of the strength that drove her to remain with her people when she could have opted to live in the safe white suburbs with any of a number of elderly women whom she had befriended while working for various animal rescue organisations over the years. Her eyes were round and gentle as a puppy's; her huge breasts could have comforted the whole of Crossroads.

After the *witdoeke* burned down her shack, Iris joined a band of angry squatters on a march to protest against the apparent collusion between the security forces and the vigilantes. The police opened fire on the marchers and hit a dog. Iris, so the story went, ran across the road, grey and smarting with teargas, to rescue the poor animal, which was squealing in pain and fear.

What must those hard men of the riot unit have thought of this bulky black mama in her threadbare jersey, African print skirt and someone's cast-off running shoes, risking her neck to save a mongrel? Even they could not bring themselves to shoot, although one, barely out of his teens, tossed a half-brick at her from the safety of his armoured vehicle. The missile struck Iris below the ribs and knocked her off her stride but she did not fall. Winded, with the dog under one arm, her eyes stinging and streaming from the chemical cloud, she bent to pick up the brick and then carried the animal to cover. When things had quietened down, she had the dog smuggled out of the sealed-off township to one of those safe white houses: another rescue by the St Francis of Crossroads.

When Jeremy asked her about her mercy dash, she told him softly that she carried the brick in her bag, hoping to bump into that policeman. She wanted to hand it back to him with dignity. She wanted to ask that young white man if he would have thrown a brick at a *white* woman his mother's age.

Iris wore a Star of David around her neck because the Jews had helped her and she liked to joke that she was Jewish. It was her lucky charm; it made her invulnerable. She could pluck wounded animals from the jaws of the beast without fearing that it would swallow her.

When the winter of 1986 passed and Jeremy once more got sucked into his profession and his white world, he inevitably lost contact with Iris and with hundreds like her, simple people whose acts of heroism would forever go unnoticed. He looked now with longing into the rough alleys between the squatters' shacks, wondering if he would see her; but of course she did not come running out, dog under one arm, a well-worn half-brick with rounded edges in the other, recognising his car. He had no idea where she was, if she was even still alive. Every week the newspapers carried articles about shacks that had burned down, either because of overturned candles or arson. Had brave Iris survived?

'Do you know any of the squatters?' he asked.

'Some,' David shrugged. 'Who d'you want?'

'A woman by the name of Iris. She helped sick animals.'

He shook his head listlessly. 'We can stop and ask.'

But Jeremy did not want to become involved any more. If he met Iris, would she see him as an equal or still as a member of that welfare organisation which daily brought bread and paraffin and milk powder to her miserable fellows? Would she resent him because Jews for Justice had run out of steam and the squatters, eventually left on their own, probably felt bitter and betrayed? Had she ripped off her Star of David in anger at being deserted? It was too complicated; and Elmarie would make his life hell if he got involved with the squatters again. He had buried that part of himself: it had been an adventure, but now it was over. He was helping in another way.

'It doesn't matter,' he said, slowing down in front of the Tshabalalas' house. 'Remember to be in court on time. Monday, 10 o'clock.'

'OK,' David said, getting out of the car as stiffly as a zombie.

Jeremy watched him slouch up the path and wearily push open the front door. Then the lawyer drove away, avoiding the potholes, past the bedraggled Port Jackson shrubs, alien vegetation that had invaded the Cape Flats, leaving the ghetto behind for the welcome folds of Table Mountain.

8

Whites

When they had finished making love, Elmarie was crying. Jeremy laid his hand tenderly on her shoulder and from there it slipped to her breast. He cupped his fingers over the smooth hot flesh, as much to comfort himself as her, and felt the velvet skin of her nipple press into his palm. A moment ago his lust had been extinguished, buried deep inside her, but now, suddenly, he felt a new stirring, brought on by her vulnerability. He pushed himself against her thigh but she was no longer interested in sex. Sobbing silently, she dabbed her eyes with the sheet.

'What's the matter?'

She looked at him with the mournful eyes and quivering lips of someone who is newly bereaved, but did not answer.

'What's wrong?'

'I'm crying,' she began, then stopped to draw the breath to continue. 'I'm crying for the loss of my birthright.'

'Why? What do you mean?'

'It's de Klerk,' she said emphatically.

'I don't understand . . .'

'He's selling out my people. We fought for this country, my . . .' she sought for the correct generation, '. . . my great-grandparents. And now he's giving it all away. All their struggles were for nothing,' she added, swallowing her tears. 'They died in vain.'

'There is no other way,' he said patiently. 'Apartheid can't go on. It's killing the country. We can't afford it.'

But she just curled up on her side, drawing her knees towards her chest, and he lay next to her, moulding his body to the shape of hers, his erection drooping and lost. She rubbed the backs of her fingers against her lips as her breathing returned slowly to normal, and the tension eased out of her tight shoulders.

'Please be kind to me,' she said softly. 'I have nightmares.'

'What about?' He put his fingers into the hollow at the small of her back and gently traced the fine golden line of hair up the groove of her backbone to between her shoulder-blades. In the lobe of her ear was a hole through which she could put an earring, a pin-prick indentation in the fleshy skin.

'The accident,' she said and her body was cold against his.

'Tell me,' he murmured when she did not go on.

'You know the story.'

'It doesn't matter. I want to hear it again.'

'Are you sure?'

'Of course.'

'All right,' she relented although he knew she wanted to tell him. 'It was Christmas Eve. My mother was drunk – she'd been celebrating all day. My father drove me to the café in Voortrekker Road to buy a Coke. I remember the bright Christmas lights; I was so very excited and happy to be in the car with my dad – he was my whole world. But then there was a terrible crash and the car screeched and spun around and for me Christmas ended ... When I looked again, the windscreen was just a hole surrounded by broken glass and the black night poured in. The front of the car had been squashed into my father and I knew they would never be able to cut him out: his body had merged with the metal. The only lights then were the flashing red lights of an ambulance. Blood blotted out my sight. All I can remember after that was the screaming ... I think it came from me. My mother visited me in hospital but she would not stay overnight – she said hospitals frightened her. So there I was, a seven-year-old child who had just lost her father, alone and scared in a hospital ward ... That's my nightmare,' Elmarie concluded, touching the scar on her forehead with the tips of her fingers, as if for reassurance that her familiar wound was still there. 'And the black driver ...' her body trembled. 'He laughed in court, that's what my mother said, when the magistrate only gave him ten years. He thought they'd hang him ... Ten years, less time off for good behaviour – that's what my father's life was worth.'

Jeremy held her tenderly, as one would nurse a wounded bird, soothing away her pain while the room began to grow dark and the lights of the city pierced the veil of night.

She sighed heavily. 'Somehow it's all right in the morning when I open my eyes. I wake up, have breakfast, and life goes on.'

'Yes, it does,' he said, and because he wanted to take her mind off the trauma of her past with news of a dynamic event, he added: 'There's a march tomorrow.' It was the first comment that came into his head but as the words passed his lips he realised he had made a mistake. Political events which excited him struck at the core of her insecurity.

'What march?' Her voice had a sudden slicing edge that made him flinch.

'To the Castle,' he answered, dragging the words out.

She sat up quickly and turned to face him. In the darkness, her milky body reflected the streetlight, creating an illusion of softness. 'Why?' she demanded. 'Why the Castle?'

'It's the army headquarters,' he said, switching on the lamp. 'The marchers are going to stand and point at it for an hour.'

She screwed her eyes against the light. Her face puckered and she pulled the sheet up over her shoulders. 'Why do you accuse the army? They keep order. Without the army, there'd be chaos.'

He took a deep breath and spoke slowly as if he were explaining to a child. 'The army provokes the trouble,' he said. 'They take sides as they did in Crossroads. Their policy is to divide the blacks into factions, to set them against one another, to bribe one warlord so that he'll attack the next one down the road. The army looks good keeping order when the blacks start killing each other. And they make sure their side wins, so they have a puppet leader in place . . .'

'Have you got proof of this?' she snapped back. 'You're a lawyer and I'm a journalist. We both know that such wild claims must be backed by evidence.'

'The proof will come out,' he promised, resigning himself to the inevitable argument. 'The dirty tricks, the political murders, the disappearances . . . And we'll all be surprised at where the orders came from, how high up.'

'You can't blame the army and the police for everything,' she said. 'Surely the blacks must take some responsibility for themselves? If you don't believe that, you're as patronising and racist as all those other white liberals.'

'They're driven to do things to one another that we, whites living in our safe suburbs, could not comprehend. I know. I take the cases. The point is that anyone, no matter what colour, would behave like that in those conditions. And apartheid is to blame.'

'Well go and protest then.'

'I can't,' he said and the words came out as a bark. 'I'm in court tomorrow. I've got a murder case.' He swung his legs out of bed; all the love that had existed between them five minutes earlier had evaporated in a sudden cauldron of accusations.

'Why don't you go and live in Crossroads with the squatters?' she taunted. 'You want to help them so much.'

But he was pulling on his trousers, hopping and tripping in his haste to get dressed, and he did not accept the bait.

'Apartheid is over,' she sneered. 'Mandela is free. The ANC is unbanned. Black drivers can kill as many people as they want. I can't understand what you're still protesting about.'

'It's not over yet,' he was driven to retort. 'You don't have to worry about your birthright. White privilege is still intact. The army is making sure of that.'

'And what's wrong with that?'

'The army should defend the country, not make war on fellow citizens.'

'Open your eyes! You're so obsessed with the blacks that you ignore your own people.'

'Who are my people?'

'Everyone is complaining about how bad things are. The Jews I meet are opening import-export businesses and leaving their money overseas. The Afrikaners are grumbling because they have to work sixteen-hour days just to make ends meet. And what do the blacks do? They go on strike! That's why I'm so worried. What happens if they strike at the printers and we can't bring out the magazine? The staff will be laid off and I may lose my job. It doesn't matter to you: no one can kick you out. No wonder the English say to me: "You guys were right all along. The blacks *are* pigs."'

'You certainly know how to wreck any intimacy,' he said bitterly as he tied his shoelaces and made for the door. 'I won't put up with racism. Even if it's from the mouth of someone I love.'

'Kiss me before you go,' she pleaded in a small voice. She knelt on her bed and, closing her eyes, tilted her face towards him, her lips slightly open, her expression as pure as an angel's.

His resolve melted, his anger dissolved as the child in her appealed to the father in him. How could he punish her when she had suffered

141

so much already? When, in fact, her hurt would rebound on him and he would return to his lonely house, knowing that there was unresolved anger between them. How would he be able to concentrate on his job, on defending David Tshabalala? Helpless before her machinations and his own weakness, he turned back. His lips rested for a moment on the scar on her cold pale forehead. When he lifted his head, her eyes were still closed.

'Maybe we should quit,' she suggested, not for the first time.

'Maybe,' he answered reluctantly, not wanting any more unpleasantness.

'We don't even live together,' she said, 'and we fight all the time. How on earth could we be married?'

He shrugged, frozen, wondering how to contain this latest outburst.

'And I'd have to become Jewish,' she said. 'No, it'll never work.'

'My mother wants it,' he said, trying to sound apologetic. 'She's got a ghetto mentality . . .'

'So when mummy cracks the whip, you dance? Is that it? Or do you want it too?'

He squirmed under her accusation but he hid behind his advocate's mask and gave nothing away. 'What I want,' he said, 'is for us to have values in common. That would make it easier for us to live together.'

'Then why don't you become Christian?' she lashed back and he dropped his chin to save himself from the blow. 'You're as racist as I am,' she said smugly. 'You will only marry a Jew. You people keep to yourselves. You're worse than the Afrikaners and you pretend to be liberals.' She was enjoying herself. 'When the going gets rough, you'll run away to Israel.'

'Israel's hardly an alternative,' he said wearily. He should have gone when he first intended to: after every reconciliation came another fight; life with her was a mad roller-coaster ride. 'I wouldn't go to Israel to escape. The life there is even harder than here. And more dangerous.'

'Well I can't become a Jew,' she said flatly. 'I believe in Christ. I can't change my religion like slipping on another pair of shoes, just as you can't. And you don't have to worry. I don't want to get married to you.'

Their arguments had become like joints in which the cartilage had worn down. Without insulation, the smallest jar went straight to the bone. They now needed to cover far less verbal territory to achieve the same hurtful effect.

The doorbell rang like the gong at the end of a round and the fighters separated and moved to their corners.

'Please pass me my dressing gown,' Elmarie said in a neutral voice, wiped completely clean of the stains of her anger, as if no harsh words had passed between them at all. Caught off guard by this new mood-swing, yet relieved that the argument was over, he did what she asked. She hurried into the lounge, shuffling her feet into her slippers, followed stiffly by Jeremy, his head held high. Elmarie peered through the peep-hole then unlatched the door and stepped back. Her mother swaggered in, beaming.

'Hello all!' Marie Coetzee challenged. 'Guess what happened to me today?'

'What, Ma?' Elmarie asked, pulling her robe across her waist and retying the knot of the belt. 'Come, sit down.'

But Marie was too excited. She hardly paused for breath, she was so keen to get her story out. Her face creased like dry earth during a drought. Her inevitable cigarette left a grey trail marking her passage into the room. 'Today,' she said, her eyes bright with the thrill of the frontier, 'today I shot someone.'

'What?'

'Ja, let me tell you,' she said triumphantly. 'A *skollie* got into my backyard and I found him standing next to the dustbin. I asked him what he thought he was doing and he started walking towards me. So I shouted and then he got a fright and he tried to jump over the wall. I had my gun in my bag, and I pulled it out and I aimed it at him. Then he came at me.' She lifted her hands, imitating the action of shooting, her cigarette the smoking pistol, and pulled back an imaginary trigger, clicking her tongue as she did so. 'I got him in the hips and he dropped like a stone.' She flicked her fingers to show how the intruder had gone down.

'Ma! Are you all right?' Elmarie exclaimed, rushing over to her mother and putting her hands on the old woman's shoulders: it was the first time Jeremy had seen them touch.

'Ja,' she laughed. 'I'm OK. I don't know about him though. Bloody *kaffir* had it coming.' She flopped back deeply into one of Elmarie's armchairs with the satisfaction of one who has done a job well. She slapped her bag on the floor; Jeremy wondered if the gun was still inside.

'Disgusting people!' Elmarie snorted. '*Etters!*'

'I called the police and they came in three minutes. Two very nice youngsters. They phoned for an ambulance from my house when they saw how bad he was.'

'Are you in any trouble?' Jeremy asked.

For a moment Marie looked blank. 'What kind of trouble?'

'With the police.'

'Why should *I* be in trouble?' she asked uncomprehendingly.

'Because you shot a man.'

'*Ag* no,' Marie shrugged. 'They took a statement from me, but that's all. Gert sorted it out. He knows them all at the station. They arrested the *kaffir*.'

'It was self-defence,' Elmarie bristled. 'What are you implying?'

'Well at one point the guy was running away,' Jeremy said.

Marie looked from one to the other in bafflement; she was not interested in the niceties of the law. She knew she had done the right thing.

'Well Ma, if you need a lawyer . . .' Elmarie began, again wrapping the robe tightly round her chest as if she had suddenly caught a chill.

'Yes, thanks Jeremy,' Marie said, shutting the trapdoor on that line of conversation.

'Why didn't you phone me?' Elmarie asked.

'*Ag* you know, it was so busy, with the police, and then the ambulance took him away. And the neighbours all came to see what was happening. I hosed down his blood,' she added. '*Jislaaik*, but he bled a lot.'

'Rather his blood than yours,' Jeremy observed.

'They hate us,' Elmarie said. 'After all we've done to them. It'll take years before it can come right. I don't know if I want to live here during that time.'

'Do you mean you want to emigrate?' Jeremy asked.

She did not reply directly; all she said was: 'Crime has rocketed since the ANC was unbanned. And it's not just robberies. But there's violence too. They don't just rob you; they rape and murder you as well.'

'A *kaffir* will always be a *kaffir*,' Marie Coetzee said, clearly thrilled to be the centre of attention, the one who has made the news. She jabbed her cigarette into an ashtray so that the sparks flew.

'I'll get you something to drink, Ma. You must be in a state of shock.'

'I'm fine, but a cup of tea would be nice.' She opened her bag and fished in it for her packet of Lucky Strikes. She turned to Jeremy. 'You know,' she mused. 'Gert has a lot of faults but I'll say this for him. He taught me how to shoot. Always go for the lower part of the body, he told me, otherwise they can still get you. If you shoot them in the chest, they can still move. It's not like in the bioscope.' She lit her new cigarette with a plastic lighter and hungrily breathed in the smoke.

'As long as you're OK,' Jeremy heard himself saying, dutifully, as a potential son-in-law, giving the support that in these circumstances would come naturally from an Afrikaner. He blinked away an absurd picture of his own mother, dangling a smoking revolver, an intruder bloodied and crippled on her balcony.

'*Ag*, I'm a tough old bag,' Marie cackled, vigorously blowing a blue cloud into the room.

'Excuse me,' Jeremy said, 'I just want to see how Elmarie's doing,' and he escaped into the kitchen.

Elmarie was filling the sugar bowl. Her three fluted antique cups were ready on a tray. The kettle had not yet boiled. Wordlessly, he walked towards her and took her in his arms. She smiled, put down the bowl, and wrapped her arms around his back. They held each other in a silent, still dance and she grunted softly in pleasure as he squeezed her breasts under his elbows. Their bodies were as one; their distress at each other was neutralised, they were made whole again.

'I can't stay for tea,' Jeremy said, brushing her hair gently away from her ear. 'I've got a case starting tomorrow, so I should get an early night.'

'OK,' she whispered, kissing him on the lips and he tasted her want. 'I'll see you to the door.'

'Goodbye,' he said to Marie Coetzee. 'Remember to give me a ring if there's any trouble with the police.'

'OK, 'bye!' she called, her voice still inflated with excitement.

Elmarie kissed him again in the passage outside her flat, out of sight of her mother, and then he left, allowing the night to swallow him.

◆

The possibility that the violence would force him from the country of his birth, the land that he loved, filled him with hurt and anger. Gunmen hid in ambush, murder at their fingertips, fuelled by a hatred of whites who had driven them into the ground. Now that Mandela was free, they had risen up to avenge their indignities and suffering against their former leaders. And, in their turn, the whites were kitted out in their neo-Nazi frames of reference, hot with vengeance of their own.

The lid was off the pot; Elmarie had warned against what would come out of those poisoned depths. Her scar, a third eye, had peered through the mirror dividing present from future; she had seen what he would not.

He dreamed that he opened his briefcase and inside was sand and a gun – symbols of a violent, ravaged land.

9

Trials

The sound of spilled water jerked Jeremy Spielman from his early morning reverie as he crossed Keerom Street. Sitting on an upturned crate between Rembrandt House and the Court Restaurant, a milkman was washing his hands, pouring water from a milk bottle on to first one, then the other, kneading them together carefully. He put the bottle down on the pavement with a glassy clink, and lifted a syringe and vial from the trouser pocket of his white overalls. He tapped a crooked finger against the syringe, then popped the needle, visible only as a sliver of sunlight, into the lid of the vial. Cross-eyed with concentration, his leg stuck out like a rudder across the pavement for balance, the milkman slid the fine metal point into his wrist. Jeremy realised he had been standing and gawking as if at a carnival side-show, although the man, in his booth of milk crates, gave no sign of caring that he was being observed. His operation over, he pulled out a sandwich from a red lunch box, and chewed slowly and thought-fully, staring at nothing in particular. The lawyer entered the res-taurant and bought a box of gum to keep his mouth moist in court. When he left, the milkman was sipping coffee from a glass mug.

◆

David Tshabalala stood in the dock, tense as a cocked crossbow, gripping the rail in front of him as if his life depended on it. He was wearing an old brown suit that smelled of mothballs and was slightly too small, revealing an inch or so of wrist and sock. His eyes were bloodshot, as if he had not slept the night before. Facing him was Jan Botma, a bright young prosecutor, very thin, with black hair Bryl-creamed flatly over to one side. His black pencil moustache and blue suit under his court gown identified him unmistakably as a civil servant.

'You are accused of the murder of Gloria Kekana,' Botma was saying. 'How do you plead?' His words rolled slickly, almost thoughtlessly, off his tongue: for David this was the most crucial time of his life; for Botma it was just another day at the office, another case in what would be a long career.

David opened his mouth, but no sound emerged.

'How do you plead?' Botma repeated patiently.

David's eyes implored his lawyer to help him. Then he remembered what to say. The words were born in great pain. 'Not guilty,' he blurted out, and Jeremy smiled in encouragement.

'And on charge number two, you are accused of the attempted murder of Edward Kekana. How do you plead?'

'Not . . . not guilty,' David stammered, brushing his hand over his face and clearing his throat.

Jeremy stood. Unlike Botma, he was not feeling professional nor confident: he still bore the bruises of the night before, even though he and Elmarie had eventually parted in love rather than in hate. 'My Lord, the plea is in accordance with my instructions. The accused is prepared to make certain admissions. He admits stabbing the deceased and the person assaulted with a pocket knife. But he denies that he had the intention to kill or to injure. He avers that he was acting out of provocation . . .'

The judge, formidable in his red robes, looked down from under bushy eyebrows which framed dark eyes grown cynical in the criminal courts. His thin lips had a built-in sneer. Jeremy had appeared before him previously and knew that the scorn was not reserved for the evidence of the accused, but was dished out equally to the State witnesses. He bent his long torso over his desk, making notes as if from too great a height.

'The accused admits that the deceased, named in the charge sheet, died from the wounds he inflicted with a knife?' the judge asked, aggressively, as if he felt that Jeremy was conceding too much and was putting his client at a disadvantage.

'That is correct, my Lord,' the lawyer replied with all the authority he could instil in his voice: he had to command respect, to show that he was not just another junior stumbling through a *pro deo*; he knew precisely what he was doing. 'It would seem that the only contest between the accused and the State is over the accused's state of mind at the time of the stabbing.'

The judge scowled. 'Is the identity of the persons named in the charge sheet correct?' He knew that the senior advocates did not want *pro deos* which did not pay, whereas the younger members of the Bar grabbed at any work they could get; this led to the anomalous situation that the most serious cases were often handled by the most inexperienced lawyers. Judges sometimes had to keep an eye on the defence and protect the accused from their own counsel.

'Yes, my Lord.'

'Very well, Mr Spielman, I'll note those admissions. The accused may be seated.'

Again David glanced at his lawyer for confirmation. Jeremy nodded and his client sat down gingerly, as if frightened to entrust his weight to the wooden bench. Jan Botma handed in as exhibits the list of admissions, the post-mortem report and a photograph of the scene of the killing: Jeremy doubted whether his adversary had done a personal inspection; Botma would not have any ghosts to exorcise.

Flanking the judge, the two elderly assessors eagerly pecked at their copies of the exhibits. One was a retired magistrate with a receding hairline which accentuated his predatory nose. The other was an advocate whose increase in years had brought a corresponding decline in the number of attorneys who briefed him; he had turned his energies to writing, and had produced a series of law books. He popped a monocle into his right eye and, with a red handkerchief flowering out of the top pocket of his dark jacket, he had an air of worldliness which the narrow civil servant did not.

'My Lord, the first witness I am calling is Dr Frisch.'

A wizened old man who looked as if he had been pickled in formalin stepped up into the witness-box and swore to tell the truth. He was thin and dry and wore a dusty suit. He carried a bundle of papers which he dropped on the stand before him.

'You are a qualified medical doctor and a specialist in pathology?' the prosecutor asked.

'Correct,' the old man said, tugging at his goatee as if this were the mechanism to open his mouth, although he spoke with the authority of one who has testified in many such trials: his voice was too big for his shrivelled frame.

'Could you tell the court your findings in the post-mortem you conducted in this case?'

'Yes,' he said, adjusting his spectacles as he read from his report.

'The chief post-mortem findings were an incised and penetrating wound of the posterior torso which penetrated the chest, cut into the aorta and caused death . . .'

The terminology was the familiar medico-legal jargon that marked the interface between the two disciplines. When David plunged the knife into Gloria's back to end the torment into which their relationship had degenerated, he could not have known that one day this ugly little man would be analysing its passage through her internal organs. He sat dumbly as a butcher while the pathologist verbally splayed out her insides in a ritual the whites had invented to help determine innocence or guilt. Was it any more comprehensible to David than throwing the bones would be to Jeremy?

'The height of the deceased was measured . . . and the mass,' Frisch was saying as if he were discussing the carcass of a cow rather than the remains of a human being. 'The body was well developed and the nutrition was good. Rigor mortis was fully developed and the body was cold to touch. The eyes had been removed in accordance with the Human Tissues Act of 1983 . . .'

Jeremy glanced up at the gallery, a floor above. A scattering of people sat there, probably relatives of the parties, listening intently to language they were unlikely to have understood.

'So there was only one serious wound, Doctor?' Botma asked.

'That is correct.'

'Doctor, evidence will be presented that when this wound was inflicted the attacker was kneeling next to the deceased while she was lying on her stomach in the street. Is the wound consistent with that?'

'Yes. It could well fit in.'

'And now, Doctor, please turn to the hospital report dealing with the injuries inflicted on Mr Edward Kekana . . .'

The court orderly, an old white policeman, dozed on a bench beside the door, quietly enjoying his last few years of duty. The cushy jobs still go to the whites, Jeremy thought. On his way to the office that morning, he had driven past court. Sitting on the cold, grey steps, shotgun propped against his leg, was a black *kitskonstabel*, one of the 'instant policemen' created from the townships to deal with the unrest there, and now seconded to guard this place of white law. His brown belt and boots went uneasily with his bright blue overalls – a paramilitary clown who appeared none the worse for wear after

150

spending the night in the open. He had answered the lawyer's scrutiny with a pimply smile. I might be about to plant a bomb, Jeremy had thought, and still he'd smile at me, because I'm white: that's his training. When the lawyer arrived later at court, the black policeman had gone home to sleep. And here, inside this wood-panelled room, the pampered old man was nodding off like a dog beside a fireplace.

'I have no more questions,' the prosecutor said.

'Doctor,' Jeremy asked, getting slowly to his feet, 'can you say if these wounds were carefully planned, or were the result of wild stabbing without direct aim?'

'Mr Spielman,' the judge butted in impatiently, 'How can he possibly tell you that?'

'As your Lordship pleases,' Jeremy conceded, stinging from the rebuke. 'I have no further questions.' It was just as well that there were no attorneys in court and that the people in the gallery were too unsophisticated to understand the relevance of his blunder.

'I now call Mr Edward Kekana,' Botma announced and the usher, emaciated and stooped as a vulture, pounced into the corridor and returned with the new witness under his wing: a portly man with a full fleshy face and slanted oriental eyes.

'Before he goes into the box, my Lord, may I ask that he stands next to the accused so the court can compare the height of the two?'

'Very well.'

Kekana opened the door of the dock and stepped in. He did not look at David and the accused edged away as if he were being confronted by a poisonous toad.

'If the two can stand still,' Botma said, addressing them in the third person.

'The top of the witness's head comes to just above the bottom of the accused's chin,' the judge commented for the benefit of the court record. 'He is a head shorter. Are you happy with that, Mr Spielman?'

'Yes, my Lord.'

Kekana wore a navy jacket with grey trousers which strained around the tops of his plump thighs. He left the disreputable world of the dock and strutted to the witness-box with the assurance of a man who is a leader in his community. Jeremy felt sorry for David. What chance did the uneducated labourer have against this important man? Love had wrecked his life. He had been pushed to the point where a

151

knife was his only voice. Jeremy could feel no pity for the father who, because of his bullying, had lost a daughter. He could not allow himself sympathy for a desperate father, trying to get the best for his only daughter who had made a bad choice.

'On the 17th September 1989 you were at your home in Nyanga?' Botma asked. He spoke with the assurance of a stage magician who knew the rabbit would come out of the hat, as it usually did. 'And your daughter, the deceased, arrived?'

Kekana wiped the corner of his eye with a fat hand. He did not answer immediately. He bit his lip and struggled for the words. 'That is so,' he managed at last. He had won his battle against the intruder who had stolen his daughter – but at what cost!

'And she told you that the accused had snatched her baby away?'

'Yes.' Kekama rocked a little as he spoke. He took a clean white handkerchief from his jacket pocket, unfolded it and dabbed his brow. He kept it in his hand, where it flapped like a flag of surrender.

'What did you do?'

'We . . . we got into my car and drove to look for Themba . . .'

'Themba?'

'I am sorry.' The witness glanced up at the judge; he was sweating. 'Themba is the accused. Then my daughter shouted: "There they are!" I stopped the car and we got out and we approached the accused. I said: "Give me back the baby." The next thing, he walked towards me with the child in his hands, and then he stabbed me, two blows . . .'

'Where were you stabbed?'

'On my arm. It went right through my arm and penetrated into my chest. The other was on the back of my neck . . .'

The judge, hardened by his years of listening to the stories of killers and victims, exhaled with a noisy rush of air. 'You say the blow went right through your arm into your chest?'

'That's correct, my Lord.'

The judge shook his head, signalling with his imperious mane of white hair his amazement at the ferocity of the attack. 'Has it left you . . .?' he began, leaning into the microphone, obviously choosing his words carefully so as to be as tactful as possible. 'Is there any permanent damage?'

'My Lord, I can't straighten my fingers,' Kekana said, lifting his arm and showing a partly-clenched fist. 'It cut through something inside here; I don't know what.'

'Is it painful?'

'Sometimes, especially in the cold.'

Botma stood back from the microphone with a slight smile of pleasure that the judge was sympathetic to the complainant. Then the white head nodded. 'Go on.'

'Very well, my Lord.' Immediately, the prosecutor slotted in the next question, but it was a weak one; his concentration had been disturbed. 'Did you see what he stabbed you with?'

'No, my Lord, but I think it was a knife.'

Botma's eyes squeezed a fraction, the closest he got to a wince, then he bounced back. 'What happened to the baby?'

'Themba . . . I mean the accused, he gave me the child while he was stabbing me. I handed her over to someone else who was standing nearby.'

'Where is the baby now?'

'At my house. My wife is looking after her. She is well . . . but she has no parents.' Kekana gave a pointed look in the direction of the dock.

'Did you go to hospital?' Botma was back in his stride.

'Yes. For a week. My wife watched over the shop. Then I asked them to let me out so I could attend my daughter's funeral.' Kekana's head drooped and his shoulders shook as he tried to stop himself from weeping. 'She was our only child,' he said in a broken voice. 'I miss her so much.'

'Thank you,' the prosecutor said, allowing his lips to turn up in a smug grin. 'No more questions.'

'Mr Kekana,' Jeremy said, standing and squaring his shoulders as he prepared to throw the first punch. He had to strike quickly to dissipate the court's sympathy for this man who had suffered so much. 'Was the accused married to your daughter?'

'No.'

'Well then, did the accused ever pay you *lobola* for your daughter?'

'He paid me money, but it was not *lobola*. It was for making Gloria pregnant.'

'How much did he pay?'

'It was a thousand rand.'

'When did he pay this money?'

Kekana thought for a minute before replying. 'He paid it in 1986.'

'And you accepted the money then?'

'Yes.' Kekana shuffled in the witness-box, not sure what to expect or how to answer it.

'How old is the baby?'

'She is a year now.'

'Let me see . . . That means the baby was born in March 1989. So your daughter must have fallen pregnant about the middle of 1988?'

Kekana was beginning to see the trap that the lawyer was setting, but he realised he already had one foot over the pit and he had committed himself to the fateful step. 'Yes.'

'Well, Mr Kekana, that is very strange. How could the money be damages for making Gloria pregnant when you accepted it two years before your daughter actually fell pregnant?'

Kekana shook his head. Botma's face was impassive; he just listened intently and jotted down the occasional note.

'I put it to you that the accused was married to your daughter and you knew it and accepted it.' Jeremy turned – he was now performing for the gallery – and saw that David was smiling. A little skill in cross-examination was worth more than a townshipful of People's Courts.

'No,' Kekana said stubbornly but Jeremy knew the witness was wounded.

'They lived in the same house as husband and wife?' the lawyer persisted.

'They argued a lot.' Kekana responded, mopping the sweat that was now running freely down his cheeks.

'Like any married couple,' the judge remarked drolly, and giggles rippling round the room aroused the court orderly from his stupor. He looked up groggily for a moment before letting his head fall back on his chest. Jeremy felt the thrill of knowing that the judge was on his side – for now.

'You called the accused and his mother to a meeting?'

'Yes, we had a meeting.' Kekana's voice had lost its confidence. He spoke more hesitantly now, weighing his words, trying to gauge where the new trap was being laid on the path ahead.

'And at the meeting, you told them the thousand rand was not *lobola* but was damages for making Gloria pregnant?'

'Yes I said that!' Kekana blurted out. 'It was true.'

154

'And David, the accused, got angry and said you were a thief?'

'He's a rude boy!'

'So what did you do?'

'I reported him to the People's Court.' Kekana shook his permanently clenched fist; he felt he had justice on his side now. Without concern for the barbs of his tormentor, he charged on. 'That boy had no manners! I am a respected man. I am an elder in my church! How can he talk to me like that?'

'Did the People's Court treat him harshly?'

Kekana's eyes narrowed, as if he realised too late the implications of his outburst. 'They gave him a hiding for insulting me.'

'In fact,' Jeremy said gravely, 'they sentenced him to sixty lashes and Gloria, your daughter, intervened after about thirty and made them stop.'

'Yes,' Kekana replied quietly.

'And the Comrades running the People's Courts warned the accused never to see Gloria again nor to give you any more trouble?'

'Yes, they told him.' Kekana seemed to blow himself out like a puffer fish but Jeremy was remorseless: he thrust in his dart, determined to puncture this man's self-righteousness. Or was it a protection against the relentless questioning?

'So, when David snatched the baby and you went after him, did you threaten to report him again?'

'Yes,' Kekana said, in little more than a whisper, perhaps compelled by his religious beliefs not to commit perjury but hardly able to muster the strength to utter the word.

'You know that the People's Courts have a reputation in the townships for instilling terror? They have sentenced their victims to the most violent punishments, as we saw in David's case. Some of those who had the misfortune to be tried by these courts were killed. You must have been aware of this?'

Kekana did not answer.

'Were you?'

'Yes.'

'So David had every right to be upset and concerned when you made this threat?'

Kekana hung his fleshy head, mortified that he, the complainant, had been turned into the guilty party.

155

'And you, a church elder, were happy to have your son-in-law punished this way?'

'He was rude to me.'

'I have no more questions, my Lord.'

'The court will adjourn,' the judge announced.

'All rise!' the policeman bellowed, and, as everyone stood, the judge and his assessors filed out for lunch.

◆

The pavement outside the court smelled of detergent. Jeremy bought a newspaper and a toasted sandwich from the café in the arcade below Chambers. What a country this has become, he thought, as he chewed slowly through the oily bread, the newspaper spread across his desk. On an inside page with a small-type headline was a two-paragraph article declaring that only one person had been killed in unrest-related incidents in the past twenty-four hours: a black man had been hacked to death in a township that no one had heard of. In any civilised country, a death as horrific as this would have made headline news. But in South Africa, it was just another dead black. Any newsworthiness in the article lay in the fact that only one person had died. Usually the toll was higher. Cynically, Jeremy thought that certain of his brethren might even welcome the country's violence: every new death brought the prospect of more work for the hungry young advocates, rapacious ambulance-chasers.

No briefs had come in during his morning in court but he could not allow himself to dwell on the negative: he had to concentrate on the case of David Tshabalala. His hand strayed to the phone but then he pulled it back. He did not need to hear any complaints from Elmarie either. Nothing should detract from the mood of controlled aggression that he had to effect for his afternoon in court.

He really should bring fruit to the office like some of his healthier colleagues, he mused. This sandwich, made of cardboard and grease, couldn't be doing him any good.

◆

The woman in the witness-box wore a nurse's uniform and spectacles with thick black frames which gave her an air of permanent disapproval. Her face was angular, dropping away sharply from wide cheekbones to a narrow jaw. She had a thin mouth that turned down at the corners as if she were calculating the measure of every word before dispensing it.

Botma half crouched, leaning on his elbow, stalking her, like Batman pursuing his prey through the shadows of Gotham City. As a boy, Jeremy had identified with the 'darknight detective', had devoured tales of the sinister champion of justice who prowled the night in his long black cape. When Jeremy first put on a court gown, he was amused at how the outfit resembled that of his childhood hero. He had paraded before a full-length mirror, Esta and Selwyn watching proudly, the caped crusader of the Magistrate's Court. But ironically he had ended up defending the criminals. It was Botma, the prosecutor, who more accurately reflected the comic-book avenger.

'So, Mrs Maponya, you saw Mr Kekana approach the accused?'

'Yes. He shouted at the accused to give him the child. The accused handed over the child, then stabbed him.' She spoke unemotionally as if she were reading a hospital report on a patient.

'Where were you then?'

'I live in the house you see in the photograph, opposite where the stabbing took place. I came out when I heard the shouting. Then I saw all this.'

'What did you do?'

'When Mr Kekana fell down, I was standing behind him. I took the baby from his hands.'

'What happened next?'

'The accused ran after Mr Kekana's daughter. She was screaming. He threw her down and he kneeled on the ground and he stabbed her in her back.'

'Was she threatening him?'

'No, my Lord. Not at all.'

'And the streetlight we can see in the picture. Was it on?'

'Yes, my Lord. I could see everything clearly.'

'Did you try and give first aid to the victims?'

'Yes I did. My sister took the baby from me and I stopped the blood from Mr Kekana's wounds. But his daughter was already dead. I couldn't do anything for her.'

'Where was the accused?'

'He ran away.' The nurse gave a discreet cough into the back of her hand and then put a finger behind her spectacles to rub her eye.

'Thank you,' Botma said. 'That is all.'

Jeremy stood up. The witness had created a very good impression: she had answered directly without evasion; she had no axe to grind in this incident and, to make it worse, she was a nurse. But the lawyer had a scalpel to slice at her credibility. 'Mrs Maponya, when the quarrel started, where were you?'

'I was inside my house,' she said. A gulley opened between the tendons of her throat, betraying a hitherto unrevealed tension. She held her blue handbag tightly, like a swimmer in trouble clutching a buoy.

'What brought you out?'

'The shouting.'

'What did you see?'

'I saw Mr Kekana and his daughter running towards the accused.'

'Did you know them before?'

'No. None of them. But I had seen Mr Kekana in church.'

'And while they were running, they were shouting at him?'

'That is correct.'

'So they were already shouting by the time you came out of your house?'

'Yes,' she said guardedly.

'In that case,' Jeremy struck, 'you did not hear everything they said to him?'

She was silent. She rubbed her fingers in her hair which was greying at the temples. So often a witness created a story, based partly on observation, the missing pieces supplied by imagination. The witness believed the story: through repeated tellings, the fiction melted seamlessly into the greater narrative. The skill of the cross-examiner was to pare the lie from the truth.

'My client will say that both the deceased and her father threatened to report him to the People's Court if he did not hand over the baby. You testified that Gloria made no threat at all. Perhaps you did not hear the threat because it was made while you were still in the house?'

'It is possible,' she conceded, reluctant to make any admissions that would impugn her credibility.

The warm glow of another small victory settled in his stomach, like a glass of good port. But the problem he could not cross-examine away was that David Tshabalala had stabbed his wife after the danger contained in her threat had passed because he had already handed over the baby; and that he had chased her- to do so. Whether provocation was a complete defence against the murder charge was up to the court to decide. Like a surgeon operating on a patient with a malignant tumour, there was a limit to what Jeremy could achieve for his client.

Botma did not call any more witnesses and closed his case before the tea break. He was either confident of a conviction or no one else would come forward to testify. Perhaps he accepted that the truth was out. As the court emptied, he was joined by a coloured policeman, probably the investigating officer, Cupido. They stood together, part of a team, discussing the case. Botma said something and Cupido laughed, the restrained laugh of a man who is secure enough not to have to show that he is grateful to the white Afrikaner for sharing a joke with him.

◆

Jeremy collected his post at Fatiema's desk – a boring accumulation of accounts, bank statements and junk mail which he threw in the bin. Was it the destiny of late twentieth century *Homo sapiens* continually to have to tear open unwanted envelopes?

In an attempt to clear his head, the lawyer took the lift downstairs, crossed Queen Victoria Street and entered the Botanical Gardens. He walked along the winding paths between magnificent banks of flowers, past exotic old trees and fish ponds in which lazed enormous white and gold koi. Lovers lay entwined on the lawns, ignoring the KEEP OFF signs; an earnest young man slouched on a park bench, his nose buried in a novel with a cover picture of a dead cat, hanging by its neck, with milky eyes and outstretched paws. But Jeremy hardly noticed the beauty and the activity around him. Head down, he replayed the morning's evidence, analysed the prosecution's strengths and weaknesses and wondered how David would hold up in the

159

witness-box. Only the screeching of the squirrels, as discordant as grinding gears, made the lawyer look up briefly.

Two of the rodents were scampering up and down the trunk of an algae-covered oak tree, squabbling over an acorn. An urchin with glue-intoxicated eyes stood and watched them, a little smile on his child's lips. He bent to pick up a piece of blue chewing gum that someone had left in a crack in the paving and popped it in his mouth. Then he lay down on the hot grass, drawing his knees up to his thin chest for the comfort that a mother should have given him.

Streaked by seagull droppings, the statue of Cecil John Rhodes, ancestor of the inventors of apartheid, pointed a weighty arm to the north, exhorting conquest, blind to its consequences to future generations of oppressed and oppressors alike.

From his shadow, a tall black man wearing dark glasses lurched over to Jeremy; he had a portable phone jammed between his shoulder and his ear. It started ringing and the man brought himself to a halt, a smile melting across his bony face. He pushed the instrument towards the lawyer and slurred: 'Hey, man. It's from Washington DC for you. You're a very important person. They want to ask what they must do about South Africa.' Jeremy fixed him with a frozen stare of incomprehension and the man reeled away, apparently unoffended. His phone was ringing again. It's probably Elmarie, the lawyer thought, checking up on me.

◆

The air in the courtroom, grown musty by mid-afternoon, seemed to have sapped the strength of David Tshabalala. His eyes bulged mournfully from his shaven head, his scar was a dark brown knot on his forehead.

'When Gloria came to live with me, her father was very angry,' he muttered and the judge strained to hear, his neck taut as he leaned forward. Tufts of white hair grew from his large fleshy ears.

'Why was he angry?' Jeremy asked.

'Because he wanted her to marry a rich man from his church.'

A Mills and Boon novel lay on the table next to the stenographer. The plump fingers of her left hand kept inching towards it as if she were trying to escape the sordid horror of township violence in the

160

book's predictable, comforting pages. A set of earphones framed her short brown curls, feeding the court proceedings directly into her head. Her small mouth, a bright red flower, repeated certain words of the evidence; her right hand jotted down loops and squiggles of shorthand, skilfully avoiding being tripped up by her long, red nails. A tent-like dress of blue polka dots enveloped her podgy shoulders and wide back, yet she wore a wedding ring; someone must have found her attractive enough to marry.

'Now where was the People's Court held?' Jeremy was asking.

'It was in a school yard.'

'Who was there?'

'Four or maybe five Comrades and Mr Kekana and Gloria and me.'

'No schoolchildren?' the judge interrupted.

'No, it was on Sunday.'

'And what happened?' Jeremy continued when the judge nodded him on.

'Mr Kekana said I was rude to him and they sentenced me to sixty strokes.'

'Please repeat that. You said *sixty* strokes?'

'Yes. Sixty.'

'Did you get a chance to tell your side of the story?'

'They listened to me, but they'd already made up their minds. Mr Kekana is very rich and important.'

'How did they give you these strokes?'

'They pushed me over a table and said that we were in school and they would teach me a lesson.'

'Did you have any clothes on?'

'Only my underpants.'

'What did they hit you with?'

'*Sjamboks*.'

'Did they give you the full sentence?' Jeremy asked and when David looked blank, added: 'Did you get all sixty strokes?'

'Gloria stopped them after about thirty, I think. I was almost unconscious by that time. One of the Comrades, he told me later that Gloria stood between me and them. She was ashamed of what her father had done.'

'Will you show the court the marks?'

David took off his jacket and hung it over the rail of the witness-box. Then he unbuttoned his shirt. The stenographer's eyes lingered on the massive, labourer's body which loomed above her – forbidden fruit – and, when he turned his back to reveal the network of welts, she – battle-hardened in the courts – could not help but gasp. The judge and his assessors studied the scars with an air of detachment as if they were inspecting a specimen under a microscope. Groans escaped from the gallery and were stifled when the judge raised a warning eyebrow.

'Thank you,' Jeremy said. 'You can get dressed now.'

The stenographer's cheeks were flushed and she kept her eyes fixed on her notepad.

'Now,' the lawyer continued, 'on the night of the killings, you arranged to meet Gloria at the witchdoctor?'

'Yes, my child was sick.'

'Go on. Tell the court the full story.'

'The witchdoctor gave us some medicine for the baby and I paid her. It was good to be with my family again. That's what I wanted. I started to walk home and I asked Gloria to come with me. But she would not. She said she had choir practice. I pulled the child out of her hands because I wanted her to follow me, but she ran away.' David gave his evidence in an uninterested sing-song voice as if he were merely reciting words that he had prepared in advance, as if he had withdrawn from the events in this courtroom and was standing in for someone else. He closed his eyes for a moment and rubbed the scar above his eyebrow with the heel of his hand.

'How did you feel about what you had done?'

'I was very unhappy. While I was walking down the street, I felt depressed and confused. Then I heard a car coming from behind me. I heard people getting closer and I was afraid because the situation in Crossroads was very tense. I thought they were coming to attack me. I pulled out my knife and turned round and saw Gloria and her father.'

Jeremy hesitated for a moment at this new version of David's story – that he did not know who was following him – but it was a small point and the lawyer could not bring his client's credibility into question by challenging it. He continued: 'Did they say anything to you?'

'They were shouting together. They said I must hand over the child

162

or they would report me to the Comrades again. I got scared. Then something snapped inside my head. I stabbed him and before I knew what I was doing, I stabbed Gloria too.' David was staring at his hands with a glazed expression as if he could not recognise them, instruments of death.

The judge leaned back and yawned. He pulled a piece of loose skin from his bottom lip and examined it closely on his fingertip as if it were the only object of any importance in the courtroom.

'I know that I have done a terrible thing,' David said miserably. 'I have killed the person I love.'

◆

The lawyers swarmed out of court like bats from a cave. In Keerom Street lurked a yellow police van with wire mesh over its windows and a yellow police car, its aerial as thin and menacing as the milkman's hypodermic syringe. Moustachioed policemen in blue riot outfits lounged beside their vehicles, thick as thugs, drinking Cokes and watching the court. Then another yellow van, smaller than the others, nipped down the road and screeched to a halt. Trigger fingers twitched, but more out of habit than necessity; eyes searched for the source of danger but never relinquished their laughter. Out of the van jumped a paunchy plainclothes driver, who strode to the back and pulled open the swing doors. He heaved and grunted and then removed a bundle of washing. Jeremy suppressed a chuckle: stencilled on the side of the small van was the logo: BRIAN'S LAUNDRY, in black letters with a red dot on the 'i'. Brian had better not collect laundry in the townships, Jeremy thought. The one-eyed mobs might well mistake his vehicle for a police van.

Lewis Singer waddled down the grey steps, his black gown billowing clownishly in a gust of wind that jerked to attention the South African flag on the court's roof. The brown box-like suitcase in which he carried his law books banged awkwardly against his leg.

'So I see Mandela's been kissing Arafat,' he said sarcastically. 'Between the blacks and the Afrikaners it doesn't look so good for the Jews, does it?'

Jeremy tried to flatten his hair against the fumbling breeze. 'Who knows? We'll have to wait and see.' He was too wrapped up in his case to discuss Lewis's favourite subject.

Dust from a construction site had got into one of Singer's eyes and his face contorted as he tried to dislodge the grit with his stubby forefinger. 'Are you doing a *pro deo*?' he asked when he could see again.

'My staple diet. Killed his girlfriend.'

'Over another man, I suppose.'

'Something like that.'

'The problem as I see it,' Lewis said, 'is that three million whites just cannot support thirty million blacks. Their need is too great. Even if the politics come right, the economics are against us. With the best possible scenario, I give this country four to five years. We're going to end up like a third-rate Kenya.'

A conduit of builders unloaded bricks from the back of a truck and stacked them on the pavement in front of the office block they were putting up.

'Credit cards for the ANC's next march,' Singer quipped. 'The bricks I mean.'

But Jeremy shrugged off the comment irritably and Lewis had to lengthen his stride to keep up with his shorter colleague. They passed the security guard at the entrance to Huguenot Chambers and Jeremy pressed the button for the lift.

'It's these People's Courts I don't like,' he said at last as Lewis got in.

Singer was struggling again with the dust in his eye and he was not listening properly. 'What?'

'My accused was beaten up by a township court.'

'What do you expect from them?'

'They fascinate and terrify me,' Jeremy said. 'They're our Khmer Rouge.'

'It's all part of the ANC's plan to undermine the Government,' Singer replied. 'I may not be active in politics like you, but I can put two and two together.'

Jeremy looked at him sharply. 'That's hardly a correct assessment,' he responded as the lift stopped at their floor and they stepped out. 'Not everyone who isn't going to Australia is active in politics.'

'Australia ...' Singer mused, with a gleam in his eye. 'It's very

164

similar to South Africa you know – vegetation, climate, lifestyle. Except that it doesn't have our problems: there are no blacks. Is that paradise or not?'

'They killed all their blacks,' Jeremy shot back, but the comment ricocheted off Singer's thick skin.

'I've travelled all over the world,' he went on, 'and I wouldn't live anywhere else. Europe is too crowded and dirty, America is too loud . . . but Australia is like home away from home . . .'

'Except for the flies,' Jeremy retorted, suddenly angry, not only at his colleague but at this violent, divided country which chased away its sons and daughters in fear and anger; or murdered them.

He left Singer standing forlornly at reception and strode off to his office. He removed his court gown and hung it in the cupboard, packed up and left immediately, locking the door.

In the parking garage, a *kitskonstabel* was pushing the rusty, dented Volkswagen Beetle of a young advocate who had joined the Bar too recently to care about his image. Probably in contravention of police regulations, the black constable had left his shotgun leaning against a wall to help the white boss. He would not have dared to part with his weapon in the townships where the angry Comrades would have burned him alive as a collaborator.

'It won't start!' the driver shouted, carefree, not yet having shed his surfboard youth for the gravity which success at the Bar would demand. He tugged at his door which was still flapping open. 'I left my lights one!'

'Can I help?' Jeremy called but then the car emitted a roar, kicked into life and sputtered off down the ramp. The policeman stopped running and straightened. On his way to retrieve his shotgun, he stuck his finger, reflectively, in his nose. His motto might have been: 'Protect and serve'.

◆

A woman on television was saying: 'Afrikaners are very obsessed with eating meat. You always see programmes where they're making *braais* and *potjekos*. The English also have their cooking shows but there is an emphasis on other foods as well . . .'

Jeremy reluctantly picked up the phone and dialled Elmarie's number; calling her every evening was a bad habit but he could not kick it. He settled back in his chair, needing her, after his day in court, to be supportive, to tell him how well he was doing against all the odds. He did not want to hear of *her* trials.

'How was your day?' he asked.

'I had a bad experience,' she said and he wished he had not called; he considered ringing off and pretending they had been disconnected but she would only phone back.

'What happened?' he asked resignedly.

'I stopped at a garage to get petrol this afternoon,' she said and her voice was slurred. 'There was a black couple sitting on a low wall with a little boy. He threw a stone at my car. I got out – I was so cross – and the woman apologised. She said the boy's mother was a prostitute and his father was on the trawlers. She was looking after him. I gave her five rand because I felt sorry for them . . .' Elmarie paused, and Jeremy waited for the punch line. 'Then the man shouted at me. He said: "Fucking whiteys! You think we're trash." I just got back into my car and drove away. I was too upset to fill up.'

'That's terrible,' Jeremy clucked. 'What a nasty man.'

'There's no future for whites here,' she said. Then she laughed coarsely. 'I heard a joke today. You know why our magazines don't sell to blacks?'

'Why?'

'The pages are too glossy. They can't be used as toilet paper.'

'I have to go,' he said abruptly. 'There's someone at the door.'

'Maybe it's one of your lady friends from Jews for Justice,' she retaliated in a voice thick with alcohol. 'Why don't you leave me and go off with one of them? They would have said "shame" about those people at the garage . . . they would have said it's because of apartheid . . . we must excuse them . . . they can't help it. That's the kind of woman you need.'

The receiver slipped out of Jeremy's fingers and came to rest, trembling, across the face of the telephone, while he buried his head in his hands and wondered if Lewis Singer's decision to emigrate was the only sensible one.

◆

On the steps of the Supreme Court, groups of people had gathered, waiting for the day's proceedings to begin. A knot of black women in ANC T-shirts, probably come to support political triallists, disentangled to allow the lawyer to ascend. As usual, the police vans were in place, keeping their vigil. A white woman wearing a purple dress stood on the landing, anxiously looking at her watch and then up the road, as if the person she was due to meet was late. There was a chill in the early morning air, a hint of the winter to come.

David was sitting on a bench in the corridor outside the courtroom, his torso bent forward, his elbows resting on his knees. He kneaded his fingers with an agitation that could have come from a lack of sleep: his face was gaunt, his eyes burned, as if he had lost kilograms overnight.

'How's it going?' he asked and laughed nervously. 'Am I going to win?'

'I'll close your case after your mother has given evidence,' the lawyer said. 'Then the prosecutor and I will present our arguments. And then the judge will decide.'

'What about the doctor who asked me about my head?'

'If they find you guilty, I'll call him in extenuation.'

David did not answer and Jeremy wondered how much he understood of the mysterious and elaborate rules of this court as opposed to the rudimentary justice dispensed arbitrarily by those in the townships. In the end, both imposed severe sentences. The white man's court just had a pretence of being more civilised because its proceedings were dressed up in complicated trappings. Maybe Jeremy was just feeling cynical; of course there were safeguards in the one that were lacking in the other. But ultimately the crimes and their defences had been defined by white law-makers. Why could township definitions not be as valid for township circumstances?

They entered the court together, in silence, the tall black man depending on the small Jew for survival in this legal jungle where snares were laid by a cunning prosecutor and had to be sprung by an equally shrewd defence counsel.

'I call Mrs Thelma Tshabalala,' Jeremy announced and the stooped woman opened the door to the witness-box with the fatalism of one going to the gallows. To the assessors she probably looked like a domestic worker who cleaned their houses. Could they divest themselves of their racial and class prejudices and treat her testimony as that of a human being?

'My son, he was a good boy,' she said and her face crunched up in crying, as if she had held back all her grief for this moment; now she could do no more for him than tell his story. Her tears flowed down her thin cheeks, her frail body shook beyond control, her sobbing had the stenographer reaching for her tissues as well. The mother stood alone in the witness-box before the judge and his assessors and she wept bitter tears for the waste of her son.

◆

Jeremy undid the knot in his tie. Elmarie sat on the cream sofa wearing shorts, her firm legs curled beneath her, lighting a cigarette with the burning stub of the last one. Her hair hung in lank unwashed strands and her pretty face, devoid of make-up, was pasty except for the raw redness of her scar. A glass of gin sent its heady perfume across the room.

'I wish you'd give that up,' he said but she brushed off the admonition with an irritable wave of her hand and took another sip.

'How's your mother?' he asked. 'I hope the man she shot didn't die and that she's not in trouble with the police.'

'I have no idea,' Elmarie replied. 'I haven't spoken to her since Sunday night. I suppose I'd have heard if anything was wrong. That's the only time I do hear from her.'

Not wanting to tap any further into a well of bitterness, Jeremy picked up the newspaper. Flexing it, he tried to focus on the outpourings of distress from the black areas: things were getting worse. It was especially sad that those who had lived under oppression all their lives should now die in the cauldron that had bubbled over when the lid came off. It was ironic that those who had struggled so long for freedom should be murdered during the course of meaningless violence when freedom was at hand. Unless the violence was not as meaningless as it appeared to an innocent living in the safe white suburbs. Victims spoke increasingly of what they termed a 'third force' stoking the flames: white men in balaclavas petrol-bombing squatter shacks, silent black killers throwing commuters off trains, police standing by while Government-supporting vigilantes attacked

ANC groups at funerals. It was Crossroads all over again but magnified a hundred times across the country. Unfamiliar townships erupted in orgies of spectacular blood-letting. Roll calls of the dead were becoming commonplace in the daily newspapers. How could one comprehend the misery of one's countrymen from the bare newsprint? And what was the point of trying poor David Tshabalala when so many cold-blooded killers would never be brought before the courts? The genetic time-bomb, implanted deep within the body politic by the hatred of previous generations, was threatening to blow apart the nation inherited by their descendants, black and white. Somewhere in the dark forests of Jeremy's mind, a bell tolled like a mantra for the suffering in this beautiful country. He put the paper down and rubbed his eyes.

'How did it go in court today?' Elmarie asked.

'He was found guilty of murder and attempted murder.'

'Will he hang?'

'If there aren't any extenuating circumstances. I'm arguing tomorrow.'

'They behave like animals,' she said caustically. 'And they want to rule the country.'

'Apartheid has destroyed the social fabric ...' he began but his words felt old and tired, even to him.

'You always blame the Government.'

'I've tried to tell you,' he said patiently. 'I've tried to explain, but you refuse to understand. If *we* can't see eye to eye, what hope is there of the political leaders agreeing on a new deal.'

'The Afrikaners won't allow them to take over,' she warned. 'We were the poor whites in this country. We also suffered. Thousands of women and children died in the English concentration camps. The Afrikaners' social fabric was also destroyed. But we built ourselves up again.'

'And how brutally have you ruled! Out of your struggle came a reign of iron.'

'And unfortunately that has created a new struggle with its own tyrants,' she said. 'I don't want to live under Mandela's reign of iron.'

'Well, you'll have to leave then. Lots of South Africans are going to Australia.'

'We all may have to,' she answered. 'The quality of life here has become so diminished, the crime rate is so high . . . What's it all for?'

'You mean the quality of life for the whites,' he countered. 'For the blacks it's been like that ever since the Afrikaners put them in ghettos.'

'And before. They've been killing one another for hundreds of years. What makes you think they're going to stop now? You can have your little *pro deos* but they'll go on killing long after Mandela's taken power; they're using bush law here. Come.' She unfolded her model's legs and stood above him. 'I've made supper. Do you want to eat?'

Bending over, she kissed him on the mouth and he breathed the heavy sweet smell of gin. 'I'm sorry I snapped at you,' she whispered. 'I've just been so tense. I was really upset about what happened at the garage yesterday.'

'It's all right.'

'And I'm sorry about what I said last night. We've got such different outlooks and I worry so much that you'll go off with someone else who shares your views . . . Please forgive me.'

'Sure,' he mumbled, overwhelmed yet again by her sudden change of mood, unable to match her ups and downs with suitable mood swings of his own.

'Good,' she said cheerfully and he followed her sullenly to the table. Her fingers, when she served the food, were very red, as if engorged with blood. They ate in silence: lamb chops, baked potatoes and peas. He hadn't realised how hungry he had been, and how irritable that hunger had made him.

'Did you have a good day?' he asked after he had helped her take away the last of the dishes and they faced each other over coffee.

'Yes,' was all she said, but an inflection in her voice hinted that there was more.

'What did you do?' he enquired dutifully.

'I defrosted the fridge,' she said. 'I hate an iced-up fridge. It reminds me of an old fat woman.'

'I mean, what did you do at work?'

'I went out to Crossroads.'

His cup froze halfway to his mouth. 'What?' The sharp word and his puckered forehead indicated his amazement and consternation.

'I'm researching an article on how the squatters decorate their

170

shacks,' she said, pretending to be nonchalant, exhaling smoke out of her mouth. 'I saw some wonderfully inventive interiors today. One shack had walls covered entirely by labels from tins of tomato paste, another had pages of a magazine . . .'

'But,' he stuttered, 'but you don't just go to Crossroads!'

'Why not? Are *you* the only white allowed in?'

'No, I don't mean that. It could be dangerous . . . you don't know anyone there . . .'

'I went with Thandi. She's our receptionist. Her cousin lives in the shack with the tomato labels.'

'But it's what you fear most, the black-white thing . . . Yesterday you were freaked out when a child threw a stone at your car, today you drive into one of the most unstable areas in Cape Town. I don't understand you at all.' He swallowed the coffee in one gulp, hardly noticing the heat of the liquid as it burned its way down his throat. 'You've got this love-hate relationship with the blacks, like your great-great Afrikaner grandparents. You've got a fascination with them that you try to suppress but sometimes it gets the better of you . . .'

She shrugged. 'I'm a journalist and it was a good story. There was no trouble. Everyone we met was very friendly to me.'

'Did you two go alone?' He did not know what to say; he was trying to encapsulate all the questions that were buzzing in his head into one.

She laughed. 'Not a chance. We went in the firm's car with a driver and a photographer. I don't want my car burned out. Anyway, why should you be so concerned? Didn't your woman friends go into Crossroads when you were helping the squatters?'

'I wasn't having a relationship with any of them,' he said testily. 'That makes a difference.' His breath caught in his throat as he imagined her forced out of the car by a black man whose grudge against whites had overcome his reason, a distorted man with a lifetime of hatred against whites for all the indignities he had suffered. Of course apartheid was to blame. It had ruined the country. It had turned the people against each other and poisoned the well of goodwill. It had made heroes of murderers and fools of peacemakers.

'This is the first time you've taken my side against them,' she said.

'I don't see it as siding for or against anyone. I'm worried about you. Since Mandela's release, expectations have soared. People expected to become rich overnight, to be freed from their poverty and squalor. And that did not happen. Their frustrations have made the townships very volatile. You know that . . .' As he spoke, he realised again how the situation in the country had deteriorated. What a way to live! 'I hope you didn't go to Crossroads to show me you could be like my "woman friends".'

'Come on,' she interrupted putting on a dazzling smile, changing the subject before he could cross-examine her any further. 'I don't want to discuss it. Let's go to a movie. We haven't been out together in ages.'

'I can't,' he answered. 'I've got to prepare for tomorrow.'

Disappointment brought the shutters down over her face and as she picked up his coffee cup – one of the fluted set – it rattled because her hand was shaking so much, and he feared she would drop it.

'You only think of yourself,' she said resentfully. 'You're cold. Even colder than François.'

'Who's François?' he asked, distracted and confused by her sudden hostility.

'They guy I left for you.'

'What do you want me to do? A man's life depends on my performance. It's my duty to do my best for him. Even if he did behave like an animal.'

'So you're going home now?'

'I've got my papers with me. I can work here.'

'Rather go.'

'What will you do?"

'I don't know. Read my book by Lowry, or write my article . . . or,' she added spitefully, 'visit a friend.'

He pulled on his jacket and stuffed the newspaper into his briefcase, his cheeks burning from this new flare-up. As he closed the door of her flat, he reflected that these conflicts were never resolved; they were simply buried, like skin growing over a splinter while the festering took place hidden inside.

The leaves of the rubber plant in the foyer had collapsed. The caretaker had forgotten to give it water and the harsh summer heat had sucked out the last of its juice. The leaves hung, parallel to the stem, pointing to the Underworld, an inverted Tree of Life.

Jeremy drove home too fast, his pulse thudding in his ears. The cottage was dark but friendly and he let himself in with relief, comforted by the familiar warm smells. How ideology bedevils relationships in South Africa, he thought. Would things be any better between us if we lived in Australia?

◆

The man in the witness-box had sandy hair and a soft smile. A homely old blue suit hung on his scarecrow frame, slightly too big, as if he had bought it second-hand and it had been badly altered. A plastic model of a human brain nestled in the palm of his left hand. As he spoke, the long fingers of his right hand caressed its wrinkled walnut surface, stopping from time to time to indicate a specific place.

'Dr Higgins,' Jeremy asked, 'you examined the accused and compiled a report. What did you find?'

'Yes, I did,' the psychologist answered, speaking quickly and fluently as if he were lecturing a class. 'David Tshabalala received a hammer blow to his head about eight centimetres above the right eye. The frontal lobe lies immediately above and behind the eye socket.'

'And, Doctor, what are the consequences of injury to this area of the brain?'

'If there is injury to the orbital cortex on the lower surface of the frontal lobe, there may be changes in personality and social functioning, most notably involving a loss of those inhibitory functions whose operation make civilised standards of behaviour possible. Patients suffering from frontal lobe damage typically show irritability and a lack of perseverance. They are demanding, disinhibited and aggressive. There may be anti-social conduct and the patient may come into contact with the law. He has little insight into the changes which occur.' The psychologist's index finger moved over the model in his hand, stroking it as one might rub behind a dog's ear. 'Typically, the patient is subject, under minor provocation, to sudden explosions of violent behaviour.'

'And how does this relate to the accused, Doctor?' Jeremy's throat was clogged with phlegm this morning, perhaps as a result of two consecutive nights spent arguing with Elmarie. He licked his dry lips then sipped from his glass of water. His career would not survive too many further upheavals with her. The lance, which she plunged into

173

him every time she felt insecure, would surely kill the goose that she hoped would ultimately provide the security she craved.

David Tshabalala sat in the dock, examining the nails on his killer hands, while the white men discussed his brain as if he were not even present: the enemy that lived in his head, that had, through malfunction, forced him to destroy himself.

'I have studied the medical records,' Higgins answered, 'and I would say the accused's behaviour, the loss of control on the night of the killing, was consistent with damage to the orbital cortex of the frontal lobe . . .'

'Thank you, Doctor.'

One of the assessors yawned and put his fist into the hole of his mouth but the judge was watching the psychiatrist closely. His spectacles dangled like the scales of justice from his big fingers. Jeremy turned to look at the cast of characters who had brought him here: Thelma and Kekana sat at opposite ends of the gallery, each one wrapped in a cocoon of misery; tears rolled down David's cheeks and fell, unchecked, on to the impartial courtroom floor.

◆

It was late afternoon and Jeremy was staring at the mountain framed in his big picture window. His feet were crossed on his desk and he took a swig from the bottle of beer which he allowed himself at the end of a trial. He lifted the receiver and dialled.

The voice at the other end was distracted. 'Yes, hello Jeremy.'

He was tempted to put the phone down without saying any more but he knew it would make him feel worse.

'My case is finished,' he said. 'Another day in court, another two hundred rand.'

'And?' Elmarie asked. He imagined her dividing her attention between him and her article on decorating squatters' shacks.

'He got seven years.'

'No death sentence?' she asked, excitement creeping into her voice.

'No, just seven years in jail . . . don't ask me why it was seven and not six or eight . . .'

'You won!' she cried. 'You saved him!'

'In a way,' he replied heavily. 'I should have done better.' The same sense of hopelessness that he had felt at the plight of the squatters was closing in on him: he had tried again and failed. 'Maybe if someone more senior had handled it . . .'

'Nonsense!' she exclaimed. 'You saved his life. It's better than he would have got from his own courts. You can't just wave a magic wand and everyone's problems will go away.'

'I know,' he said. 'But now he loses his job. And his mother is destitute. She isn't eligible for a pension. She depended on him for money . . . what's she going to do?' He jammed the bottle to his lips. 'That was part of my argument in mitigation but they didn't listen to me.'

'It's not your problem,' she said and her voice exuded concern for him. 'You can't get too emotionally involved in your cases. You've done your job and now it's over, time for the next case.'

'I know,' he said wearily. 'When I get another one . . .'

'Will you appeal?'

'Yes. I'll apply for leave to appeal against the sentence. I won't have much luck with the conviction.'

'Would you like me to write a story about the case?' Elmarie asked. 'I can ask our readers to help the mother.'

'That's an idea,' he said, no less surprised than he had been the previous night when he learned of her trip to Crossroads. 'I'll give you Thelma's phone number.' Perhaps Elmarie could get a better result than he, ironic as that might seem. 'You'd have to let me read it first.'

'OK,' she said. 'You can give me the details. It would make a nice human interest story. Now, how about that movie tonight?'

'Yes, why not?' he answered. 'It should cheer me up.'

'Fine,' she said. 'I'll see you at my place at seven.'

'I dreamed about you last night,' he admitted, not wanting her to go, trying to keep her on the line for as long as he could.

'What about?'

'It must have had to do with you going to Crossroads,' he said. 'I dreamed you were at a cocktail party. You were hiding in a closet – I don't know why – and you opened the door and stuck your face out. You were very beautiful.'

He imagined her smiling at this and her smile brought back to him a feeling of the beauty of her face in the dream.

'Nelson Mandela was walking past. He saw you and he was so

captivated that he stepped inside the closet and took you in his arms and started to waltz with you.'

'Weren't we cramped?' she asked.

'The closet was as big as a dance hall.'

'What did I do?'

'You were surprised but went along with him good-naturedly. He was very urbane and charming and gentle. Then suddenly he stopped as though he had come to his senses and realised that he had gone beyond the bounds of decency. He fumbled in his pocket and brought out his ID book, as if that was why he had accosted you, to show you something, and he opened it. One of the details on the front page besides "name" and "address" and "height" was: "alive".' Jeremy paused then, enveloped in the sensation of the dream as fully as if he were still asleep.

'What did you feel?' Elmarie asked. 'About me dancing with another man.'

'I was slightly jealous. But in a way he was so like a father that he was hardly threatening.'

'What a strange dream,' she said, then: 'I've got to go. Someone's waiting to see me.'

'OK,' he answered. 'I'll be at your flat at seven.'

He put the phone down but did not move. Another client, another trial, and people scarred by the events in a violent society. Was this what he went to university for? Was this how he would spend his life: going through the motions of an elaborate game?

David had not spoken to him when he was led away. He did not even say thank you for saving his life. His withering glance showed that he knew his was simply another case, another few hundred rand for this hungry young lawyer. It showed that he did not believe Jeremy had tried hard enough for just another poor black sheep going through the white meat-packaging system.

Perhaps the People's Courts with their instant justice were better: sixty lashes and then if you survived it was all over. They served the community's needs: punishment without removing the breadwinner – unless he died.

The blood flowed freely down the face of the Magritte as it had flowed down David's face when he was beaten by a hammer and turned into a murderer; as it had flowed down Elmarie's face when

176

she was split open in the car accident that killed her father and marked her for life. As it flowed out of the wounds of this beloved country. But the lips of the death mask in the paintings were turned upward: she was smiling, a bitter smile of memory.

Jeremy poured the last of the bottle's contents into his mouth and felt his head spinning. He remembered that he had not eaten, and too late he pushed the bottle away from him: he still had to get home. With fingers slightly muddled from the alcohol, he pushed buttons on the intercom.

'Hello Jeremy,' came Fatiema's voice, caring as a mother's.

'A cup of coffee, please,' he said. 'Urgently.'

'Coming up,' she said chuckling and added: 'You know, you must either drink regularly or not at all. Once in a while is no good.'

'The coffee, please,' he said. 'Give me the lecture tomorrow.'

'It's on its way,' she replied, 'and I will.'

◆

TWENTY DIE IN NATAL CARNAGE was the headline in the newspaper Jeremy bought from a vendor who danced through car fumes between the lanes of traffic at the top of Long Street. The story, which he skimmed while he waited for the lights to change, told of a blood-bath in Natal's 'valley of death' during savage fighting between supporters of the ANC and the rival Zulu-based Inkatha organisation. Hundreds of people had been injured and hundreds of houses burned down as bands of warriors, armed with guns and knives, settled old scores or created a myriad new ones. Survivors were streaming into refugee centres and relief agencies were hard pressed to cope. A Red Cross official said that refugees had not slept for the past three nights and were close to hysteria. A police patrol had come under heavy fire in an ambush. Even the monosyllabic journalese could not disguise the horror.

What a mockery of the hope and exultation that had greeted the unbanning of the ANC and the release of Mandela. 'Now sanctions must end,' Lewis Singer had said that day. 'There's nothing to stop investment from flowing into the country.' It was only five weeks ago, but it seemed a lifetime. Who now would want to invest in this mad country?

Jeremy drove up Kloof Street in bumper-to-bumper late afternoon traffic while a hot wind whipped down from the mountain, buffeting his car. Heat is death, he reflected. Trapped by the seat belt, he could not manoeuvre out of his stifling jacket; nor would the violent gusts allow him to open his window. In this grim new South Africa, one's horizons narrowed: you couldn't go into the townships, or drive on this road, or visit that part of the country, until the only safe place left was the small space within the *laager* of your home – and you lived in constant fear that it, too, would be violated. Singer had the answer to that question: leave the whole mess behind and emigrate to Australia. But it was hard enough making a living here: how could Jeremy possibly contemplate starting again in a foreign country? He could not leave his mother and what would he do with Elmarie?

It happened in a second. A gap opened between his car and the one in front, and, in frustration, he trod hard on the accelerator to make up space and time. As he did so, a dove dropped into the road before him. Too fast to stop, cars behind him, he drove straight into the swooping bird. There was a clunk on his bumper, then a ragged bundle of heat and feathers whacked into the windscreen. Jeremy dodged instinctively, averting his eyes, but the dove had already catapulted over the roof and landed in the street behind. He could not even see whether it was dead and the gridlock prevented him from stopping. Trembling with shock, he drove on past the post office and the park, turned into Ivy Street, and switched off the ignition. He sat behind the steering-wheel without moving, catching his breath, recovering.

Mr Pretorius was fighting against the gale to close his front gate. He did not see Jeremy. Hat jammed over his ears, his fox terriers at his heels, he strode up the garden path towards his front door, almost bent double into the wind. He disappeared into the dark house, firmly closing out the world.

When Jeremy got in, the answering machine was blinking furiously. He pushed the play button and the frenzied voice of Vivian, his mother's maid, escaped: 'Mister Jeremy, Mister Jeremy! Please come quick.'

His fingers dialled the number automatically, remembering the digits independently of his brain which had frozen. The line was engaged. He dialled again; he became aware that he had dropped his jacket and case on the floor. He got through. The phone rang interminably and the sweat burned from his pores, soaking his white shirt and stinging his eyes. And then someone lifted the receiver on his mother's side but said nothing: there was only the sound of laboured breathing.

'Hello!' the lawyer demanded. 'Mom, is that you?'

'Mister Jeremy . . .' Gusts of sobbing blew away Vivian's words. 'It's the madam . . .'

'What about the madam? What's the matter?' he shouted, trying verbally to slap the maid out of her hysteria.

'She's . . . I found her . . . she's . . .' Vivian could not say it.

The blood thudded in his head, as if forced through by a pile-driver. 'How?' he squeezed out of his locked jaw. 'What happened? Was she attacked?'

'I phoned the doctor,' Vivian managed. 'Here he is.'

And then a man's plummy voice replaced the maid's: 'This is Dr Levine, Jeremy. I'm afraid your mother is gone.' He used the present tense with the euphemism to soften the blow. 'She must have had a heart attack.' His words were as calm and modulated as if he were diagnosing a case of tonsilitis in his comfortable Sea Point rooms: there was no trace of panic, just misplaced reassurance.

Jeremy's fingers throttled the receiver. He grunted as he pushed his face into the sweaty white plastic. Time had forgotten to move; he was in an eternal present, created between the doctor and the telephone, from which there was no escape.

'She did not suffer,' Levine added, in his soothing bedside tone. 'She must have gone immediately . . . Jeremy, are you still there?'

But numbness had seeped from the top of his head through his eyes and into his mouth – he was blind and he could not prise open his lips. It went down his shoulders and into his fingertips. He could no longer feel the ache in his elbow from the constriction of holding the phone.

'Jeremy. Do you want me to come over?'

A disembodied voice replied: 'No, Doctor. I'm all right.'

'I've called the *Chevra Kadisha*. They'll take the body away. Do you want to see her before she goes?'

Jeremy did not answer. The veil that Dr Levine would have drawn over her face now covered his too. When he opened his mouth to breathe, to talk, he sucked in the cloth of the shroud and it clogged his mouth, suffocating any sound he might have made.

'You'll have to arrange the funeral with them . . . but you can do that on the phone.'

He was an orphan, he realised with sudden fear. He was alone now. Who did he have left in the world? No brothers or sisters to share his grief, to face this new future without parents. There were only a few distant relatives like Uncle Hymie who meant nothing to him. For an absurd moment, it occurred to him that his mother had got the death sentence from which he had saved David Tshabalala. But what was her crime? Inability to accept the new South Africa? Old Mr Pretorius battled on, sick and alone, behind his fence in the corner of the street; he had a resilience bequeathed by generations before him who had hewed their living out of this inhospitable land. But Esta was too European; she could not adapt. She had given up the struggle at the first sign of adversity.

'I'll be there now,' he said, forcing himself back to reality.

Then his room was gone and he was flying over Kloof Nek and his mother's face shimmered on the grey cloud that filmed the mountain. Her silver lips pleaded with him: 'Help me, my son. Please help me. I am in pain.' But he knew he had left it too late. He had helped others in situations where he could control the amount of help he gave. But her need was so great that one either ignored or was consumed by it. He had opted for the former and now it was too late. The sea was bright blue; the sun had sprinkled gold dust on its placid surface. As he drove down the lush winding road of the Glen into Sea Point, he was overwhelmed by the beauty of the mountains and the sea: it was a day meant for celebration, not for dying.

Vivian loomed in the doorway, a weighty black presence, dabbing the tears from her eyes with the hem of her clean blue overall. When she saw Jeremy, she erupted with sobbing: for a moment he could not understand why she was upset; surely this death would release her from the insufferable domination of a racist employer. Yet Vivian and Esta must have formed a bond over the years: they must have loved each other with a mutual dependence that no one else had understood, that had grown out of their incarceration together in this little flat.

Without thinking, Jeremy put his arms around her shoulders and embraced her, breaking through the racial barrier that had separated them all the years he had known her, and he sank into the huge softness of her African bosom. She folded her hands around his back and they held on, a mighty animal, not moving, taking and giving solace, the one to the other.

'What happened?' he asked at last, aware that he was also crying, his tears flowing uncontrollably down his cheeks. He pulled back and wiped the sides of his nose with the back of his hand as he might have done when he was a child in the arms of a black nanny.

'I came back from my lunch and I didn't hear nothing from her room. I called "Madam" but she did not answer. So I went to her room and she was lying on her bed on her stomach. I thought she was sleeping so I left her . . .' Vivian sniffed and blew her nose into her tissue. 'When I came to wake her for tea she still did not move, so I shook her and then I knew . . . I got such a fright I phoned your work but they said you went home, so I phoned your house and I spoke to that machine . . .'

That was while I was stuck in the traffic in the murderous heat, he thought, killing birds. 'And before you went out for lunch, how was she?'

'She said she was tired and she had a pain in her arm. I didn't think anything . . .'

'I told her to see the doctor about that pain,' he said forlornly, 'but she wouldn't listen. Is the doctor still here?'

'Dr Levine, he went back to his surgery. He said you can phone him.'

'I want to see her.'

Vivian turned back into the flat and Jeremy walked past her, guiding his reluctant footsteps up the endless passage to the bedroom with its fearful burden that used to be his mother. The late afternoon sunlight dropped bars across the blue carpet which caught the soles of his feet and tripped his progress as he passed the bathroom. At the end of the corridor, the walls suddenly tilted inwards, leaving a small gap that was almost too narrow for him to squeeze through but which gave Vivian no trouble. The room was as white as a morgue.

Esta lay on her back, her blue death mask removed from the pain of the world as serene as the Magritte print, Memory, in her son's office. She was so peaceful she could have been sleeping but her features had a waxen abandon that put her undoubtedly beyond sleep. Her mouth would have fallen open were it not for the pillow the doctor had positioned under her chin. Her naked face, unmade-up and deeply crevassed, was exposed in a way she would never have permitted while she was still alive. Someone had thoughtfully drawn a blanket up to her chest. Her lifeless hands that had once frolicked over piano keys, bringing smiles to the faces of so many 'old people' as she called them, were folded across her breast. The fingers had become stubs of meat. They would give no more pleasure. Her fleshy ears would never again hear the opulence of the symphony orchestra that she loved.

This was the organism that had brought him into the world and now it was gone; the umbilical cord has been severed. You only really cease to be a child when your parents are dead he thought, even though she had infuriated him rather than given him motherly love, especially since her husband had died.

Jeremy stood at the bedside above the husk of his mother. He did not move any closer. He could not bring himself to touch the body, to put his lips to the cold flesh or hold the corpse's hand. His mother had left this decrepit hunk of meat behind: she was gone. What remained did not need to be embraced.

The sun was sinking into the sea and shadows began to consume the room but he did not switch on the light: it was right that Esta should lie in darkness. He thought of pulling the blanket over her face but that seemed too final. This way he could still pretend that she was not dead, that the ashen, sunken features might flicker again to life, that the eyes would open from sleep and the mouth would emit its old raucous grumblings.

He turned away and Vivian went with him. He flopped down into one of the hideous jaw-like armchairs in the room that doubled as dining room and lounge. Now the practical problems would begin: burying his mother, finding her will – if she had one – and disposing of her estate. It was just as well that he was not busy at work. If he had inherited – and there was no reason to doubt it – he would sell the flat and buy Vivian a house. He would give her enough money so she did not have to work again – some reward, or guilt money, for the abuse she had endured so loyally over the years. And he was now free to escape to Australia without worrying how to take his mother with him.

Suddenly he wanted to be in Elmarie's arms. He needed her to comfort him like she had done when his father died, as he needed her to share his joy when Mandela was released. He wanted to draw her heat into his body, to feel her breath on his neck, to lie on top of her and have her take him inside her pulsing, alive, vagina. The vagina that had been his gateway into the world was dead. He needed to make love intensely to reaffirm his own life.

'My mother did not suffer,' he said hopefully to Vivian who carried in a tea tray with assured, untrembling fingers and put it down on the table. She handed him a cup and took the other and sat beside him in an intimacy that she might have adopted when alone with Esta but not when visitors came and she reverted to her role as servant. She sat, his equal for the first time, and sipped tea from a white china cup – his surrogate mother. But her eyes were bloodshot and sunken; her gums, he noticed absently, had receded from her white teeth, increasing their length.

'I was only away for an hour,' she replied. 'Miss Esta died quickly.'

'If she'd been in pain, she'd have tried to phone,' he reasoned, trying to make the death feel more tolerable than his father's which had been horrible. The fingers of the hand that was not holding the cup tapped absently on the armrest of the chair. Jeremy put his thumb to his mouth and bit off a piece of nail. 'What do you plan to do now?' he asked, then added hurriedly: 'I'll help you, of course.'

As if she had not heard his offer she said: 'I will go back to the Transkei to my children. There aren't any jobs here. All the whites have run away because there's too much fighting. Maybe I'll come back to Cape Town next year.'

Somewhere a bell was tolling stridently: *'Dolente! Dolente! Dolente!'* demanding that the dead be grieved for, warning against the impending civil war, urging all reasonable people to step back from the pit that would swallow them. The sun went away then and a chill of sudden night gripped the room.

Jeremy's glance snagged on a headline in a newspaper sprawled across the blue sofa where his mother used to spread herself out: PIG'S HEAD FOUND AT SYNAGOGUE. The paper was a day old. He leaned over and retrieved it with shaky fingers and read: 'A pig's head was found on the porch of a synagogue in Johannesburg. The walls were spray-painted with swastikas and graffiti, including: "DEATH TO RACE MIXERS" and "VIVA MANDELA".'

Did Esta read this article? Were the Nazi connotations of white hatred the final straw for her, terrified as she already was of the blacks? Perhaps he had taken her fears too lightly, perhaps he should have helped her emigrate to Australia as Lewis Singer was helping his mother.

But he could not allow himself to fall into the trap of that guilt: his life had been dominated by the guilt that she had engendered; it must not survive her. Esta had found freedom from her fears of a new South Africa, from her loneliness at the absence of her husband. The death was a release, not an uninvited guest. Had her son found the freedom to progress into the new South Africa without the yolk of his mother's aspirations for him?

He reached out for the phone and dialled Elmarie's number. 'Hello?' She was there; they had an arrangement to go to a movie, he remembered. 'My mother . . .' he faltered, 'my mother . . .'

'What!' she demanded. 'Tell me.'

'My mother . . . died this afternoon.'

Her silence was as intense as his had been earlier on the phone to Dr Levine. 'They're different from us,' his mother had said. 'They take what they can but when the going gets tough, they call us "bloody Jews".' Would Elmarie rejoice now that her adversary was dead?

'Where are you?' she said at last.

'At her flat.' His words were stones. They plummeted from the tenth floor into the street below.

'I'll be there now.' The phone clicked off.

The tramp grinned as the assassin's knife ate into his internal organs: it was a savage death grin, braced by his yellow wolf teeth. He grinned because, in that moment, he recognised the killer's face, clearly through the cracked mirror that divided them: the killer was Jeremy Spielman, his host who, with the death of his mother, had been able to murder the weakness within him.

Jeremy stood up and his grief began to overwhelm him. He pushed past the blue settee and went out on to the balcony and stared down at the furious traffic below. And, finally, he asked himself, how was it possible for the overwhelming majority of the citizens of a country to want peace and yet be pushed into bloody war by a minority of madmen? Could it be that, within each one of us, there is a small destructive force that secretly applauds when the warlords rattle their *pangas* and incite us to hate the blacks, the Afrikaners, the Zulus, the ANC, the Jews? Is this force in us so disproportionate to the civilising influences that govern the rest of our lives that it can overcome our reason and allow us to be led by the rabid demands of the fanatics to whom we have surrendered our power? And is this force allied to the self-destructive behaviour which will, if turned inward instead of out, topple a man from his pedestal in the social hierarchy and plunge him into the abyss? If this is so then the guilt is within us all, then the soldiers and the tramps are merely opposite sides of the same coin. And we must guard, for all we are worth, against the terrible enemy that lives within us.

As the dark clouds hovered over the red band of sunset splayed across the horizon, and the calm black sea yielded the first twinkling lights from the ships in its grip, Jeremy Spielman held tightly on to the railing and sobbed into the gathering night. A bell was tolling inexorably, from where he did not know: 'Dolente! Dolente! Dolente! Dolente!'